W. H. Davenport Adams

Stories of the Lives of Noble Woman

W. H. Davenport Adams

Stories of the Lives of Noble Woman

ISBN/EAN: 9783337736705

Printed in Europe, USA, Canada, Australia, Japan

Cover: Foto ©Andreas Hilbeck / pixelio.de

More available books at **www.hansebooks.com**

STORIES OF THE

LIVES OF NOBLE WOMEN.

By

W. H. DAVENPORT ADAMS.

" The woman's cause is man's: they rise or sink
Together, dwarfed or godlike, bond or free ;
For she that out of Lethe scales with man
The shining steps of Nature, shares with man
His nights, his days, moves with him to one goal,
Stays all the fair young planet in her hands.
......O we will walk this world,
Yoked in all exercise of noble end."

TENNYSON.

London:

T. NELSON AND SONS, PATERNOSTER ROW.

EDINBURGH; AND NEW YORK.

1898

PREFACE.

——•——

HE object of the present volume is to illustrate from the Lives of Noble Women those higher qualities which elevate the character of the sex, and brighten and purify our daily life.

In selecting the subjects of his biographical sketches, the author has endeavoured to fix upon women who have been not less distinguished by their domestic than by their public virtues; upon women who have been Christians "faithful to the end," and patriots firm in their loyalty to their country, as well as upon women illustrious as wives, mothers, daughters, or sisters. The sphere in which woman influences us for good is much wider than society sometimes supposes; and the pages of history record innumerable examples of her heroic devotion and constancy to a great purpose. It is well that these examples should be kept before the eyes of the younger female members of our families; and that they should be encouraged to aspire to a high standard of duty, while not forgetting that their true happiness will always lie within the home circle.

The author has sought to give as much variety as

possible to his sketches, and to avoid subjects which have been well worn by previous writers. It is thought that for most young readers the following pages will have a certain air of freshness. They are founded on the best and latest authorities; and at the risk of rendering them less entertaining, the author has scrupulously refrained from exaggeration of detail or depth of colouring. All sensational devices have been eschewed, and he has strictly adhered to the sober truthfulness of history.

In dealing with such themes as the mental and moral qualifications of women, it is almost impossible to say much that is new, and the chances are that what is new may not be true. The author, therefore, has had no ambition to startle his readers with ingenious paradoxes, while he has had as little desire to weary them with venerable platitudes. He has aimed at telling his story simply but clearly; and with the exception of a few brief observations prefixed to each chapter, has left his young readers to discern for themselves the obvious moral which every good and noble life presents, assured that it will not fail to impress itself upon their quick wits and bright intelligences.

This little book was originally issued under the title of "The Sunshine of Domestic Life," and passed through several editions. On again reprinting it, the author thought it desirable to christen it with a title which should more clearly indicate its leading aim.

CONTENTS.

A PERFECT WOMAN

'I saw her upon nearer view,
A spirit, yet a woman too!
Her household motions light and free,
And steps of virgin liberty ;
A countenance in which did meet
Sweet records, promises as sweet;
A creature not too bright or good
For human nature's daily food,
For transient sorrows, simple wiles,
Praise, blame, love, kisses, tears, and smiles.

And now I see with eyes serene
The very pulse of the machine;
A being breathing thoughtful breath,
A traveller 'twixt life and death;
The reason firm, the temperate will,
Endurance, foresight, strength, and skill;
A perfect woman, nobly planned,
To warn, to comfort, and command;
And yet a spirit still, and bright
With something of an angel light.'

WORDSWORTH

Steadfastness to the Truth.

THE STORY OF ANNE ASKEW.

I.

HOLY WRIT has warned us that we cannot serve two masters, God and Mammon, and that the claims of heaven and the world are incompatible. We must make our election to abandon the one, if we follow the other; and the reader needs not to be told how awful an influence her choice will exercise upon her life here and her happiness hereafter. May she choose the better part, and ever keep before her eyes the prize of her high calling, looking to an incorruptible crown, and the 'fadeless amaranthine wreath' of immortal love! So will she contribute to the happiness of her home, by the brightness and beauty of her daily example, by the steadfastness of her devotion, the gentleness of her character, and the nobility of her self-sacrifice.

We say, advisedly, self-sacrifice, for she will be required to endure much, to forgive much, to yield much. The soldier must be faithful to his colours in the hour

of disaster as in the flush of triumph, and even if not
called upon to receive the baptism of battle, will be
sorely tried on the march, in the camp, at the bivouac,
in the routine of his daily life.   And so for the Christian
lady, there will be trouble, and suffering, and tempta-
tion, though the dark days are past when the believer was
often compelled to seal her faith with her blood, and. to
proclaim her devotion to the truth amid the fires of
Smithfield.   There are martyrs, now-a-days, however,
though their martyrdom is never witnessed by human
eyes, nor hallowed by human sympathy; domestic
martyrs, whose sufferings are more protracted, if less
terrible, than those of Cranmer, Latimer, or Ridley;
martyrs who serenely smile while the heart is wrung with
unutterable sorrow, and mutely bear the ills of the
present, looking forward to a glorious and unclouded
future! Neither stone nor tree shall bear any record of
their thoughts, their woes, or their prayers, but angels
look forth upon the silent struggle, and whisper approval
when the victory is won.   It is thus that thousands, un-
cheered by the applause or sympathy of their fellows,—

' Have made an offering of their days,
  For truth, for heaven, for freedom's sake,
  Resigned the bitter cup to take,
  And silently, in fearless faith,
  Bowing their noble souls to death.'

How the sharpest trials and keenest agonies may be
bravely borne, and the oppression of the persecutor
made to yield the crown of eternal glory, let us learn
from the life of a noble martyr, who perished for God's
cause in the very springtime of a prosperous career, and
shed her youthful blood

' In confirmation of the noblest claim,—
    Our claim to feed upon immortal truth,
    To walk with God, to be divinely free,
    To soar, and to anticipate the skies.'

Anne Askew, who sacrificed her life 'for the witness of Jesus, and for the Word of God, and because she would not worship the beast, neither his image, neither would receive his mark upon her forehead, nor in her right hand,' was sprung from an ancient and honourable English family which had long been settled at Kelsey, in Lincolnshire.   She was born in 1520, the second daughter of Sir William Askew, but of her early life and education neither history nor tradition has preserved any particulars.   She is said to have been a lady of great beauty, gentle manners, and warm imagination,* and, as we shall hereafter see, her taste was refined, and her power of poetical expression considerable.   Her temper seems to have been naturally quick, but her firm judgment and steadfast will controlled it.   Her intellect was acute, and she loved to examine an opinion for herself before she accepted it.   Once convinced of its truth, she never abandoned it, for her firmness and inflexibility were not less conspicuous than her quickness and amiability.   In a word, she appears to have been gifted with a well-balanced mind, and to have realized, in many respects, Wordsworth's beautiful ideal of

' A perfect woman, nobly planned,
    To warm, to comfort, and command.'

It was not her fortune, however, to play so bright a part in social life, and her excellent virtues served but to throw a sunshine over her last hours.   In the days of

---

* Lord Campbell, 'Lives of the Lord Chancellors.' 644.

Henry VIII. daughters were dutiful and fathers stern, and considerations of domestic happiness were but little esteemed if they clashed with worldly interests. A friend and neighbour of Sir William Askew was a Mr. Kyme, a man of great wealth and extensive local influence. To cement their friendship and unite their families by matrimonial ties became the desire of both these Lincoln-shire magnates, and, accordingly, it was arranged that the son and heir of Mr. Kyme should wed the eldest daughter of Sir William Askew. But the lady died before the scheme could be carried out. Anne Askew was then put forward in her sister's place, and her happiness sacrificed to her father's worldly ambition. As her proposed husband was notably her inferior in mental qualities, and his character sullied with the fly-blows of country scandal, Anne warmly protested against the match. But her father insisted, and she learnt her first hard lesson of duty by obeying his commands.

Anne Askew's married life was not unworthy of her; but so incongruous an union could not be crowned with domestic happiness. Between her husband and herself rose the impassable barrier of a superior intellect and a firmer will, and though she bore him two children, they brought no love into the cold and dreary home.

It was about this time that a copy of the Scriptures fell into this unfortunate lady's hands. Tyndale had just completed his translation of the New Testament into English (A D. 1525–6), and Henry VIII. had sanctioned its publication. The waters of life, so long sealed up to the many, poured their brightening and fertilizing flood over the whole land. Ah, and how eagerly the thirsty spirits— fed for ages by a jealous priesthood on the husks and shells of the truth—drank of this new river of life! Not the least avid among these was the quiet woman who, in the solitude of an unsatisfied heart, had pined for the song of consolation. She read the word devoutly, and her quick intelligence soon perceived the grossness of the errors in which she had been educated. She was too honourable, and of too resolute a will, to remain member of a church which based its doctrines upon misrepresentation and falsehood. Though fully aware of the obloquy she would incur by such a step, and of the bitterness of the persecution it would assuredly entail, she boldly renounced the creed of Papacy, and embraced the 'new heresy'—the doctrines of the Lollards or Wickliffites. Nor, thenceforward, did she waver in her allegiance to the truth, even in the agonies of the torture or the last fiery ordeal of the stake.

Her renunciation of Popery brought down upon her head the thunderbolts of priestly wrath, and the fierce indignation of her husband. But neither menaces nor bribes, neither ill-usage nor cajolery, could shake her belief in God's Word, and her husband, as ignorant as he was intolerant, expelled her from his house. A woman not easily dismayed, she straightway proceeded to London, and took the steps necessary to secure a divorce, acting, as she explained, on the Apostolic doctrine,—

'If a faithful woman have an unbelieving husband, which will not tarry with her, she may leave him, for a brother or sister is not in subjection to such' (1 Cor. vii. 15).

In the metropolis she soon made the acquaintance of many distinguished Lollard ladies, and, it is said, was

appointed one of the maids of honour of the Queen,
Katherine Parr. She does not appear to have carried
her divorce suit into the courts of law—probably because
she was too soon involved in the furnace of persecution—
and undoubtedly her labours would have been unsuccessful, as neither justice nor equity was obtainable by a
heretic. She dropt her husband's name, however, and
once more signed herself 'Anne Askew.'   *

It is necessary here we should enter into a brief ex-
planation of the penal statute under whose sanguinary
provisions Anne Askew's enemies hunted her to death.

The Parliament summoned in 1539, appointed a com-
mittee to draw up a bill against diversity of opinions in
matters of religion. After a long-continued theological
discussion, in which Bishop Gardiner warmly advocated
the doctrines of the Papal Church, and prevailed over
the counsels and influence of Cranmer, six articles were
agreed to as representing the fundamental tenets of the
English Church. These were:—*

1. That in the Sacrament is present really, under the
form of bread and wine, the natural body and blood of
our Saviour Jesus Christ, conceived of the Virgin Mary;
and that after the consecration there remaineth no substance of bread or wine, or any other substance but the
substance of Christ, God and man.

2. That Christ was entirely in each kind, and therefore
communion in both was not necessary.

3. That priests by the law of God may not marry.

4. That vows of chastity or widowhood, taken after
the age of twenty-one, ought to be observed by the law
of God.

* Fuller, 'Church History of Britain,' ii. 98, *et seq.*

5. That private masses might be lawfully used in the English Church, as by them good Christian people receive godly consolation and benefit.

6. That auricular confession was expedient, and ought to be retained, used, and frequented in the church of God.

These articles were burdened with sanguinary penalties. Those who should ' by word, writing, printing, or otherwise, publish, preach, teach, affirm, argue, or hold any opinion' contrary to the first, were declared heretics, and condemned to suffer death by burning, even without the benefit of abjuration. To dispute the other five articles was declared a felony, and, on the first occasion, the criminal was to forfeit all his goods and possessions, and be imprisoned during the king's pleasure; on the second, he was doomed to suffer death. The marriages of priests contracted before this Parliament were declared null; and the same severe penalties were pronounced upon women who married priests, as upon priests who wedded women.

To secure the effectual working of this Act, commissioners were appointed in every shire, of whom three were to form a quorum, and who were to sit four times at least in the year, with full power to receive informations, accusations, and evidence, before a jury of twelve men, upon oath, and to declare sentence. In the commission was included the archbishop, or bishop, or his chancellor, or a commissioner named by him. Similar powers were bestowed upon the justice of peace in their sessions, and every steward, under-steward, or deputy, in his law-days, so that England might fairly be described as suffering under a reign of religious terror.

The Act of the Six Articles was afterwards so far modified as to allow the offender an opportunity of recanting; but if he offended a third time, the full penalties of the law were to be inflicted without mercy. Some other alterations, designed to render it more moderate, were introduced by Parliament in 1544. Nevertheless, it still remained a terrible engine of persecution, and fully deserved its popular appellation—the whip with the six strings; a whip which, wherever it fell, drew blood!

But Truth derives fresh life and potency from the endeavours which ignorance and cruelty make to crush it. Vainly break the storms and billows of fraudful force against its immutable Rock!

> ' Truth divine for ever stands secure,
> Its head as guarded as its base is sure,'—

and in spite of sanguinary penalties and unjust judgments, the doctrines of the Reformation were embraced by hundreds of eager and inquiring spirits.

It was soon suspected by the myrmidons of Popery that Anne Askew was a heretic; and one Wadloe, a cursitor of the Court of Chancery, and a Papist, took lodgings next to her own temporary residence in the Temple, in the hope he might obtain sufficient evidence to warrant her incarceration. But he who goes down to curse is sometimes compelled to bless, and Wadloe found himself obliged to acknowledge to Sir Lionel Throgmorton, that she was the devoutest woman he had ever known; 'for,' said he, 'at midnight she begins to pray, and ceases not for many hours, when I and others are addressing ourselves to sleep or to work.'* Such

---

* Strype, ' Ecclesiastical Memorials,' vol. i., pt. i., p. 597, *et seq.*

excellence of character and purity of life could not dis-
arm the persevering hostility of her own husband and
the Romish priests. An ungrounded expression or two
furnished them, at last, with the means of compassing
her destruction. Thus she had, on one occasion, denied
that the character or belief of the priest in any wise
diminished the efficacy of the sacrament of the Lord's
Supper ; in other words, that, whether administered by
Lollard or Papist, it was still the emblem of Christ's
blood and body. She had also contemptuously affirmed,
that she would rather read five lines of the Bible than
hear five masses in the chapel. On these grounds she
was accused of heresy, and straightway arrested.

Her first examination took place in March 1545. A
jury, or inquest, under the presidency of Christopher
Dare, was held for the purpose at Sadler's Hall. His
questions pressed her closely as to the exact nature of
her opinions on the great popish dogmas of the Mass,
Transubstantiation, Auricular Confession, and the connection of the office of the priest with the administration
of the Eucharist. In her replies she displayed a wonderful acuteness of penetration and solidity of judgment.
During her imprisonment she wrote a full account of the
examination, which remains a remarkable monument of
womanly constancy and Christian courage.*

II.

The first examination ran as follows :—

Christopher Dare. ' Do you believe that the sacra-

---

* This account was published by Bishop Bale, with an introduction, in 1547,
with the title of ' First Examinacyon of Anne Askewe, lately martyred in Smyth-
felde by the Romish Pope's Vpholders, with the Elucydacyon of Johan Bale.
Marp. in Hessen, 1546.' It was reprinted by the Parker Society.

ment upon the altar is the very body and blood of Christ?'

Anne Askew refused to be entrapped, answering this insidious question by another,—

'Please inform me why Stephen was stoned to death?'

Christopher Dare. 'I cannot tell.'

Anne Askew. 'Neither will I tell you whether I do or do not believe the sacrament upon the altar to be the very body and blood of Christ.'

Christopher Dare. 'A woman has testified that you have read how God was not in temples made with hands.'

Anne Askew. 'As to this I would refer you to the seventh chapter of the Acts of the Apostles, verses 48–50, where Stephen says: "Howbeit the Most High dwelleth not in temples made with hands; as saith the prophet, Heaven is my throne, and earth is my footstool: what house will ye build me? saith the Lord: or what is the place of my rest?" and to the seventeenth chapter of the same book, verse 24, "God that made the world and all things therein, seeing that he is Lord of heaven and earth, dwelleth not in temples made with hands."'

Christopher Dare. 'Why did you say that you would rather read five lines in the Bible than hear five masses in the church?'

Anne Askew. 'I confess that I said no less, because the one greatly edifies me, the other nothing at all. And St. Paul doth witness,' she continued, 'in the fourteenth chapter of his First Epistle to the Corinthians, wherein he saith, "If the trumpet giveth an uncertain sound, who will prepare himself to the battle?"'

Christopher Dare. 'You also said, that if an ill priest ministered, it was the devil, and not God.'

Anne Askew. 'I deny that I ever said or thought so. What I said was, that whoever ministered unto me, his ill conditions could not injure my faith, but in spirit I received nevertheless the body and blood of Christ.'

Christopher Dare. 'What think ye concerning confession?'

Anne Askew. 'That, as St. James saith, every man ought to confess his faults to others, and the one to pray for the other.'

Christopher Dare. ' And what say you as to the king's book?' (namely, 'The Erudition of a Christian Man,' compiled by various bishops and divines, and published by order of Henry VIII.)

Anne Askew. 'As I never saw it, I can pronounce no judgment on it.'

Christopher Dare (scornfully). 'Have you the Spirit of God?'

Anne Askew (humbly). 'If I have not, then am I but a reprobate and castaway.'

A priest now made his appearance on the scene, and proceeded to interrogate her upon the sacrament of the Eucharist; but perceiving that he was a papist, and that his design was to wring from her some unguarded admission which might imperil her life, she refused to make any answers to his questions. He then inquired, whether she did not think that private masses were of great help to departed souls? 'It is great idolatry,' said she, 'to believe more in these than in the death which Christ died for us.'

She was now removed from Sadler's Hall, and brought
before the Lord Mayor, Sir Martin Bowes, who examined
her in much the same strain, and was equally foiled by
her prompt, vivacious answers. She incurred a rebuke
from the Bishop of London's chancellor 'for uttering
the Scriptures.' St. Paul, he said, forbade women to
speak or talk of the Word of God. She replied, that she
knew the apostle's meaning as well as he, which was,
that a woman ought not to speak in the congregation by
way of teaching: and then she asked him, how many
women had he seen go into the pulpit and preach? He
replied, None. Then, retorted she, you ought to find no
fault with poor women, unless they have offended against
the law.

Baffled by her woman's wit, the Lord Mayor now committed her to prison, and, in direct defiance of the law,
refused the application of her friends to bail her. She
was flung into the Compter, and for eleven days was
allowed to see no friendly face, to hear no friendly
tongue. A priest, however, was sent to her by Bonner,
to examine her, and give her good counsel. He began
with a pretence of humane feeling. For what cause, he
said, was she put in the Compter? She told him she
knew not. Then, said he, it was great pity she should
lie in so loathsome a place without cause, and he was
very sorry for her. But the cloven-foot soon showed
itself. He charged her with denying the 'sacrament of
the altar.' She answered, indifferently, that what she
had said she had said. He then asked her if she were
content to be shriven. Even so, she replied, if she
might have one of three ministers to shrive her—either
Dr. Crome, Sir Guillam Whitehead, or Huntington,

whom she knew to be men of wisdom. 'As for you, or any other,' she added, 'I will not dispraise, because I know you not.'

The priest, somewhat chafed, exclaimed, 'Think not but that I, or any other who may be brought you, shall be as honest as they; for if we were not, you may be sure the king would not suffer us to preach.' To this she answered, in the words of Solomon, 'By communing with the wise I may learn wisdom, but by talking with a fool I shall take scathe.' Confounded by her wit, the priest changed his course, and asked, 'If the host should fall, and a beast did eat it, whether did the beast receive God or no?' 'Seeing that you have taken the pains to ask the question, I desire you also to answer it yourself; for I will not, because I perceive you are come to tempt me.'

On the 23rd of March she was visited in the Compter by her cousin Brittayne, who immediately afterwards repaired to the Lord Mayor, for the purpose, if possible, of obtaining her release on bail. The Lord Mayor intimated his wish to befriend her, but declared that the sanction of a spiritual officer was necessary, and requested him to wait upon the bishop's Chancellor. For as he could not commit her to prison without the order of a spiritual officer, no more could he release her without that spiritual officer's consent. Brittayne repaired to the Chancellor, who, however, could not act without the permission of the Bishop. He undertook to intercede with Bonner on the subject, and requested Brittayne to see him the next morning, and he would let him know his lordship's pleasure.

Brittayne returned on the morrow, and found Bonner with the Chancellor. The Bishop declared that he was well contented she should come forth to communication; and appointed her to appear before him for examination on the following day, March 25, at three o'clock. He also expressed a desire that such learned men as she esteemed should attend the examination, that they might see and report that she was treated with no rigour. Brittayne answered that he knew no man whom she preferred to another. 'Yes,' said Bonner, 'as I understand, she prefers Dr. Crome, Sir Guillam Whitehead, and Huntington, that they might hear the matter, for she did know them to be learned and of a godly judgment.' This he said from no wish that she should obtain the advantage of their counsel, but that he might secure an opportunity of arresting them and flinging them into prison.

On the 25th she appeared before Bonner, and underwent a similar verbal persecution to that which she had endured at the hands of Christopher Dare. The Bishop exercised all his subtilty to entrap her into some direct expression of her faith, but found her prepared and guarded on every point. It was no weak woman contending with a superior mind, but a calm and ready intellect foiling the astuteness of a practised 'man of the world.' Bonner, with a great show of friendship, besought her to unburthen her mind, for that she did not need to stand in doubt or fear. Neither he, nor any man for him, should take her at advantage of any word. Therefore, he bade her speak fearlessly. She replied that she had nought to say, for her conscience was burdened with nothing. 'Then,' exclaimed Bonner,

'I can give you no good counsel.' 'My conscience,' she replied, 'is clear in all things.' 'You drive me,' rejoined the angry Bishop, 'to lay to your charge your own report, which is this: You did say, he that doth receive the sacrament by the hands of an ill priest, or a sinner, receiveth the devil, and not God.'

'I never spake such words,' she answered indignantly; 'but, as I said before, that the wickedness of the priest did not hurt me, but in spirit and faith I received no less than the body and blood of Christ.' 'What saying is this, *in spirit?*' demanded he; 'I will not take you at the advantage.' She answered, 'My lord, without faith and spirit, I cannot receive him worthily.'

What was her belief with reference to the presence of Christ's body in the consecrated host?

'I believe,' she replied, 'as the Scripture doth teach me.'

'But what if the Scripture doth say,' continued the Bishop, 'that it is the body of Christ?'

'I believe,' she said, 'as the Scripture doth teach.'

Then he repeated his query, 'What if the Scripture doth say that it is the body of Christ?'

Again she answered. 'I believe as the Scripture informeth me.'

Anxious to embarrass her, and force her into some entangling admission, he continued to perplex her with subtle questions; but her straightforward simplicity completely defeated him. 'I believe therein,' she concluded by saying, 'and in all other things, as Christ and his apostles did leave them.'

The Bishop grew wroth at her brief and direct answers. 'Why have you so few words?' said he.

'God,' she replied, ' hath given me the gift of knowledge, but not of utterance; and Solomon saith, that a
woman of few words is the gift of God.' He then
accused her of having said that the mass was supersti-
tious, wicked, and no better than idolatry. She denied
that she had made any such statement, adding, ' I was
asked whether private mass did relieve departed souls or
not, and I answered, O Lord, what idolatry is this, that
we should rather believe in private masses than in the
death of the dear Son of God!'   Then said Bonner,
'What an answer is that?'   'Though it be but mean,'
she rejoined, 'yet is it good enough for the question!'

Finding himself worsted in this wordy war, the Bishop
angrily exclaimed: 'There are many that read and know
the Scripture, and yet follow it not, nor live thereafter.'
With all the loftiness of innocence, Anne Askew repelled
the insinuation: 'My lord, I would wish that all men
knew my conversation and living in all points; for I am
sure myself, this hour, that there are none able to prove
any dishonesty against me.*   If you know that any can
do it, I pray you bring them forth.'

Thereupon the Bishop retired, to commit, as he pretended, some of her meaning to writing, which she was
required to subscribe as her confession of faith. The
document which he drew up, and which totally misrepre-
sented her principles of belief, ran as follows† :—

' Be it known of all faithful people, that, as touching
the blessed sacrament of the altar, I do firmly and undoubtedly believe that, after the words of consecration

---

* The old meaning of *honestus* was (from the Latin) *honourable* or *becoming*;
and Anne Askew uses the word " dishonest" in a similar sense.

† Foxe, ' Acts and Monuments,' vol. v., p. 553 (8vo edit.)

be spoken by the priest, according to the common usage of this Church of England, there is present really the body and blood of our Saviour Jesus Christ, whether the minister that doth consecrate be a good man or a bad man; and that, also, whensoever the said sacrament is received, whether the receiver be a good man or a bad man, he doth receive it really and corporally. And, moreover, I do believe, that whether the said sacrament be then received of the minister, or else reserved to be put into the pyx, or to be brought to any person that is impotent or sick, there is the very body and blood of our said Saviour. So that, whether the minister or the receiver be good or bad; yea, whether the sacrament be received or reserved, always there is the blessed body of Christ really. And this thing, with all other things touching this sacrament, and other sacraments of the Church, and all things else touching the Christian belief, which are taught and declared in the King's Majesty's book, lately set forth for the erudition of the Christian people, I, Anne Askew, otherwise called Anne Kyme, do truly and perfectly believe, and so do here presently confess and acknowledge. And here I do promise, that henceforth I shall never say or do anything against the promises, or against any of them. In witness whereof, I, the said Anne, have subscribed my name unto these presents.'

Having read to Anne Askew this curious declaration of principles, which she did not entertain, he demanded of her whether she did not agree with it? She replied, 'I believe so much thereof as the Holy Scripture doth agree unto; wherefore, I desire that you will add to it this sentence.' Bonner furiously exclaimed that a woman

should not dictate to him what to write; and thereupon
he went forth ' into his great chamber, and read the
same bill before the audience, which inveighed and
willed her to set to her hand, saying also that she had
been favoured, and that she might thank others, and not
herself, for the favours she found at his hand; for he considered that she had good friends, and that she came of
a good family. Never sure,' observes Foxe, the zealous
old martyrologist, ' never sure did a Bishop show favour
to a lady with so ill a grace.'

At length, on the importunity of her friends, she appended to the pretended confession her signature, thus:
' I, Anne Askew, do believe all manner of things contained in the faith of the Catholic Church.' The
Catholic, mark you, not the *Roman* Catholic. Bonner
appreciated the understood distinction, and breaking
forth into ungovernable passion, rushed into an adjacent
apartment, followed by Anne Askew's cousin Brittayne,
who besought him, for God's sake, to be a good Bishop
to her. Bonner answered, that she was a woman, and
that he was nothing deceived in her. ' Then,' said
Brittayne, ' treat her as a woman, and do not set her
weak woman's wit against your lordship's great wisdom.'

After a while the Bishop's wrath was appeased, and he
was persuaded to come out of his chamber, and take her
name, with the names of her sureties—her cousin Brittayne, and one Master Spilman of Gray's Inn. It was
then supposed she would have been immediately released; but Bonner ordered her to be detained in prison
until the next day, when he willed her to appear in the
Guildhall. This she did; and on the following day she
was dragged to Paul's Church, and much delay was again

exhibited; but, at length, the influence of her friends prevailed, and she was set at liberty.

Thus ended Anne Askew's first persecution.

III.

She was not allowed, however, any long interval of peace, for Bonner and Gardiner had determined, unless she recanted her Lollard doctrines, to make a terrible example of her. Accordingly, in 1546, she was again apprehended, and brought before the King's Council at Greenwich. And as she was firm in her profession of the faith, she was remanded to Newgate, to remain there and answer to the law.

On the 25th of June she was formally examined, her examination lasting about five hours. The following account of it is given very nearly in Anne Askew's own simple and graphic language :—

My Lord Chancellor, she says, asked of me my opinion in the sacrament. My answer was this: I believe that so oft as I, in a Christian congregation, do receive the bread in remembrance of Christ's death, and with thanksgiving, according to his holy institution, I receive therewith the fruits also of his most glorious passion. The Bishop of Winchester bade me make a direct answer. I said, I would not sing the song of the Lord in a strange land. Then the Bishop said I spake in parables. I answered, it was best for him, for if I showed the open truth, they would not accept it. Then he said I was a parrot. I told him again I was ready to suffer all things at his hands, not only his rebukes, but all that should follow besides; yea, and all that gladly. Then had I divers rebukes of the council, because I would not ex-

press my mind in all things as they would have me
But they were not, in the mean time, unanswered for all
that, which now to rehearse were too much, for I was
with them about five hours.

The next day I was brought again before the council,
and was questioned what I said respecting the sacrament.
I answered that I had already said what I could say.
After many words they bid me go aside. Then came
Lord Lisle, Lord Essex, and the Bishop of Winchester,
requiring me earnestly that I should confess the sacrament to be flesh, blood, and bone. I told these noblemen that it was a great shame for them to counsel contrary to their knowledge; whereunto, in a few words, they
said that they would gladly all things were well. The
Bishop said he would speak with me familiarly. I said,
'So did Judas when he betrayed Christ.' He then desired to speak with me alone, which I refused. He asked
me the reason of my refusal. I said, that in the mouth
of two or three witnesses every matter should stand, after
Christ's and Paul's doctrine.

My Lord Chancellor then re-examined me upon the
sacrament. I asked him, How long would he halt on
both? He asked where I found that. I said in the
Scripture. He then departed. The Bishop said I should
be burnt. I answered that I had searched all the Scriptures, yet could I never find that either Christ or his
apostles put any creature to death. 'Well, well,' said
I, 'God will laugh your threatenings to scorn.' Then
was I commanded to stand aside; after which came Dr.
Cox and Dr. Robinson to me; but in conclusion we could
not agree. After striving to convince me, they drew out a
confession respecting the sacrament, urging me to set

my hand thereunto; but this I refused. On the following Sunday I was so extremely ill that I thought death was upon me; upon which I desired to see Mr. Latimer, but this was not granted. In the height of my illness I was conveyed to Newgate, where the Lord was pleased to renew my strength.

On my being brought to trial at Guildhall, they said to me there that I was a heretic, and condemned by the law, if I persisted in mine opinion. I answered, that I was no heretic, neither yet deserved I my death by the law of God. But as concerning the faith which I uttered and wrote to the council, I would not deny it, because I knew it to be true. Then would they needs know if I denied the sacrament to be Christ's body and blood? I said, 'Yea; for the same Son of God, who was born of the Virgin Mary, is now glorious in heaven, and will come again from thence at the latter day. And as for that you call your God, it is a piece of bread. For more proof thereof, mark it when you list, that if it lie in the box three months it will grow mouldy, and so turn to nothing that is good. Whereupon I am persuaded that it cannot be God.'

After that they willed me to have a priest, at which I smiled. Then they asked me if it were not good? I said I would confess my faults unto God, for I was sure that he would hear me with favour.

And so I was condemned.

And this was the ground of my sentence:—My belief, which I wrote to the council, that the sacramental bread was left us to be received with thanksgiving in remembrance of Christ's death, the only remedy of our soul's recovery; and that thereby we also receive the whole benefits and fruits of this most glorious passion. Then

would they know whether the bread in the box were
God or not. I said, God is a spirit, and will be wor-
shipped in spirit and truth. Then they demanded, Will
you plainly deny Christ to be in the sacrament? I answered, That I believe faithfully the eternal Son of God
not to dwell there; in witness whereof I recited again the
history of Bel, Dan. xix.; Acts vii. and xvii., and Matt.
xxiv., concluding thus: ‘I neither wish death, nor yet
fear his might; God have the praise thereof with thanks.’

After this examination Anne Askew addressed a letter
to the King himself, and forwarded it by the hands of the
Chancellor. It is admirable for its simplicity and straight-
forwardness. We cannot refuse to adorn our pages with
it:—

‘I, Anne Askew, of good memory, although God hath
given me the bread of adversity and the water of trouble,
yet not so much as my sins have deserved, desire this
to be known unto your grace, that forasmuch as I am by
the law condemned for an evil doer, here I take heaven
and earth to record that I shall die in my innocency, and
according to that I have said first, and will say last, I
utterly abhor and detest all heresies. And as concerning
the Supper of the Lord, I believe so much as Christ hath
said therein, which he confirmed with his most blessed
blood. I believe so much as he willed me to follow, and
believe so much as the Catholic Church of him doth
teach. For I will not forsake the commandment of his
holy lips. But look what God hath charged me with his
mouth, that I have shut up in my heart. And thus
briefly I end for lack of learning.’

Neither arguments nor protestations availed her aught
with her sanguinary persecutors. Yet could they not

darken her spirit, nor deprive her of her hope and trust in God, as is sufficiently evidenced from the strain to which she gave utterance while languishing in the dreary solitudes of Newgate.

ANNE ASKEW'S PRISON SONG.

Like as the armed knight,
  Appointed to the field,
With this world will I fight,
  And faith shall be my shield.

Faith is that weapon strong
  Which will not fail at need:
My foes, therefore, among,
  Therewith will I proceed.

As it is had in strength
  And force of Christ's own way,
It will prevail at length
  Though all the devils say nay.

Faith in the fathers old
  Obtainèd righteousness:
Which makes me very bold
  To fear no world's distress

I now rejoice in heart,
  And hope bids me do so:
For Christ will take my part,
  And ease me of my woe.

Thou say'st, Lord, whoso knock
  To them wilt thou attend:
Undo, therefore, the lock,
  And thy strong power send.

More enemies now I have
  Than hairs upon my head:
Let them not me deprave,
  But fight thou in my stead.

On thee my care I cast,
  For all their cruel spite:

I set not by their haste,
　For thou art my delight

I am not she that list
　My anchor to let fall,
For every drizzling mist,
　My ship substantial.

Not oft use I to write
　In prose, nor yet in rhyme:
Yet will I show one sight
　That I saw in my time.

I saw a royal throne,
　Where Justice should have sit,
But in her stead was one
　Of moody, cruel wit.

Absorbed was righteousness,
　As of the raging flood;
Satan, in his excess,
　Sucked up the guiltless blood.

Then thought I, Jesus, Lord,
　When thou shalt judge us all,
Hard is it to record
　On these men what will fall;

Yet, Lord, I thee desire
　For that they do to me,
Let them not taste the hire
　Of their iniquity.*

After a few days of captivity in Newgate, **Anne Askew** was removed to the sign of the Crown, where she was beset by Mr. Rich and the Bishop of London with assiduous cajolery, and who, by alternate threats and promises, endeavoured to turn her aside from her profession of faith.

These were succeeded by one Nicholas Shaxton, who advised her to recant even as others had done. She re-

* Foxe, 'Acts and Monuments.' vol. v., appendix, No. 19.

plied, ' It had been good for you never to have been born,' with many other words, chiefly from the Book she had so zealously and lovingly studied. She was then remanded to the Tower, where she remained until three o'clock, when Mr. Rich and one of the king's council attacked her with urgent demands that she should show unto them if she knew any man or woman of her sect. Her answer was, ' I know none.' They then endeavoured to betray her into accusations against Lady Suffolk, Lady Sussex, Lady Hertford, Lady Denny, and Lady Fitzwilliam. She answered, If she should pronounce anything against them, yet should she not be able to prove it. Then said they unto her: The King is informed that you could name, if you would, a great number of your sect. She answered, That the King was as well deceived in that behalf as he was dissembled with by them in other matters.

They then commanded her to show how she was maintained in the prison, and who willed her to adhere to her religious opinions. She told them that she derived support and consolation from no human source. All the help she had received in the Compter was from her maid; who, as she fared through the streets, narrated her mistress's sad circumstances to the London 'prentices, and they assisted her with money, though who they were she never knew. But her persecutors insisted that several ladies had sent her money. She replied, That a man had certainly placed ten shillings in her hand, with the information that they came from the Lady Hertford; while another had given her eight shillings, and said it was a gift from the Lady Denny. Whether this were true or no, she could not tell, as she only spoke from what her maid had said. 'There are some of the council, they exclaimed, 'who maintain you;' but this she earnestly denied.

Not satiated with persecution, her enemies now re solved to put this noble woman to the torture, in the hope they might wring from her agony some implication of other heretics. They kept her on the rack for some time, but she uttered neither word nor moan. She neither accused others, reproached her enemies, nor bewailed her own sufferings. Silent and calm she lay, as on a bed of repose, so angering her persecutors by her inflex ible courage that Rich and the Lord Chancellor actually put their own hands to the rack, and tortured her until she was nearly dead, an act of cruelty unusual even in an age of horrors. The lieutenant then ordered her to be removed from the rack, when she immediately swooned. On her recovery, she was kept sitting on the bare floor for two hours, disputing with the Chancellor, who, despite his brutal inhumanity, insulted her with professions of goodwill, and urgently entreated her to renounce her faith. 'But,' said she, ' my Lord God, I thank his everlasting goodness, gave me grace to persevere, and will do so, I hope, to the very end.'

After these hours of unutterable suffering, she was brought to a house and laid on a bed, 'with as weary and painful bones as ever had patient Job,' yet still ex pressing her gratitude to God. The Lord Chancellor then sent her word that if she would abandon her opinions she should want for nothing; if she would not she should forthwith be flung into Newgate, and burned. She re plied, with all a martyr's enthusiasm glowing in her soul,

That she would rather die than desert her faith; praying that God would open his eyes, so that the truth might have free course and be glorified.

Touching the order of her torture in the Tower, says Foxe, it was thus:—First, she was led down into a dungeon, where Sir Anthony Knevet, the lieutenant, commanded his jailer to pinch her with the rack; which being done so far as he thought sufficient, he was about to remove her, supposing that she had suffered enough. But Wriothesley, the Chancellor, displeased that she was so speedily released, when she would make no confession, commanded the lieutenant to bind her on the rack again. And when Knevet, less brutal than his superior, refused, and urged the weakness of the poor victim as a reason, the Chancellor threatened to report his disobedience to the King. And he and Mr. Rich, throwing off their gowns, must needs play the tormentors themselves, first inquiring, whether she were with child. To which she nobly answered, ' Ye shall not need to spare for that, but do your will upon me;' and so—'quietly and patiently praying unto the Lord, she abode their tyranny, till her bones and joints were almost plucked asunder, so that she was carried away in a chair.' When the torture was ended, Wriothesley and his worthy colleague left.

I confess that there is something in the story of this noble woman which nerves me greatly. Was ever courage greater than hers? Was ever steadfastness more glorious? Did ever hero, plunging into the thick of the battle, and carrying his country's ensign triumphantly through the 'imminent breach,' surpass the heroism of Anne Askew?

Meantime, while they were making their way to the

royal palace by land, the good lieutenant, immediately
taking boat, sped to the Court in all haste to speak with
the King before the Chancellor.   And addressing Henry,
with 'bated breath,' he desired his pardon, and explained
every incident of the scene lately enacted in the Tower;
adding that the Lord Chancellor had threatened him because at his commandment, not knowing his Highness's
pleasure, he had refused to rack her, which he for compassion could not resolve in his heart to do, and therefore
humbly desired his Highness's forgiveness.   Even Henry's
obdurate soul seems to have been touched by the lieutenant's story; he expressed his anger at the extreme
torture to which Anne Askew had been subjected; and,
granting Knevet the pardon he craved, willed him to
return and attend his charge.   Great was the excitement
in the Tower among warders and jailers to know how
their lieutenant had fared, and great was their joy when
he came so cheerfully, and declared how favourably he
had been received by the King's majesty.   From whence
we may conclude that persecution was more in favour
with peers and statesmen than with humbler officials.

It was about this time that Anne Askew addressed the
following reply to a letter which she had received from
one John Lascels, a fellow-martyr :—

'O friend, most dearly beloved in God!   I marvel
not a little what should move you to judge me in so
slender a faith as to fear death, which is the end of all
misery.   In the Lord, I desire you not to believe of me
such weakness; for I doubt it not, that God will perform
his work in me, like as he hath begun.   I understand
the council is not a little displeased that it should be
reported abroad that I was racked in the Tower.   They

say now, that what they did there was but to fear me
(to terrify); whereby I perceive they are ashamed of
their uncomely doings, and fear much lest the King's
majesty should have information thereof, wherefore they
would no man to noise it.   Well; their cruelty God forgive them!'

Having been falsely accused of beginning to waver in
her faith, she thus disposes of the calumny:—

'I have read the process, which is reported of them
that know not the truth to be my recantation.   But, as
the Lord liveth, I never meant a thing less than to
recant.   Notwithstanding this, I confess that in my first
troubles I was examined by the Bishop of London
about the sacrament.   Yet had they no grant of my
mouth but this, that I believed therein as the Word of
God did bind me to believe.   More had they never of
me.   Then he made a copy, which is now in print, and
required me to set thereunto my hand; but I refused it.
Then my two sureties did will me in no wise to stick
thereat, for it was no great matter, they said.   Then,
with much ado, at the last I wrote thus: "I, Anne
Askew, do believe this, if God's word do agree to the
same, and the true Catholic Church."   Then the bishops,
being in great displeasure with me because I made
doubts in my writing, commanded me to prison, where
I was awhile, but afterwards by the means of friends I
came out again.   Here is the truth of that matter; and
as concerning the thing that ye covet most to know,
resort to the sixth of John, and be ruled always thereby.
Thus, fare ye well.'

While in Newgate she drew up a Confession of Faith,
which she probably designed to leave to posterity as a

memorial of her unshaken steadfastness in what she believed to be the truth. We subjoin this interesting document for the benefit of our elder readers. The juniors may pass on to our narrative of this heroic woman's latest trials.

CONFESSION OF FAITH OF ANNE ASKEW.

' I, Anne Askew, of good memory, although my merciful Father hath given me the bread of adversity and the water of trouble, yet not so much as my sins have deserved, do confess myself here a sinner before the throne of his heavenly Majesty, desiring his eternal mercy.   And forasmuch as I am by the law unrighteously condemned for an evil-doer concerning opinions, I take the same most merciful God of mine, who hath made both heaven and earth, to record that I hold no opinions contrary to his most holy Word ; and I trust in my merciful Lord, who is the giver of all grace, that he will graciously assist me against all evil opinions which are contrary to his blessed verity; for I take him to witness that I have done, and will, unto my life's end, utterly abhor them to the uttermost of my power.

' But this is the heresy which they report me to hold, that after the priest hath spoken the words of consecration, there remaineth bread still.   They both say, and also teach it for a necessary article of faith, that after these words be once spoken there remaineth no bread, but even the self-same body that hung upon the cross on Good Friday, both flesh, blood, and bone.   To this belief of theirs say I, Nay.   For then were our common creed false which saith, that he sitteth on the right hand of God the Father Almighty, and from thence shall come to judge the quick and the dead.   So, this is the heresy that I hold, and for it must suffer the death.   But, as touching the Holy and Blessed Supper of the Lord, I believe it to be a most necessary remembrance of his glorious sufferings and death.   Moreover, I believe as much therein as my eternal and only Redeemer Jesus Christ would I should believe.

' Finally, I believe all these scriptures to be true which he hath confirmed with his most precious blood ; yea, and as St. Paul saith, those Scriptures are sufficient for our learning and salvation that Christ hath left with us; so that I believe we need no un-written verities to rule his Church with. Therefore, look what he hath said unto me with his own mouth in his holy gospel, that I have, with God's grace, closed up in my heart; and my full trust is, as David saith, "That it shall be a lantern to my footsteps." There be some that say I deny the Eucharist, or Sacrament of Thanks-giving; but those people untruly report of me, for I both say and believe it, that if it were ordered as Christ instituted it and left it, a most singular comfort it were unto us all. But as concerning your Mass as it is now used in our days, I say and believe it to be the most abominable idol that is in the world. For my God will not be eaten with teeth, neither yet dieth he again; and upon these words that I have now spoken, will I suffer death.'

To this admirable Confession she appended the following

PRAYER.

' O Lord, I have more enemies now than there be hairs on my head; yet, Lord, let them never overcome me with vain words, but fight thou, Lord, in my stead, for on thee cast I my care. With all the spite they can imagine, they fall upon me, who am thy poor creature. Yet, sweet Lord, let me not set by them which are against me, for in thee is my whole delight; and, Lord, I heartily desire of thee that thou wilt of thy most merciful good-ness forgive them that violence which they do, and have done unto me. Open thou also their blind hearts, that they may hereafter do that thing in thy sight which is only acceptable before thee, and to set forth thy verity aright, without any vain fantasy of sinful men.

' So be it, Lord, so be it.' *

Anne Askew having resolved to embrace the crown

* See Bishop Bale's valuable and interesting store-house of historical records, 'De Scriptoribus Britannicis' (vol. ii.); Foxe's 'Acts and Monuments' (vol. v.); Foxe's 'Book of Martyrs;' Strype's 'Ecclesiastical Memoirs;' and Southey's 'Book of the Church' (vol. ii.) These references are intended for the use of those of our older female readers who may wish to consult the original authorities.

of martyrdom, rather than be false to her God and
Saviour, the day of execution was at length appointed.
It is strange, however, that much discrepancy of statement prevails in reference to the exact date of an event
which may fairly be called historical. Foxe says that
she suffered in the month of June; Bishop Bale, on the
16th of July. The latter is probably correct.

Torture and imprisonment had so racked her limbs
and weakened her frame, that they were compelled to
carry her to the place of execution in a chair. Three
other heretics suffered with her—Nicholas Belenean, a
priest of Shropshire; John Adams, a tailor; and John
Lascels, a gentleman of Nottinghamshire, and of the
King's household. The four martyrs were chained to
three separate stakes; Anne to one stake; one of her
fellow sufferers to a second; and the two others to the
third   In this final hour of trial they nobly encouraged
one another with words of hope, faith, and consolation;
Anne setting before them a glorious example of constancy, which they could not choose but attempt to
rival.

After they had been bound to the stake, and when all
things were ready for the fire, Dr. Shaxton, the preacher
appointed for the occasion, began his sermon. For the
Papal Church did not cease from its efforts to convert
the heretic even in the supreme moment of their greatest
sufferings. Anne Askew listened to him with reverent
attention, approving him when he spoke well; and when
he spoke amiss, firmly expressing her dissent, saying,
' He speaketh without the book.'

The sermon being finished, the martyrs began their
prayers—Anne Askew with ' an angel's countenance.

and a smiling face.' The multitude of the people was exceeding great, and the excited crowd rolled to and fro, like a wind-driven sea. Upon a raised platform, undei St. Bartholomew's Church, sat Wriothesley, Chancellor of England, the venerable Duke of Norfolk, the aged Earl of Bedford, the Lord Mayor of London, and divers other eminent personages. Before the fire was kindled, one of them hearing that the martyrs had gunpowder about their bodies—humanely placed to shorten their sufferings —and fearing that its explosion might drive the fagots about his ears, did not scruple to make known his apprehensions; but the earl assured him that, as the gun- powder was lodged about the persons of the martyrs, no danger could possibly exist.

Then the Lord Chancellor once more tempted Anne Askew with the offer of the King's pardon if she recanted. A letter, said to be written by the King himself, was placed in her hand. But she, boldly refusing even to look upon it, exclaimed, 'I came not hither to deny my Lord and Master.' Similar letters were offered to the other martyrs, who, however, emulated the constancy of their sister, and cheering and encouraging each other with hopeful words, converted the place of execution into a place of triumph, and showed themselves worthy of the crown of glory that was even then descending upon their heads. Thereupon the Lord Mayor exclaimed, with a loud voice, *Fiat justitia!* Let justice be done ! *Justice!* Alas, what crimes have been committed undei the shelter of this holy name ! 'Let justice be done !' Let the innocent perish because they love the truth better than life !

Then, as the fire kindled, the sky all of a sudden

veiled itself in darkness ; a peal of thunder broke above
the heads of the startled multitude; and the rain descended.   'The sky,' says Bale, quaintly, ' abhorring
so wicked an act, suddenly altered colour, and the
clouds from above gave a thunder-clap, not at all unlike
to what is written in Psalm lxxvi. 8: "Thou didst
cause judgment to be heard from heaven ; the earth
feared, and was still."   The elements both declared
therein the high displeasure of God for so tyrannous a
murder of innocents, and also expressly signified his
mighty hand present to the comfort of them which
trusted in him.'   While such was the interpretation put
upon these natural phenomena by the friends of the
martyrs, the Papists regarded them from a very different
point of view.   They looked upon the darkness and the
thunder as emblematical of God's wrath against heretics,
and cried out, in furious exultation, 'They are damned!
they are damned !'

Thus were these blessed martyrs, says Foxe, compassed
in with flames of fire, as holy sacrifices unto God and
his truth.

Anne Askew, at the time of her martyrdom, was in the
28th year of her age, in the very summer and glory of
her life.   The advantages of wealth and rank were hers,
and she might reasonably have anticipated a long career
of worldly prosperity, which her refined taste and cultivated intellect would have adorned with all gentle
womanly graces.   But these bright hopes and radiant
prospects she willingly resigned, that she might give a
noble example to the world of Christian heroism—of
steadfastness unto death—of a weak woman's nature so
elevated and inspired by devotion as to be capable of

the greatest sacrifices, and triumphant over the most terrible sufferings. We are not called upon to endure the same trials, but nevertheless let us strive to inform our lives with the same noble virtues. She who would brighten home, and make a sunshine in a shady place—who would dissipate the clouds of domestic sorrow, and promote a genial spirit of household love—must learn, like Anne Askew, to be

'Faithful unto the end.'

Her name, says Froude,* was written among those who were to serve Heaven in their deaths rather than their lives. Let it be for us to make our *lives* a faithful and devout service unto Heaven!

* Froude, 'History of England from the Fall of Wolsey.' iv 499.

II.

Matronly Excellence.

THE STORY OF LADY VERE.

' Eyes not down-dropp'd, nor over-bright, but fed
With the clear-pointed flame of chastity :
         Locks not wide dispread,
Madonna-wise, on either side her head ;
Sweet lips, whereon perpetually did reign
The summer-calm of golden charity,
Were fixèd shadows of thy fixèd mood
Reverèd Isabel, the crown and head,
The stately flower of female fortitude,
Of perfect wife-hood and pure lowlihood.
    . . . Through all her placid life,
The queen of marriage—a most perfect wife. '
                       TENNYSON

THE Lady Vere, whose life we are about to narrate, was the wife of the famous general, Lord Vere, Baron Tilbury, who commanded the English forces in the Netherlands during the great struggle of the Dutch against the oppression of Spanish tyranny. He was not unworthy, as we shall incidentally show, of such a wife ; nor was the wife unworthy of such a husband. And, owing to their combined virtues and mutual love, their home was blest, from first to last, with surpassing happiness ; was brightened within, whatever the clouds without, by the pure sweet sunshine of domestic life.

Mary Tracey, the youngest of fifteen children, was born on the 18th of May 1581. She was the daughter of Sir John Tracey, of Toddington, in the county of Gloucester, and of Anne Throckmorton, of the Throck-mortons of Corfe Court. Her mother died three days after her birth, having given her life that her child might live; and when about eight years of age she lost her father. Orphaned at so early an age, she nevertheless was so well supported and maintained through the grace of the Most High, that in token of her gratitude she afterwards adopted for her motto the phrase, *God will provide.* This motto she inscribed in most of the books of her library.

In her nineteenth year she was married to William Hobby, Esq., son of Sir William Hobby, privy councillor to Henry VIII. She bore him two sons, both of whom died in their youth.

After the death of Mr. Hobby, she chose for her second husband one of the greatest soldiers of the age, Sir Horatio Vere, afterwards Baron of Tilbury. Of this illustrious man a brief notice seems desirable.*

Sir Horatio was the fourth and youngest son of Geoffrey de Vere, of Kirby Hall in Essex, third and youngest son of John de Vere, fifteenth Earl of Oxford. Manifesting in his early years a strong passion for chivalric pastimes and military exercises, he accompanied, ere yet he had arrived at manhood, the contingent despatched by Queen Elizabeth in 1585, under the command of the Earl of

---

* Motley, 'History of the United Provinces;' 'Biog Britannia,' vol. vi

Leicester, to assist the United Provinces in their rebellion against the yoke of Spain. Side by side with his elder and scarcely less famous brother, Sir Francis, he fought gallantly in numerous engagements, and especially distinguished himself, in 1596, in the Earl of Essex's bold attack upon Cadiz.

In 1600 he first attracted attention as a soldier of ability no less than of gallantry by the great repulse which he administered to the Spaniards at Nieuport. He next displayed his skill and prudence as a tactician by successfully withdrawing his small army of 4000 men, in the face of an overpowering Spanish force under the command of the Marquis of Spinola (A.D. 1600).

On the death of his brother, Sir Francis (August 28, 1609), he was appointed Generalissimo of the English Forces in the Low Countries. He was shortly afterwards nominated Governor of the Brill, by letters-patent under the Great Seal of England. In May 1616, he restored the Brill to the Dutch government by order of James I., receiving in exchange a yearly pension of one thousand pounds, and the reversion of the Mastership of the Ordnance.

In 1625, Charles I., on his accession to the throne, signified his approval of the merits of this famous soldier by elevating him to the peerage, under the title of Lord Vere, Baron Tilbury, of Tilbury, in the county of Essex.

Vere was a gallant gentleman, an accomplished soldier, a knight *sans peur et sans reproche*, and a devout Christian. He had more meekness than, and as much valour as, his illustrious brother; and so pious, says quaint old Fuller, 'that he first made his peace with God before he went out to war with man.' 'One of an excellent temper, it

being true of him what is said of the Caspian Sea, that
it doth never ebb nor flow, observing a constant tenour,
neither elated with good success, nor depressed with the
reverse of fortune. Had one seen him returning from a
victory, he would, by his silence, have suspected that he
had lost the day ; and had he beheld him in a retreat, he
would have collected him a conqueror, by the cheerfulness of his spirit. No doubt but he was well prepared
for death, seeing such was his vigilancy, that never any
enemy surprised him in his quarters.' *

After her marriage, Lady Vere accompanied Sir Horatio abroad, and resided for a considerable period in
Holland. Their eldest daughters, Elizabeth and Mary,
were born abroad, and afterwards naturalized by Act of
Parliament, in the 21st year of the reign of James I. The
influence exercised upon her mind and character by the
austere simplicity and unadorned ritual of Dutch Presby-
terianism was considerable. The ministers whom she
admitted into her society, and in whose prelections she
took the greatest pleasure, were either Puritans or at
least partial to Puritanism. She frequently rendered
them pecuniary assistance, was ever liberal to their
widows and orphans, and showed herself eminently
charitable in deed as in thought and word. Thus, Dr.
Ames, pastor of the English church at Hague, wrote
to her in 1616, after her return to England: ' Your kindness towards me and mine I do with all thankfulness
acknowledge ; but your respect unto my poor ministry I
do much more joy in than in all the rest.' †

* Fuller, ' Worthies of England,' i. 331.
† MSS. Brit. Mus., Bibl. Birch, 4275, No. 5. Cit. by Anderson

In January 1616/7, Lady Vere lost her youngest son by her first husband, Philip, who died in the fourteenth year of his age.

Soon afterwards she gave birth to another child, and was seized with a violent fever, which brought her to the very brink of the grave. Her recovery was for some time very doubtful, being much retarded by her brother's death; but Time, the consoler, brought healing to the heart and strength to the body, and the clouds that had long rested upon her gradually cleared away. All her hopes and prayers now centered in her eldest and only son, who seems to have inherited his father's manly virtues and his mother's Christian graces. He was despatched, for the completion of his education, to Emmanuel College, Cambridge, notorious then for its Puritan proclivities; and his industry and talents speedily secured him the favouring notice of its Principal. In a letter to Lady Vere, dated January 11, 1618/9, while acknowledging a New Year's gift which her generous bounty had bestowed, he says : ' The more experience I have of your son, the better I like and love him, for I find his inclination to be unto any good of learning and virtue, besides his true and sincere affection to pure religion, whereby he hath gained my resolution to further him in all these, so much as in me lieth.'

But this goodly promise was fated never to ripen to maturity. This youth, on whom so many glowing hopes and proud ambitions reposed, died in 1623, when only twenty-two years old. His mother's grief was great, but she knew where to look for consolation. And a true and trusty friend addressed to her in her hour of trial such words of noble encouragement and admirable feeling, that we cannot refrain from transferring them to our pages.*

'God hath taken away your well-beloved and only son. I confess this is such a cross as must needs affect the heart of a loving mother. But remember that he hath given you his own and only Son, to be your wisdom, righteousness, holiness, and redemption. He hath adopted you to be his daughter and heir, and fellow-heir with Jesus Christ. He hath given you his word, his Holy Spirit, and hope and assurance of eternal life. Besides these unspeakable mercies, the Lord hath blessed you with a gracious and worthy husband, with many hopeful children, and good likelihood of having more, with a good name, a plentiful estate, and a healthy body, unless you hurt it with sinful and worldly sorrow.

'We all confess that we and our children are subject to death, but all the question is, which is the fittest time for every man's death. If flesh may be judge, it will think it unfit and unseasonable for any of our friends to die while we live. But the Holy Scriptures will teach us that whensoever it pleaseth the most wise and righteous God to call any out of this life, that is the most season-able and fit time for his death; for the Lord knoweth best when his corn is ripe, and when to gather his fruit, and he doeth all things in fulness of time.

'If you had put your son to be nursed abroad, and should afterwards send for him home to possess his in-heritance, you would think the nurse should deal unjustly and unwisely if she would go about to keep your heir from you. God is the father of your child; he gave him his life, and breath, and being; you were appointed to

* Mr. Dod's Letter. Brit. Mus. MSS. Cited by Anderson.

he his nursing mother, and that for a few days; which
now being ended, he hath taken him into his own kingdom; and therefore you should not be so much grieved
that you part with him now, as thankful that you enjoyed
him so long, and that he now enjoyeth everlasting life in
the heavens, whither yourself also shall come within a
while.   All the afflictions that befall God's children in
this life are the cups which their Father giveth them to
drink (John xviii. 11).   Now he, being the father of all
mercy, and the God of all wisdom and comfort, will put
no ill ingredients into his cup, but will have that care of
the quantity, quality, and measure of the potion, that it
shall surely work for our great good at the last, though
for a while it be distasteful to our flesh.'

The influence which Lady Vere derived from her social
position and her high character was largely employed in
securing the appointment of devout and faithful pastors
to vacant benefices. One of these appointments is worthy
of special notice, that of the celebrated Usher to the
Archbishopric of Armagh and Primacy of Ireland.   It
was due to her urgent solicitations and earnest recom-
mendations that her brother-in-law, Mr. Secretary Con-
way, bestowed this valuable preferment upon a person
absolutely unknown to him, but who afterwards became
one of the greatest ornaments of the English Church.
When his nomination was assured she wrote to him a
congratulatory letter, and at the same time solicited his
prayers for her husband, her children, and herself.
Usher replied in the following terms:—

'March 17, 1624-5.

' My most honoured Lady,—I had need to beg pardon

of your ladyship for neglecting my duty so long in giving
you thanks for the effectual means which you have used
in furthering the obtaining of that preferment, for which
you now send me so kind a congratulation. The best
thanks that I can render for this great love of yours, is
that which you specially desire, and which, if I myself
did not remember, I should much forget myself: even
the earnest recommendation of your noble lord, yourself,
and those sweet olive plants that stand about your table,
to the protection and benediction of our great and
gracious God.

'And I most earnestly entreat your ladyship that you
would not be behind in performing the like pious office
in my behalf; that God of his mercy would be pleased to
uphold and direct me in these slippery times and dangerous days, that I may finish my course with joy, and
keep that good thing which is committed to me until the
day of Christ. I would show myself a very ungrateful
man, likewise, if I did not beseech you, in the most
effectual manner, to thank Mr. Secretary for the extraordinary kindness that he hath shown unto me, being a
mere stranger, and no otherwise made known unto him,
but by what you (out of the abundance of your affection)
have been pleased to deliver concerning me. I intend
to make my personal repair unto his honour, and to
make an acknowledgment of that duty which I do owe
unto him, whensoever it shall please God to grant me
health.'

Towards the close of the year 1627, Lady Vere passed
over to Holland to rejoin her husband, who was still
discharging his duties as commander of the English

forces in the service of the States-General. Both there and
in England, whither she returned about 1630, she passed
some years of prosperity, calm enjoyment, and religious
usefulness, everywhere extorting applause as a model of
all matronly excellences and Christian graces. But a great
blow fell upon her in 1635—the death of her admirable
and illustrious husband, in the ripeness of his fame, and
at the mature age of seventy. While dining with Sir
Harry Vane at Whitehall, he dropped down suddenly,
stricken with apoplexy, and in two hours had ceased to
be. His funeral was celebrated on the 8th of May, with
great pomp, and a grave provided for him in the English
Valhalla—Westminster Abbey.

For many years after this severe bereavement, Lady
Vere resided at Hackney, near London, but finally
took up her abode at Kirby Hall, in the parish of
Castle Hedingham, in the county of Essex. 'Here,'
says Dillingham,* 'the truly religious and honourable
the Lady Vere doth still survive, kept alive thus long
by special providence, that the present age might more
than read and remember what was true godliness in
eighty-eight.' The lamp of her life burned brightly,
as a beacon-light in a dark and cloudy time. Within
her modest dwelling was peace—the peace which pass-
eth understanding—though all England was convulsed
with the storm of civil war; and her heart was never
cold to the cry of distress, her hand never wearied
of liberally ministering to the needy. 'Her charity,'
says the quaint old divine, Gurnall, 'was so great, that
it may well be admired how this tree should not long ago
have killed itself with overbearing. She had silver for

* Commentaries of Sir F. Vere, ed. by Dr. W. Dillingham (Camb. 1657).

the penniless, food for the hungry, medicaments for the sick, salves for the wounded. Abundance of good she wrought this way, both in town and country; she did not only give, but devised liberal things.'

The same writer draws a pleasing picture of her well-ordered household. 'If ever any private dwelling,' he says, 'might be called a chapel, a little sanctuary,. her house was such. There you might find her and her family twice every day upon their knees, solemnly worshipping the great God: there you might see them humbly sitting at his feet to hear his most holy Word read unto them, concluding constantly their evening service with singing one of David's Psalms.

'And if strangers were present, there was no deferring the worship of God to a more convenient season. They, too, were expected to become members for the time of this Church in the House. On the Lord's Day you might hear the sermons preached in public repeated to the family, the servants called to give an account before her of what they remembered, and the high praises of God sounded forth by the whole family together. After supper, again, you might hear the servants in their room exercising themselves in the same heavenly duty of singing psalms. And no sooner did the good lady hear them strike up, but away she would go to join with them in that duty. And yet are we not at an end of this good lady's devotions, for every night she would herself pray with her maidens before she went to bed.'

Her later life was cheered by much domestic happiness. Her daughter Anne married Thomas Fairfax—a marriage which proved as fortunate and felicitous as had been her own. Thomas Fairfax rose to fame as the leader of the

armies of the Commonwealth, and as a man of re
markable singleness of purpose and incorruptible honesty.
Their society proved a great comfort to Lady Vere in
her declining years.

A popular novelist has written the 'Diary of a Quiet
Life.' Lady Vere's was a quiet life, unmarked by any
startling incidents, any signal reverses, any heavy
shadows ; and, as such, presents few passages on which
the faithful biographer can enlarge. Yet is it worth
studying as the life of a noble English matron, and as an
example of the happiness that attends the cultivation of
the domestic virtues. Such women exercise a great, if
to some extent an unseen influence, and mould the character and inclinations of the generation that succeeds
them.

About thirteen months before her death she fell into a
swoon, which lasted for half an hour without any appearance of her recovery. When at length she came to
herself, her first words were, 'I know that my Redeemer
liveth ;' and upon her being carried to her apartment, she
exclaimed, 'I know in whom I have believed, and am
persuaded that he is able to keep that which I have committed to him against that day.'

Towards the close of the year 1671 she was seized
with her last illness. Her agonies were severe, but from
within she derived a strength and a patience which conquered all mere physical pain. No complaint, no murmur escaped from her lips; and if she was filled with no
sense of triumphant joy, she confronted the last change
with that peacefulness which springs from the assurance
of a well-founded hope.

Two days before her death she fell into the lethargy of

exhaustion, under which she rapidly sank, passing away from this temporal life into the bliss of eternity on the 25th of December 1671, in the ninety-first year of her age. The last words she uttered before the state of syncope came on, were in admirable harmony with the tenor of her pure and devout career,—' How shall I do to be thankful? How shall I do to praise my God?'

The funeral took place on the 10th of January 1672, when a funeral sermon was preached to the large assemblage that attended the remains of this noble lady to their last resting-place, by the eminent author of ' The Christian's Armour,' William Gurnall, M.A., minister of Lavenham in Suffolk. He chose for his text the 58th verse of the 15th chapter of the First Epistle to the Corinthians,—' Forasmuch as ye know that your labour is not in vain in the Lord.' It was afterwards published under the title of ' The Christian's Labour and Reward,' with the mottoes :—

' The memory of the just is blessed ;'

' By humility and the fear of the Lord are riches, honour, and life ;' and

' Nobilis genere, sed multo nobilior Sanctitate ' (Noble by birth, but nobler far by sanctity). •

To the sermon are added elegies by nine different authors, abundantly showing the high esteem in which she was held by her contemporaries. Thus, one begins:—

' Noble herself, more noble 'cause so near
To the thrice noble and victorious Vere ,'

another, ' On her sleeping three days together before she died,' says quaintly :—

' Death's brother, Sleep, her senses tied
Three days, and then she waking died.

Sleep was the essay of Death's cup,
Which first she sipped —then drank all up
Thus swimmers first with foot explore
The gelid stream, then venture o'er.
Thus Martyr, for a trial first,
Into the fire his finger thrust,
To snip a pattern of the flame,
Then clothes his body with the same.
Thus spies to Canaan's land are sent
To view the countries ere they went.
Sleep was the mask in which she saw
The promised land *incognita*,
Which done she only wak'd to tell
By-standers that she liked it well.'

According to the fashion of that age, her memory was also honoured with several anagrams. Thus,

'*Marie Vere....Ever I arme*,"

afforded the anagrammatist an opportunity of panegyrising her as a heroine who had buckled on the Christian's armour, and, having won many a battle, had finally received the crown of victory from her Great Captain. Another ran as follows :—

'*Verè mira* (*Truly admirable*):
'Mirror of blessings ! for what tongue can tell,
For grace and greatness where's her parallel.'

And here we take our leave of this noble lady, commending her to all our readers as a bright pattern of Matronly Excellence.

Hospitality.

THE STORY OF LADY ALICIA LISLE.

' · Courage was cast about her like a dress
Of solemn comeliness;
▲ A gathered mind and an untroubled face
` Did give her dangers grace.'

DONNE.

HAT it is better to suffer death than betray the unhappy, when they put their confidence in you, is the lesson taught by the fate of Dame Alicia Lisle.

Alicia Beconsaw was the daughter of Sir White Beconsaw, a knight of illustrious lineage and unblemished character. She married—at what date is unknown—John Lisle, son of Sir William Lisle of Wootton, in the Isle of Wight.

John Lisle was a man of great courage, clear intellect, and no small ambition. He represented Winchester in the Parliament of Charles I.; and in the great struggle of the Civil War warmly espoused the cause of the eople. He was one of the judges of the High Court f Justice which condemned Charles I.; but, owing to he influence of his wife, did not subscribe his name to

the warrant for his execution. In 1649 he was elected
one of the Commissioners of the Great Seal, and a
Member of the Council of State, and attached himself to
the party of Cromwell, whom he thenceforward served
with zeal and fidelity. Nor did his services pass unre-
warded. He was distinguished by the Protector's especial favour, and named by him a member of his new
House of Lords. Succeeding Bradshaw as President of
the High Court of Justice, it fell to his lot to sentence
the royalist conspirators, Colonel Gerard, Vowel, Sir
Henry Slingsby, Hewit, and their colleagues.

After the restoration he escaped to the Continent, and
took up his abode at Lausanne, in Switzerland. In his
absence his estates were confiscated, and he himself was
declared an outlaw. While entering the Protestant church
at Lausanne, on the 21st of August 1664, he was attacked
by two Irish bravos, who shot him dead, at the instigation, it is supposed, of Henrietta, Duchess of Orleans,
daughter of Charles I., and in revenge of her father's
death. The murderers, being well-mounted, escaped
pursuit, and got safely into France.*

Lady Lisle, who was thus left a widow, with a son and
two daughters, retired to her house at Moyle's Court,
near Ellingham, Hampshire, living in the greatest seclusion, and devoting herself to acts of charity and munifi-
cence. To be in need was the only passport required to
her generous heart. So admirable was her life, that she
became the object of universal admiration and love; and
she was warmly esteemed even by the furiest Royalists of
her country, who knew that she had deeply regretted
some violent acts in which her husband had borne a part,

* Edmund Ludlow, ' Memoirs' (London, 1771, 4to).

that she had shed bitter tears for Charles I., and had protected and relieved many Cavaliers in distress.

The poet tells us that our vices often become the whips to scourge us. In the work-day world, our very virtues are sometimes made the instruments of a hostile fate. So it fared with Lady Alicia Lisle. In the rebellion of Monmouth she took no share, either actively or orally, either by expressions of sympathy or contributions of money, for she meddled not with the strifes and struggles of an unquiet time, living a life-within-life, brightened by the exercise of an untiring benevolence. When the rebellion collapsed on the fatal field of Sedgemoor (July 6, 1685), James II. showed how great had been his alarm by the cruelty with which he pursued even the meanest and most ignorant of Monmouth's deluded followers. They were hunted from town to town, from village to village, as the Spaniards hunted their fugitive slaves; and, when caught, were treated with the utmost rigour. Hampshire had not participated in the rebellion, but many of the vanquished rebels fled thither for safety, and thither they were followed by the sleuth-hounds of a sanguinary government. Two of these unfortunate men, John Hicks, a Nonconformist divine, and Richard Nelthorpe, a lawyer, who had been outlawed for complicity in the Rye-House Plot of Charles the Second's reign, aware of the Lady Lisle's reputation for generous charity, sought refuge at her house. It would appear, from the evidence recorded in the State Trials, that Hicks was personally acquainted with this benevolent woman; and in the course of his flight, having reached Warminster, bethought himself of appealing to her for protection.

Accordingly, on Friday, July 24, 1685, he despatched a

messenger to Dunne, a baker who resided in the neighbourhood of Warminster, and requested him to go to
Lady Lisle's house, which was about twenty-six miles
distant, and inquire whether she could provide a temporary asylum for an old friend. Dunne executed his
mission. Lady Lisle inquired of him whether Hicks
had been in Monmouth's army. He told her that on
this point he could afford her no information. She then
asked whether Hicks had with him any other person.
He had, was Dunne's reply. Moved to compassion by
the story of their suffering and their need, Lady Lisle
then agreed to share her hospitality with them, and appointed them to come to her house on Tuesday evening.

There would seem to be little doubt but that Lady
Alicia thought Hicks was in danger on account of his
religious profession. If, however, she knew her guests
to have been concerned in the insurrection, she was
undoubtedly guilty, says Macaulay,* of what, in strict-
ness, was a capital crime. ‘For the law of principal
and accessory, as respects high treason, then was, and is
to this day, in a state disgraceful to English jurisprudence.
In cases of felony, a distinction founded on justice and
reason is made between the principal and the accessory
after the fact. He who conceals from justice one whom
he knows to be a murderer, is liable to punishment, but
not to the punishment of murder. He, on the other hand,
who shelters one whom he knows to be a traitor, is; according to all our jurists, guilty of high treason. It is
unnecessary to point out the absurdity and cruelty of a
law which includes under the same definition, and visits
with the same penalty, offences lying at the opposite

* Macaulay, ‘History of England,' ii. 219, 220

extremes of the scale of guilt. The feeling which makes
the most loyal subject shrink from the thought of giving
up to a shameful death the rebel who, vanquished,
hunted down, and in mortal agony, begs for a morsel of
bread and a cup of water, may be a weakness; but it is
surely a weakness very nearly allied to virtue, a weakness
which, constituted as human beings are, we can hardly
eradicate from the mind without eradicating many noble
and benevolent sentiments. A wise and good ruler may
not think it even right to sanction this weakness; but he
will generally connive at it, or punish it very tenderly
In no case will he treat it as a crime of the blackest dye.
Whether Flora Macdonald was justified in concealing
the attainted heir of the Stuarts, whether a brave soldier
of our own time was justified in assisting the escape of
Lavallette, are questions on which casuists may differ;
but to class such actions with the crimes of Guy Faux and
Fieschi, is an outrage to humanity and common sense.

‘ Such, however, is the classification of our law. It is
evident that nothing but a lenient administration could
make such a state of the law endurable. And it is just to
say that, during many generations, no English government,
save one, has treated with rigour persons guilty merely of
harbouring defeated and flying insurgents. To women
especially has been granted, by a kind of tacit prescrip-
tion, the right of indulging, in the midst of havoc and
vengeance, that compassion which is the most endearing
of all their charms. Since the beginning of the great
Civil War, numerous rebels, some of them far more important than Hicks or Nelthorpe, have been protected
from the severity of victorious governments by female
adroitness and generosity. But no English ruler who

has been thus fulfilled, the savage and implacable James alone excepted, has had the barbarity even to think of putting a lady to a cruel and shameful death for so venial and amiable a transgression.'

With these explanatory remarks from the pen of our most brilliant English historian, we resume our narrative.

On their arrival at her house, Hicks and Nelthorpe were received by Lady Lisle with a cordial welcome. But early on the following morning, Colonel Penruddock, acting on information communicated by one Barter, who had acted as their guide, and now turned traitor for the sake of the reward offered for their apprehension, took with him a company of soldiers, surrounded their asylum, and demanded instant admittance. Half an hour elapsed before any answer was made to his summons. At last some ladies, whom Penruddock supposed to be Lady Lisle's daughters, upon hearing the noise and clamour, looked out of window. 'There are rebels in the house,' cried Penruddock; and demanded, in the King's name, that they should be delivered to him. The steward, Carpenter, then came out. Penruddock and his soldiers immediately rushed in, and apprehended Hicks and Dunne, both of whom they found in the malthouse, whither, on hearing the alarm, they had betaken themselves, and the latter of whom had concealed himself in a small hole, and covered himself with hay. When these were arrested, Lady Lisle now made her appearance for the first time, pale but composed, and no way affrighted by the tumult which had broken in on the silence of the morning. 'Madam,' said Penruddock, 'you have done very ill in harbouring rebels, and giving entertainment to the King's enemies.' 'I know nothing of them,' said Lady Lisle; 'I am a stranger to it, that is, to the report which you make of them.' 'Pray, madam,' rejoined Penruddock, 'be so free and in-genuous with me, and so kind to yourself, as, if there be any other person that is concealed in any part of the house (for I am sure there is somebody else), to deliver him up, and you shall come to no further trouble.'

We can easily imagine Lady Lisle's mental struggle between her natural love of truth and her sense of the solemn obligations of hospitality. She felt, however, that at whatever cost to herself, she durst not betray the guest who had confided his safety to her.

'Her words were bonds, her oaths were oracles.'

She could neither falsify her word, nor break her plighted oath, nor give up a fugitive wretch to the death. She therefore denied that there was any one else in the house, and said, 'I know nothing of them.' But Pen-ruddock acted upon the intelligence he had received from the treacherous Barter. A rigid search was insti-tuted, and, finally, Nelthorpe was found concealed in the chimney.

Having secured the three fugitives, Hicks, Nelthorpe, and Dunne, Penruddock now arrested Lady Lisle on the charge of knowingly harbouring the King's enemies, and proceeded to remove his prisoners to the county jail at Southampton. With the fate of Hicks and Nelthorpe we shall not at present concern ourselves, but continue the sad story of Lady Lisle's misfortunes.

The rage of the Government against this poor woman was uncontrollable. They determined to bring her to trial without delay, though legally she could not be con-

victed until after the conviction of the rebels whom her
charity had sought to protect.   Exactly a month after
her arrest on Thursday, August 27, 1685--she was ar-
raigned before the infamous Judge Jeffreys - whose name
has become an historical synonym for brutal cruelty and
lust of blood--and the grand jury of Hampshire, including many of her neighbours and the principal gentry of
the county, at the city of Winchester.

The indictment, charging her with high treason, having
been read, Lady Lisle pleaded ' Not guilty.' *

Owing to her age and infirmities, and her dulness of
hearing, she requested that some friend might be allowed to
stand at her side, and acquaint her with what transpired
in the court during her trial.   The court granted her request, and appointed one Matthew Brown to act for her.

The jury having been sworn, they were respectively
addressed upon the crimes of which the prisoner was
accused, by Mundy and Pollexfen, the King's counsel.
Pollexfen, a Whig barrister of great note, had formerly
been counsel for Baxter, the illustrious Nonconformist,
but had been gained over by the court party, and now
appeared to prosecute an aged lady for extending the
rites of hospitality to distressed and persecuted men.

While Pollexfen was addressing the jury, Lady Lisle
rose up to speak, as if unable to endure the burden of
the false accusation with which he loaded her.   ' My
lord,' said she, ' as for what is said concerning the
rebellion, I can assure you I abhorred that rebellion as
much as any woman in the world—'

* Consult the Trial of Alice Lisle. in the Collection of State Trials, Howell's
Trials (edit. 1809-26), xi. 298-382; Burnet, 'History,' i. 648-9: and Act of 1st
year of William and Mary for annulling the attainder of Alice Lisle, widow.

Here Jeffreys interrupted her, and bade her, at that stage of the proceedings, to be silent.

Introducing Dunne as one of the witnesses for the Crown, Pollexfen informed his lordship that he gave his testimony very unwillingly, and therefore desired him to examine him a little the more strictly. Dunne, indeed, partly from his anxiety not to criminate Lady Alice, and partly from a dread of involving himself in the guilt of perjury by saying aught untrue, was in a state of great confusion and mental anxiety. Nor did the address of Jeffreys serve to re-assure him.

'Now, mark what I say to you, friend. I would not, by any means in the world, endeavour to fright you into anything, or any ways tempt you to tell an untruth, but provoke you to tell the truth, and nothing but the truth —that is the business we come about here. ("A Daniel come to judgment!" Dunne might reasonably have exclaimed). Know, friend, there is no religion that any man can pretend to, can give a countenance to lying, or can dispense with telling the truth. Thou hast a precious immortal soul, and there is nothing in the world equal to it in value. There is no relation to thy mistress, if she be so ; no relation to thy friend, nay, to thy father or thy child, nay, with all the temporal relations in the world, can be equal to thy precious immortal soul. Consider that the great God of heaven and earth, before whose tribunal thou, and we, and all persons are to stand at the last day, will call thee to an account for thy rescinding his truth, and take vengeance of thee for every falsehood thou tellest. I charge thee, therefore, as thou wilt answer it to the great God, the Judge of all the earth, that thou do not dare to waver one tittle from

the truth, upon any account or pretence whatsoever. . . .
I tell thee, God is not to be mocked, and thou canst not
deceive him, though thou mayest us. But I assure you,
if I catch you prevaricating in any the least tittle (and
perhaps I know more than you think I do; no, none
of your saints can save your soul, nor shall they save
your body either), I will be sure to punish every varia-
tion from the truth that you are guilty of'

Having thus abundantly terrified the witness, and
thrown him into a state of pitiable mental embarrass-
ment, he proceeded to interrogate him. Thinking him
too cautious and laboured in his replies, Jeffreys repeated
his warnings.

'Mr. Dunne, Mr. Dunne, have a care,' he said, his
brow as black as thunder, his face inflamed with passion;
'have a care, it may be more is known of this matter
than you think for.'

Dunne. 'My lord, I tell you the truth'

Jeffreys. 'Ay, be sure you do ; let me not take you
prevaricating'

Dunne. 'My lord, I speak nothing but the truth.'

Jeffreys. 'Well ; I only bid thee have a care. Truth
wants no subterfuge ; it always loves to appear naked, it
needs no enamel, nor any covering ; but lying, and
snivelling, and canting, and *Hicksing* always appear in
masquerade.'

The witness continued his examination, but could not
satisfy the judge, who continually interrupted him with
bursts of passion, relieved by occasional outbreaks of the
coarsest buffoonery. 'You see, gentlemen,' he exclaimed
to the astonished jury, 'what a precious fellow this is; a
very pretty tool to be employed upon such an errand; a

knave that nobody would trust for half-a-crown between
man and man; but he is the fitter to be employed about
such works. What pains is a man at to get the truth
out of their fellows, and it is with a vast amount of
labour only that we can squeeze a drop of it out of their
souls. Verily, a Turk has more title to an eternity of
bliss than these pretenders to Christianity !'

Jeffreys. ' Did you not tell Barter (the informer) that
you told my lady, when she asked whether he was acquainted with the concern, that he knew nothing of the
business ?'

Dunne. ' My lord, I did tell him so.'

Jeffreys (with an air of great sagacity). ' Ay, did you
so ? Then you and I must have a little further discourse.
Come, now, and tell us what business was that ? And
tell it us so that a man may understand and believe that
thou dost speak truth.'

Dunne. ' Does your lordship ask what that business
was ?'

Jeffreys. ' Ay, it is a plain question. What was that
business that my lady asked thee whether *the other man*
knew ; and then you answered her, that he did know
nothing of it ?'

The judge suspected that this business referred to the
connection of Hicks and Nelthorpe with Monmouth's
army, and hoped to beguile Dunne into an admission
that he had made their connection known to Lady
Lisle.

Dunne, not ignorant of the purport of Jeffreys' question, paused awhile.

Jeffreys. ' I tell thee to answer me what that business
was, thou lying Presbyterian knave !'

Still Dunne stood silent.

Jeffreys. 'He is now studying and musing how he shall prevaricate.'

Dunne. 'I cannot mind it, my lord, what it was.'

Jeffreys. 'But mind me, prithee : thou didst tell that honest man there, that my Lady Lisle asked of thee whether he knew anything of the business, and thou saidst, No. What was that business?'

Dunne. ''That business that Barter did not know of?'

Jeffreys. 'Yes, that is the business.' And he roared out, drawing together his black bushy eyebrows,—'Prithee, friend, consider the oath that thou hast taken; and that thou art in the presence of a God that cannot endure a lie, and whose holiness will not admit him to dispense with a lie.'

Dunne, alarmed and astonished, paused for five or six minutes. Then he faltered out, 'I cannot give an account of it, my lord.'

Jeffreys. 'O blessed God, was there ever such a villain upon the face of the earth? To what times are we reserved? Dost thou believe that there is a God?'

Dunne. 'Yes, my lord, I do.'

Jeffreys. 'Dost thou believe that that God can endure a lie?'

Dunne. 'No, my lord; I know he cannot.'

Jeffreys. 'And dost thou believe then that he is a God of truth?'

Dunne. 'Yes, my lord, I do.'

Jeffreys. 'Dost thou think that that God of truth may immediately sink thee into hell-fire if thou tellest a lie?'

Dunne. 'I do, my lord.'

Jeffreys. 'Dost thou believe that he does observe everything that thou thinkest, sayest, or doest; knows the secrets of thy heart; and knows whether thou tellest a lie or not, though perhaps it may be hid from us; and knows whether thou dost prevaricate or not ?'

Dunne. 'I know the Lord does know all things.'

Lashing himself into a most violent rage, Jeffreys exclaimed, as he turned his beetling brows upon the jury,—

'I hope, gentlemen, you take notice of the strange and horrible carriage of this fellow, and withal you cannot but observe the spirit of that sort of people, what a villanous and devilish one it is: a Turk is a saint to such a fellow as this; nay, a Pagan would be ashamed to be thought to have no more truth in him. O blessed Jesus ! what an age do we live in, and what a generation of vipers do we live among ! Thou wicked wretch !'— here he flashed his angry eyes at the unfortunate witness —'how dost thou appear to give testimony before even an earthly tribunal with so much impudence and falsehood, when every lie will cost thee so dear; and except a sincere hearty repentance, and the infinite mercy of the great God for this transgression of false witness-bearing, what hopes can there be for so profligate a villain as thou art, that so impudently stands in open defiance of the omnipresence, omniscience, and justice of God, by persisting in so palpable a lie? I therefore require it of you, in his name, to tell me the truth.'

Dunne, trembling and confused, faltered out, 'I cannot tell what to say, my lord.'

Jeffreys. 'O blessed God, was there ever such an impudent rascal ? Well, I will try once more, and tell thee what I mean. You said you told that honest man

preaching in private meetings (but I never heard that he was in the army, nor that Nelthorp was to come with him); and for that reason it was that I sent to him to come by night. As to Mr. Hicks, I did not in the least suspect him to have been in the army, being a Presbyterian minister that used to preach and not fight.'

Here Jeffreys broke out into one of his violent rages.

'But I will tell you,' said he, 'there is not one of those lying, snivelling, canting Presbyterians but, one way or another, had a hand in the rebellion. Presbytery has all manner of villany in it. Nothing but Presbytery could have made Dunne such a ·rogue. Show me a Presbyterian, and I'll show thee a lying knave.'

Lady Lisle (with the calm composure of an English lady). 'My Lord, I abhorred both the principles and practices of the late rebellion.'

Jeffreys. 'I am sure you had great reason for it.'

Lady Lisle. 'Moreover, my lord, I should have been the most ungrateful person living, should I have been disloyal, or acted anything against the present King, considering how much I was obliged to him for my estate.'

Jeffreys. 'Oh, then, ungrateful! Ungrateful adds to the load which is between man and man, and is the least crime that any one can be guilty of.'

Lady Lisle (resuming her defence). 'My lord, had I been tried in London, I could have had my Lady Abergavenny, and several other persons of quality, that would have testified how much I was against this rebellion, and with what detestation I spoke against it during the time of it; for I was all that time in London, and stayed there till after the Duke of Monmouth was beheaded;

and if I had certainly known the time of my trial in the country, I could have had the testimony of those persons of honour for me. But, my lord, I am told, and so I thought it would have been, that I should not have been tried as a traitor for harbouring Hicks till he was convicted for a traitor. My lord, I would take my death of it, that I never knew of Nelthorp's coming, nor anything of his being Nelthorp; I never asked his name; and if he had told it me, I had then remembered the proclamation. I do assure you, my Lord, for my own part, I did abhor those that were in that horrid plot and conspiracy against the King's life; I know my duty to my King better, and have always exercised it. I defy anybody in the world that ever knew the contrary to come and give testimony.'

Lady Lisle having paused for a minute or two, Jeffreys interjected, ' Have you any more to say ?'

Lady Lisle. ' As to what they say of my denying Nelthorp to be in my house, I was in great consternation and fear of the soldiers, who were very rude and violent, and could not be restrained by their officers from robbery, and plundering my house. I beseech your lordship to make that construction of it ; and I humbly beg of your lordship not to harbour an ill opinion of me because of those false reports that go about of me, relating to my carriage towards the old King, that I was any ways consenting to the death of King Charles I. ; for, my lord, that is as false as God is true. My lord, I was not out of my chamber all the day in which that King was beheaded, and I believe I shed more tears for him than any woman then living did ; and this the late Countess of Monmouth, and my Lady Marlborough, and my Lord

Chancellor Hyde, if they were alive, and twenty persons
of the most eminent quality, could bear witness for me.
And I do repeat it, my lord, as I hope to attain salvation, I never did know Nelthorp, and never did see
him before in my life; nor did I know of anybody's
coming but Mr. Hicks, and him I did know to be a
Nonconformist minister; and there being, as is well
known, warrants out to apprehend all Nonconformist
ministers, I was willing to give him shelter from these
warrants. I was come down but that week into the
country, when this man came to me from Mr. Hicks,
to know if he might be received at my house; and I
told him if Mr. Hicks pleased, he might come upon
Tuesday in the evening, and should be welcome; but
withal I told him, I must go away the Monday following
from that place, but while I stayed I would entertain
him. And I beseech your lordship to believe I had
no intention to harbour him but as a Nonconformist;
and that, I knew, was no treason. It cannot be imagined
that I would venture the hazard of my own life, and the
ruin both of myself and children, to conceal one that I
never knew in my life, as I did not know Mr. Nelthorp,
but had heard of him in the proclamation. And for that
white-headed man that speaks of my denying them, as I
said before, he was one of them that rifled and plundered
my house, and tore open my trunk; and if I should not
be convicted, he and the rest of them may be called to
account for what they did; for they ought not to have
meddled with my goods. Besides, my lord, I have a
witness that can testify what Mr. Nelthorp said when he
was examined before—'

Jeffreys (interrupting her). ' Look you, Mrs. Lisle, that

will signify little : but if you have any witnesses, call them, we will hear what they say. Who is that man you speak of?'

Lady Lisle. 'George Creed is his name; there he is.'

George Creed stood forth, and was interrogated by Jeffreys. 'Well, what do you know?'

Creed. 'I heard Nelthorp say that my Lady Lisle did not know of his coming, and did not know his name; nor had he ever told his name nor he named himself to Colonel Penruddock when he was taken.'

Jeffreys. 'Well, this is nothing : she is not indicted for harbouring Nelthorp, but Hicks Have you any more witnesses?'

Lady Lisle. 'No, my lord.'

Jeffreys. 'Have you any more to say for yourself?'

Lady Lisle. 'My lord, I came but five days ago into this part of the country—'

Jeffreys. 'Nay, I neither know nor care when you came into the country; it seems you came in time enough to harbour rebels.'

Lady Lisle. 'I stayed in London till all the rebellion was past and over; and I never uttered a good word for the rebels, nor ever harboured so much as a good wish for them in my mind. I know the King is my sovereign, and I know my duty to him, and if I would have ventured my life for anything, it should have been to serve him. I know it is his due, and I owed all I had in the world to him. But though I could not fight for him myself, my son did, he was actually in arms on the King's side in this business; I instructed him always in loyalty, and sent him thither; it was I that bred him up to fight for the King.'

One would have thought the sternest heart must have been melted to compassion by the earnest and simple eloquence of this address, which the gray hairs of the speaker seemed to render doubly impressive. Be sure there was scarcely a dry eye in the crowded court; only the inexorable Jeffreys remained unmoved, and burst out with the impatient query,—

'Well, have you done ?'

'Yes, my lord,' replied the prisoner, in a firm though sorrowful voice.

'Have you a mind to say anything more ?' he said, with a seeming show of impartiality.

She answered, 'No, my lord.'

'Then command silence,' said Jeffreys; and the crier immediately made the customary proclamation.

The tone and nature of his address to the jury will be inferred by the reader from the vehement scurrility of his examination of the witnesses. 'He declaimed during an hour,' says Macaulay,[*] 'against Whigs and Dissenters, and reminded the jury that the prisoner's husband had borne a part in the death of Charles I., a fact which had not been proved by any testimony, and which, if it had been proved, would have been utterly irrelevant to the issue.' He indulged in the grossest abuse of Lady Lisle, of her witness, of Nelthorp and Hicks, and wholly neglected to refer to the important statements made by the prisoner in her defence. Finally, in the face of all evidence, he declared it fully proved that she had harboured and sheltered Hicks with the certain knowledge that he had served in the rebel army.

---

* Macaulay, 'History of England,' ii. 222

At the conclusion of his harangue, Lady Lisle rose up
and began to speak to Jeffreys.

'My lord, if your lordship please—'

'Mistress,' he immediately exclaimed, 'you have had
your turn, and cannot be heard any more after the jury
is charged.'

'My lord,' persisted the prisoner, 'I did not know
Nelthorp—I declare it—before he was taken.'

'You are not indicted for Nelthorp,' said Jeffreys;
'but we are not to enter into dialogues now, the jury
must consider of it.'

The jury were evidently unconvinced of the prisoner's
guilt.   One of them said to the judge, 'Pray, my lord,
some of us desire to know of your lordship, in point of
law, whether it be the same thing, and equally treason,
in receiving Hicks *before* he was convicted of treason,
as if it had been *after ?'*

The reader will remember that Hicks had not been
tried, and as yet, in the eye of the law, was actually
innocent.

'It is all the same,' replied Jeffreys roughly; 'that
certainly can be no doubt; for if in case this Hicks had
been wounded in the rebels' army, and had come to her
house and there been entertained, but had died there of
his wounds, and so could never have been convicted, he
had been nevertheless a traitor.'

The jury now withdrew to consider their verdict. Notwithstanding the force and vehemence of Jeffreys' charge,
they entertained a strong belief in the innocence of the
unfortunate prisoner, and could not agree to convict her.
They remained a long time in consultation. Jeffreys,
accustomed to subservient juries, who brought in such

verdicts as he chose to direct, grew very wroth at this unexpected delay. 'How they could hesitate,' he exclaimed, 'in coming to a decision upon so plain a case, he knew not! Ay, they might have decided upon it without retiring!'

At length his wrath became uncontrollable, and he was about to send a threatening message that he would adjourn the court, and shut them up all night, when, after half an hour's absence, they returned. It would seem they had determined upon a verdict of acquittal, but were overawed by the menacing brows and furious glances of Jeffreys. Accordingly, they temporized.

'My lord,' exclaimed the foreman, 'we have one thing to beg of your lordship some directions in, before we can give our verdict in this case. We have some doubt upon us whether there be sufficient proof that she knew Hicks to have been in the army.'

This was the pivot on which the whole case turned; if she was ignorant of Hicks having served under Monmouth, she had committed no treason.

Jeffreys. 'There is as full proof as proof can be, but you are judges of the proof; for my part, I thought there was no difficulty in it.'

Foreman. 'My lord, we are in some doubt of it.'

Jeffreys. 'I cannot help your doubts. Was there not proved a discourse of the battle and of the army at supper-time?' (referring to an unsupported statement in Barter's evidence.)

Foreman. 'But, my lord, we are not satisfied that she had notice that Hicks was in the army.'

Jeffreys. 'I cannot tell what would satisfy you. Did she not enquire of Dunne whether Hicks had been in the army ! And when he told her he did not know, she did not say she would refuse him if he had been there, but ordered him to come by night, by which it is evident she suspected it ; and when he and Nelthorp came, she discoursed with them about the battle and the army. Come, come, gentlemen, it is a plain proof.'

Foreman (persisting in his anxious endeavour to save the accused). 'My lord, we do not remember that it was proved that she did ask any such question when they were there.'

Jeffreys. 'Then surely you do not remember anything that has passed ! Did not Dunne tell you there was such discourse, and she was by, and Nelthorp's name was named ? But if there were no such proof, the circumstances and management of the thing are as full a proof as can be ; I wonder what it is you doubt of.'

Lady Lisle (rising to protest against this bold injustice). 'My lord, I hope—'

Jeffreys (with a frown). 'You must not speak now.'

The jury retired, and after a short absence again returned, declaring themselves dissatisfied with the evidence submitted to them. For a third time* the inhuman judge sent them back, threatening them with the penalties of treason, and declaring them false to their God, their King, and their country. Thus menaced and brow-beaten, they at length, but with evident reluctance, returned a verdict of ' Guilty.'

Jeffreys could not restrain his delight at finding his victim bound, and in the toils. Addressing the jury, he expressed his surprise that any among them could have entertained a doubt as to their guilt, declaring, in his

* Rapin and Tindal, ' Hist. of England,' ii. 750.

conscience,—*his* conscience !—that the evidence was indisputably clear and definite, and that upon such evidence he would have convicted his own mother !—as probably he would, or upon still slighter testimony, if it would have pleased the King.

This judicial murder being so far perpetrated, Jeffreys adjourned the court until the following morning, Friday, August the 28th.

Lady Lisle, who throughout the trial had exhibited a courage and composure worthy of a Christian martyr, was brought to the bar, on the following morning, with several other prisoners, to receive sentence. Jeffreys made his usual profession of compassion, but concluded by condemning the noble woman, whose only crime was a generous hospitality, to be burned alive that very afternoon.

'Take notice, Mr. Sheriff,' said this callous monster, 'you are to prepare for the execution of this gentlewoman this afternoon : but withal, I give you, the prisoner, this intimation :—We that are the judges shall stay in town an hour or two ; you shall have pen, ink, and paper brought you, and if, in the meantime, you employ that pen, ink, and paper, and this hour or two well—you understand what I mean—it may be you may hear further from us, in a deferring the execution.' It has been supposed that he meant to intimate a gift of money would obtain this indulgence.

The prisoner was then removed from the bar, preserving the calm fortitude and unshrinking intrepidity she had exhibited throughout.

But the excess of barbarity which allowed her a few hours only to prepare for a terrible death moved the pity

and anger even of the class most devoted to the Crown
The clergy of Winchester Cathedral made an earnest
appeal to Jeffreys in her behalf, and he could not afford
to neglect the remonstrances of so powerful and loyal a
body. He consented to put off the execution for five
days, namely, until Wednesday, the 2nd of September.

The interval was employed by her friends in vigorous
efforts to obtain the royal mercy.

Lady St. John and Lady Abergavenny, whose loyalty
could not be doubted, addressed themselves to the King,
declaring that they had known Lady Lisle for many
years, and could bear witness to her attachment to the
Crown. James replied that he would do nothing in the
matter, having left all to the Lord Chief Justice.

Next the royal ear was besieged by a peer of great
influence, Louis de Duras, Earl of Feversham, com-
mander-in-chief of the royal forces which had defeated
Monmouth, and who had been offered a bribe of one
thousand pounds if he secured the royal pardon. But
even his intercession was in vain.

Finding that all hope of life must be abandoned, Lady
Lisle prepared to meet her fate with resignation; but not
unnaturally shrinking from a death so terrible as burning,
she addressed to the obdurate James a brief petition. It
ran as follows :—

' *To the King's Most Excellent Majesty :*

'The humble Petition of Alicia Lisle

' Humbly Sheweth,—That your Petitioner lieth under a
sentence of death for harbouring one John Hickes, and
is sentenced to be burned on Wednesday next : that she
is the daughter of Sir White Beconsaw, descended of an

ancient and honourable family, and related to some of
the best families of the nobility of this kingdom.

'Wherefore your Petitioner humbly begs your Majesty,
that execution may be altered from burning to beheading,
and may be respited for four days.

'And your Petitioner shall pray, &c.'

To this petition James replied that no further respite
could be permitted, but that in compliance with her
prayer he would commute her sentence from burning to
beheading.

The execution of Alicia Lisle took place in the afternoon of Wednesday, the 2nd of September, in the
market-place of the city of Winchester, in the presence
of an immense multitude of spectators. What reader
cannot picture to himself the details of the dread scene?
The fatal block—the headsman's axe—the scaffold, with
its drapery of woe—the glittering pikes of the guards—
the aged lady, calm and serene in the consciousness of a
well-spent life—the heaving, restless, tumultuous crowd,
swayed to and fro by the violence of its emotions—the
blow, which completed the most barbarous murder of a
barbarous time;—all are easily recalled by the dullest
imagination. Dame Alicia Lisle made no attempt to
address the crowd, but delivered to the Sheriff a paper
containing her last solemn asseverations of innocence.*

* The paper referred to was couched in the following terms:—'Gentlemen,
friends, and neighbours,—It may be expected that I should say something at my
death, and in order thereunto I shall acquaint you that my birth and education
were both near this place, and that my parents instructed me in the fear of God,
and I now die of the Reformed Protestant religion; that if ever Popery should
return into this nation it would be a very great and severe judgment; that I die
in expectation of the pardon of all my sins, and of acceptance with God the Father,
by the imputed righteousness of Jesus Christ, he being the end of the law for

Her remains were given up to her relatives, and by them deposited, with all due reverence, in Ellingham Church-yard, near Ringwood, Hampshire.

Of the unfortunate men who had unwittingly brought Lady Lisle to a doom so terrible, it is sufficient to say that Hickes was executed on the 6th of October 1685— Nelthorp on the 30th of the same month. In his last speech, the latter completely cleared Lady Lisle from the crime of which she had been accused, and in the year following the accession of William III. (1689), her attainder was reversed by Act of Parliament. Not a shadow rests upon the fair fame of this noble and generous lady.

righteousness to every one that believes. I thank God, through Jesus Christ, that I do depart under the blood of sprinkling, which speaketh better things than that of Abel, God having made this chastisement an ordinance to my soul. I did once as little expect to come to this place on this occasion as any person in this place or nation ; therefore let all learn not to be high-minded, but fear.

'The Lord is a sovereign, and will take what way be sees best to glorify himself in and by his poor creatures ; and I do humbly desire to submit to his will, praying to him that I may possess my soul in patience. The crime that was laid to my charge was for entertaining a Nonconformist minister and others in my house, the said minister being sworn to have been in the late Duke of Monmouth's army ; but I have been told that if I had denied them, it would not at all have affected me : I have no excuse but surprise and fear, which I believe my jury must make use of to excuse their verdict to the world. I have been also told that the court did use to be of counsel for the prisoner ; but instead of advice, I had evidence against me from thence, which, though it were only by hearsay, might possibly affect my jury, my defence being but such as might be expected from a weak woman ; but such as it was, I did not hear it repeated again to the jury, which, as I have been informed, is usual in such cases. However, I forgive all the world, and therein all those that have done me wrong ; and in particular, I forgive Colonel Penruddock, although he told me that he could have taken these men before they came to my house. . . .

'I do acknowledge His Majesty's favour in revoking my sentence. I pray God to preserve him, that he may long reign in mercy as well as justice ; and that he may reign in peace ; and that the Protestant religion may flourish under him. I also return thanks to God, and the reverend clergy that assisted me in my imprisonment.   'ALICIA LISLE'

IV

The Charity that Endureth all Things.

A COMPANION PICTURE TO LADY LISLE.

THE STORY OF ELIZABETH GAUNT.*

NOTHER of the victims of James the Second's jealous cruelty was Elizabeth Gaunt, wife of William Gaunt, yeoman, of Whitechapel. She was a devout woman, of the Baptist persuasion, who, with 'the peculiar manners and phraseology which then distinguished her sect, had a large charity.' She constantly visited the prisons, and her wide benevolence embraced equally those who suffered for crime as for conscience' sake. But it was with especial pleasure that she relieved the unhappy of all religious denominations, and with still greater pleasure did she minister to the wants of those who suffered by their opposition to Papal bigotry and the tyranny of the Crown.

Among the persons concerned in the Rye House Plot was a man named James Burton. By his own confession

* Trials of Fernley and Elizabeth Gaunt, in Howell's 'Collection of the State Papers,' vol. x.; Burnet, 'History of his Own Time,' i. 649; Lord Macaulay, 'History of England,' ch. v.

he had been present when the design of assassinating the King was discussed, although he declared that he had strenuously opposed the crime. His share in the conspiracy, however, was discovered by the Government; he was declared an outlaw, and a reward of £100 offered for his apprehension. He fled from his house to avoid arrest, and, in his hour of need, found an asylum under the hospitable roof of Elizabeth Gaunt. After lying for some months concealed, she procured a boat which took him down the river to Gravesend, where he was put on board a vessel bound for Amsterdam. At the moment of their parting, she did not forget his future wants, and generously put into his hands a sum of money—£5—which, for her means, was very large.

After an absence of two years in Holland, Burton returned to England, and served with Monmouth's army at Sedgemoor. About three weeks after the utter collapse of the rebellion on that bloody field, this restless and unquiet spirit fled to London, and took refuge in the house of John Fernley, a barber in Whitechapel. Fernley was very poor, and very much in debt. He knew that a reward of £100 had been offered by the Government for Burton's apprehension; but he was too honest, too noble-minded, to betray the fugitive, who, in an agony of extreme peril, had claimed the shelter of his roof.

Burton, however, was incapable of a generous thought or a grateful feeling. He heard it generally rumoured that the King's wrath was far more strongly excited against those who harboured rebels than against the rebels themselves. James had publicly declared, that of all forms of treason, the concealment of traitors from his vengeance was the most unpardonable.

Love of life and lust of gold were two powerful motives which stifled in Burton's breast every other passion.
He delivered himself up to the Government, and, with
unparalleled treachery, gave information against his bene-
factors, Fernley and Elizabeth Gaunt! They were immediately arrested.

No time was lost by the Government in sacrificing
these new victims. Elizabeth Gaunt was brought to trial
at the Old Bailey, on Monday the 19th of October 1685,
before Lord Chief-Justice Jones—of whom it is enough
to say that he was a worthy successor to Jeffreys.

Her indictment charged her, as a false traitor, with
having secretly, wickedly, devilishly, and traitorously
entertained, concealed, comforted, and sustained James
Burton, well knowing him to be an outlaw and a rebel;
and with having given him £5 for his maintenance. She
pleaded ' Not guilty.'

A jury having been duly sworn, the Attorney-General,
who acted as Crown prosecutor, opened the case with
the usual address to the jury. It was characterized by
the usual want of truth and justice—virtues which did
not flourish in our courts of law during the Stuart reigns.

Burton was then examined. The villain, says Macaulay, whose life she had preserved, had the heart and
the forehead to appear as the principal witness against
her. Other evidence was produced to corroborate the
infamous informer's testimony, but none succeeded in
proving that she knew Burton to have been a rebel. He
admitted that in all his interviews with her he had never
discussed the plot; nor had she, in any of her conversa-
tions with him, referred to the King's proclamation. It
was evident that she had assisted him out of her bound-

less charity and religious enthusiasm, and not with any knowledge of his share in a murderous conspiracy. Had she been aware of all his guilt, probably even her generous heart would have shrunk from rendering him any assistance.

It is needless to say, however, that she was convicted. A brutal judge and a subservient jury were the ready tools of a revengeful monarch. She was convicted, and sentenced to be burnt alive.

Her execution took place at Tyburn, on Friday, the 22nd of October, in the presence of an immense and sympathizing multitude. She suffered with the serene courage of a martyr, and with the cheerfulness of a Christian. She said charity was a part of her religion, as well as faith—this at worst was the feeding an enemy—so she hoped she had her reward with Him for whose sake she did this service, how unworthy soever the person was that made so ill a return for it; and she rejoiced that God had honoured her to be the first that suffered by fire in this reign, and that her suffering was a martyrdom for that religion which was all love. William Penn, who was present at the melancholy spectacle, afterwards related that, when she calmly arranged the straw about her in such a manner as to shorten her sufferings, the by-standers could not restrain their tears.

It was much noticed, observes Macaulay, that while the foulest judicial murder which had disgraced even these times was perpetrating, a tempest burst forth such as had not been known since that great hurricane which had raged around the death-bed of Oliver. The oppressed Puritans reckoned up, not without a gloomy satisfaction, the houses which had been blown down and the ships which had been cast away, and derived some consolation from thinking that Heaven was bearing awful testimony against the iniquity which afflicted the earth. Since that terrible day, no woman has suffered death in England for any political offence.

Mrs. Gaunt bequeathed to posterity a paper in which she vindicated her character. It is written in ' no graceful style,' but with great earnestness and simplicity, and produced a powerful impression on the public mind. In it she expressed her implicit faith in the goodness of God, and her entire submission to his will. She expressed no regret for the act of charity which had met with so base a requital, but said of it proudly, ' My fault was one which a prince might well have forgiven! I did but relieve a poor family, and, lo! I must die for it!' She declared her innocence of any disloyal or traitorous design against her sovereign, and that therefore she had committed no crime which called for repentance. She complained of the insolence of her judges, of the inhumanity of her jailer, and of the tyranny of the sovereign, to satisfy whose vindictive rage so many victims had been sacrificed. In so far as they had injured her, she forgave them; but in that they were hostile to the cause and law of Christ, she left them to the final judgment of the King of kings.

Thus passed away Elizabeth Gaunt, a woman whose name and memory all English girls should accept as a precious heritage.

V

Mental Energy and Self-Reliance.

THE STORY OF ELIZABETH INCHBALD.*

ELIZABETH.SIMPSON—surely a plain and un-
pretending patronymic—was born in 1753, at
Standingfield, near Bury St. Edmunds, in the
bucolic county of Suffolk. Her father, who died when
she was about eight years of age, occupied the position
of a small gentleman farmer. His means were limited,
but, owing probably to his high personal character, he
was much esteemed by his more opulent and aristocratic
neighbours. They did not continue their notice of the
family, however, after his death; their interest in the
bereaved household growing 'fine by degrees, and beau-
tifully less.' A very dull and quiet home, therefore, was
that of the youthful Elizabeth, whose quick spirit and
lively intellect soon learned to chafe at its uniformity and
inaction.

Owing to want of means, her education was sorely
neglected. In fact, she derived but little assistance from

* Our principal authorities for this sketch are Boaden's ' Life of Mrs. Inchbald,
(2 vols., 1833); and a clever article in ' Temple Bar,' vol. i. 483-495.

the instructions of others, and was emphatically 'self-taught.' Reading and writing appeared to 'come to her by nature,' so rapid was her acquisition of knowledge.

'It is astonishing,' she says, in her autobiography, 'how much all girls are inclined to literature to what boys are. My brother went to school seven years, and never could spell. I and two of my sisters, though we were never taught, could spell from infancy.' The intellect of girls is certainly more precocious than that of boys. A lass of sixteen thinks and reasons like a woman: a lad of the same age is but an overgrown boy. But left thus to herself, her choice of reading was indiscriminate. Novels, plays, poems—whatever fell into her hands—she eagerly devoured. The fare was often unwholesome, and her naturally healthy mind at length revolted from it. 'If I stay here,' she exclaimed, 'I shall die!' She longed for a wider sphere than her dull home afforded, because she felt within herself the capabilities of a higher and better existence. The romance of her young imagination, moreover, had been stimulated, not only by the course of reading she had adopted, but by frequent visits to the theatre at Bury St. Edmunds. Mrs. Simpson was an ardent votary of the drama, and being acquainted with several performers, not only presented herself before the foot-lights three or four times a week, but frequently visited 'behind the scenes.' What a world of enchantment was thus revealed to the young and ardent Elizabeth! For youth does not detect the tinsel and the paint, the falsehood and the sham. It sees on the stage a literal presentment of Fairyland. All is bright, and beautiful, and melodious! The balletines are really nymphs and oreads; yon cavalier is

not a hard-worked 'utility actor' at £2 a week, but a
gallant gentleman, gay, dashing, and triumphant! The
brook flows merrily, the fountain flashes brightly, the
green leaves wave in the evening breeze, and youth
thinks nothing of the pasteboard and the painted canvas!
Ah, happy youth, that can thus transport itself into the
'gardens of Armida' or 'Calypso's Isle' at will, and passes
all its swift and glowing hours in a 'midsummer-night's
dream!'

One might say of Elizabeth Simpson what Bulwer
Lytton finely says of his delicate Viola*:—'Oh, how
gloriously that life of the stage—that fairy world of music
and song—dawned upon her! It was the only world
that seemed to correspond with her strange childish
thoughts. It appeared to her as if, cast hitherto on a
foreign shore, she was brought at last to see the forms
and hear the language of her native land. Beautiful and
true enthusiasm, rich with the promise of genius! Boy
or man, thou wilt never be a poet, if thou hast not felt
the ideal, the romance, the Calypso's Isle, that opened to
thee, when, for the first time, the magic curtain was
drawn aside, and let in the world of poetry on the world
of prose!'

Such a training is necessarily a dangerous one, and
many a bright young life has been saddened and over-
clouded by a sudden awakening to the terrible reality of
the work-day world. Only a very strong intellect can
survive it uninjured; and, happily, such an intellect was
Elizabeth Inchbald's.

One of her brothers in 1770 obtained an engagement
at the Norwich theatre, under a manager named Griffith.

---

* Lord Lytton, 'Zanoni,' book i., chap i.

This circumstance aroused the ambition of our young heroine—we advisedly use the word heroine, for her life had really much of the heroic element in it—and though she suffered from an impediment in her speech, which most persons would have considered a fatal obstacle to success in the theatrical profession, she privately addressed herself to the manager, requesting an engagement. He replied in complimentary terms, but, as might be expected, declined her services. The correspondence, however, continued ; and it is to be supposed Mr. Griffith expressed himself with a warmth of appreciation of her epistolary talents that compensated for the rebuff he administered to her dramatic ambition, inasmuch as she speedily elevated him into a very magnificent and brilliant ideal, inscribing her pocket-books and diaries with the flattering legend :—

'RICHARD GRIFFITH.
Each dear letter of thy name is harmony.'

At Bury St. Edmunds she became acquainted with a Mr. Inchbald, an actor of no great merit, but a man of integrity and amiable disposition. Her personal charms and remarkable talents made a great impression on him, and after Elizabeth's return to Standingfield, he made a definite proposal of marriage. But Elizabeth's mind was now filled with visions of future fame, to be realized in the great metropolis, and she was little disposed to entertain the suit of a lover who was considerably her senior.

Sick of her monotonous home existence, she at length determined upon one of the boldest enterprises that ever entered the head of a girl of eighteen ;—an enterprise which, though in her case it was eventually crowned with

success, was not the less blamable on the score of imprudence, or objectionable as a breach of decorum and
the wisely ordered regulations of respectable society.

While residing with a friend at Bury St. Edmunds,
she paid a clandestine visit to Norwich, in the hope that
a personal interview with Mr. Griffith might secure her
an engagement in his dramatic company. Failing in
this attempt, she resolved upon a journey to London,
without making it known to any of her friends or family.
'On the 11th of April 1772,' she says in her *Diary*,
'early in the morning, I left my mother's house unknown
to any one, came to London in the Norwich fly, and got
lodgings in the "Rose and Crown," in (St.) John Street.'
A small sum of money, and a bandbox containing her
wearing apparel, constituted the 'capital' with which
Elizabeth Simpson embarked on her perilous venture.

Her first care after her arrival in London was to seek
an interview with King and Reddish, the guiding spirits
of Drury Lane Theatre. King promised to call on her,
but did not; and supposing him to be prevented by the
meanness of her domicile, she removed to the 'White
Swan,' Holborn. There for some days she anxiously
awaited the appearance of the two managers, occupying
herself in reading, or in excursions about the great city
—of which, however, she could have seen but little,
since she avoided the busy streets, and visited only the
least frequented thoroughfares.

After awhile, she wrote to one of her married sisters,
then living in London, and acquainted her with the step
she had taken. While expecting her answer, she ac-
cidentally met with the husband of another sister, or, as
she quaintly says in her *Diary*, 'happened of brother

Slender.' She was thus brought into contact with her sisters, and soon afterwards she wisely took up her residence with the Slenders.

She continued her negotiations with the Drury Lane potentates, but found the entrance upon a theatrical life attended with much anxiety and peril for a young, beautiful, and unprotected woman. She met with many indignities, suffered many insults, was often repulsed, brow-beaten, disappointed; until at length she found an old friend in Mr. Inchbald, and applying to him for advice, was reminded that she could only be effectually defended and supported by a husband. 'But who would marry me?' said the lady.

'I would,' replied Mr. Inchbald; 'if now you would have me.'

'Yes, sir,' said the now penitent Elizabeth; 'and would for ever be grateful.'

This straightforward answer was dictated by no impulse of romantic love, but she really appreciated his good sense, his amiability, and integrity. She felt the truth of his observation, and her heart being occupied with ambition rather than the usual womanly fancies of a young beauty, gave her hand to her prudent counsellor without regret.

On the 9th of June 1772, Elizabeth Simpson was married to George Inchbald according to the forms of the Roman Catholic religion, and in the presence of her sister and brother-in-law. The next day the marriage ceremony was again performed between them, according to the Protestant rites. The same evening the bride and her friends repaired to the theatre to see the bridegroom play the part of Sir Charles Oakley, in Hoadley's comedy of *The Jealous Wife.* The union contracted under such singular circumstances was attended by considerable domestic happiness.

Mr. Inchbald and his wife now set out on a professional tour in the north, and the romantic Elizabeth discovered how little there is to satisfy an aspiring mind or a sensible heart in the profession of a strolling player. Having been carefully instructed by her husband in elocution, she made her first appearance on any stage at Edinburgh, on the 4th of September. She performed Cordelia to her husband's King Lear.

'The discipline,' it has been well observed, 'imposed on persons who wish to overcome an impediment in their speech is not conducive to spirited or very natural elocution. There is always a perceptible drawl, and a slowness in their utterance, which can only be suitable to certain passages. Mrs. Inchbald was not exempt from these disadvantages, and her first efforts were of course more obnoxious to this reproach than was subsequently the case. Though the intelligence of her reading and the beauty of her appearance produced their natural effect, it was felt that there was a want of warmth and impulse in her impersonation, and the general impression was chilly and formal.'

While in Edinburgh, Mrs. Inchbald applied herself to the study of French, a study which unexpectedly proved of practical advantage. Her husband suddenly came to the determination to visit France, partly because Mrs. Inchbald's health needed a change, and partly because he was desirous to burst upon the world as a portrait painter.

With slender funds the adventurous couple started on

their journey. They soon found reason to regret their
rashness. They visited Paris, saw many French landscapes, made many agreeable French acquaintances, but
the portrait painter met with few patrons, and it finally
became necessary to return to England. They resided
awhile at Brighton, plunged into the very depths of
poverty. On several occasions they were without food,
and once they were compelled to seek their dinner in a
turnip-field. An engagement at Liverpool was at length
obtained, and thither Mr. Inchbald and his wife gladly
betook themselves. They made there the acquaintance
of Mrs. Siddons and her brother, John Kemble, afterwards so illustrious an ornament of the English stage.
Their society was keenly relished by Mrs. Inchbald, who
derived much intellectual profit from their refined and
graphic conversation. She studied now under John
Kemble's guidance, and familiarized herself with the
masterpieces of English literature. It was at this time
she sketched the outline of the 'Simple Story,' and in
the elegant, accomplished, and dignified Doriforth she
pleased herself by representing John Kemble.

From Liverpool we may accompany our heroine to
Leeds, where she and her husband obtained an engagement in Tate Wilkinson's company, then esteemed
second only to the dramatic corps of the metropolis.
They had thus reached the 'turning-point' in the long
struggle to which they had been condemned. Their
income was larger, their reputation steadily increasing;
friends gathered around them who could appreciate their
merits and high character. But in one day—nay, in one
moment—the shadow of death fell heavily on the brightening scene. *Sic transit felicitas mundi!* How old the

moral, yet how ever new in its pregnant truth! Inscribe
it, my friends, on your heart of hearts; weave the cypress
in your most radiant chaplets; place the angel with the
inverted torch ever at your feasts—for no man can tell
when the darkness cometh.

An affection of the heart suddenly carried off Mr.
Inchbald.   His wife's grief was worthy of his merits; for
he had been a gentle and sympathizing friend and husband.   She records the day of her bereavement in her
Diary as 'a day of horror;' and characterizes the
following week as 'a week of grief, horror, and almost
despair.'   On the last day of the year she remarks, with
emphatic sincerity, that she 'began the year a happy
wife—finished it a wretched widow.'

We find her now, at the age of twenty-six, a widow,
an actress, and a beautiful woman; in all three capacities
exposed to undeserved obloquy and unjustifiable insult. .
Her friends could not but recognize the peculiar dangers
of her position, and some of the more enthusiastic would
have had her abandon a profession which naturally exposed her to the shafts of calumny.

A lady in Edinburgh, with more zeal than discretion,
endeavoured to bring the influence of Dr. Geddes, a well-
known divine, to bear upon her, with the view of securing
her retirement from the stage.   To his honour be it
said, he showed himself too liberal and too enlightened
to join in the attempt to fix a stigma upon a respectable
profession.   'In his sensible letter,' says a forcible writer,
'in which he avows that, with François de Sales, he con-
siders a play an indifferent thing, and does not regard
actors and actresses as necessarily bad people, he

leaves Mrs. Inchbald to decide whether in her heart she conceives her avocations incompatible with her duties as a Christian, and the exact observance of her religion. It is not to be doubted that Mrs. Inchbald gave mature consideration to the arguments of her friends; and if she decided to continue in the profession of her husband, to which she had been so long attached, and for which she had endured so many sacrifices, it was in the firm conviction that her strength of character and devotion to her duties would bear her harmless through the dangers of her career.'

Mrs. Inchbald, having gained experience of the stage and improved herself in the elocutionary art, now determined to try her fortune in London. She was sensible, too, of possessing decided literary talents, and saw that the metropolis was the only arena where they could be developed. She became a member of Mr. Harris's company at Drury Lane, at the enormous salary of £1, 6s. 8d. per week, subsequently increased to the still more enormous weekly stipend of £2. When a friend of Mrs. Inchbald's remonstrated with Harris for offering so low a remuneration, he characteristically replied that, ' if she had a low salary, she did high business, and could not be paid both in consequence and money.'

Mrs. Inchbald made her début in the character of ' Bellario' in Beaumont and Fletcher's exquisite drama of *Philaster*. She afterwards played with indifferent success in various parts, not making any great impression upon the public until she appeared as ' Angelica' in the old play of *The Fop's Fortune*.

It was in this character that Harris first saw her act, and his warm expressions of approval induced her to place in his hands a farce she had written. It was refused; probably it was never read, or assuredly Mr. Harris could hardly have allowed his friends to spread a rumour about the town that it was 'indecent, and had not a word rightly spelt.' Mrs. Inchbald had a brave heart, and these checks and calumnies could not daunt her. She removed to the little theatre in the Haymarket, where George Coleman the elder—himself a popular dramatist as well as a successful manager—produced her farce, although, after having read it, he observed that 'he had never met such a cramp hand, or was so much puzzled to make out a piece.' Her defective caligraphy was the result of her self-education, though it may be added that clever men and women—wits, dramatists, poets—have from all time asserted the prerogative of writing 'a villanous hand.' *

Mrs. Inchbald's farce was called *The Mogul's Tale*, and

* On this point we may perhaps be allowed a short digression. A writer in 'Blackwood,' some years ago, made some amusing remarks on the handwriting of various distinguished authors, which, on the whole, will be found to confirm the assertion we have made above. 'Wordsworth's writing,' be says, ' was clumsy, strong, and unequal; Coleridge's, beautiful, but very quaint and eccentric. Jeffrey, the distinguished reviewer, wrote as if against time "with a stick dipped in ink "—never was such a hideous, unintelligible scrawl—yet with a power and vivacity about it not unlike the man. Gifford had the slow, precise, and elaborate fingers of a commentator; Hogg's autograph was stiff, rigid, scraggy, as if it had never been designed but for the "chronicling of small beer." Peel wrote a sober, scholar-like hand; Croly with a "furious, rambling, excursive, but most vigorous paw." Sir David Brewster *scratched*, as with a hen's foot, his lined sentences; Chalmers wrote like a madman; Leslie, the great chemist, as if he were "a duck spluttering out of a dubble."'

Everybody knows how extravagantly bad was the writing of the first Napoleon; and Byron would never have obtained a medal for penmanship at any 'Ladies' Seminary.' Charles Dickens writes with nerve and force; Bulwer Lytton, a small and singularly irregular hand. Sala's writing is exquisitely legible, but very small and precise; Millais dashes down his strokes as he does his colours; and Lord Brougham splutters a very unreadable hand. Thackeray wrote clearly and vigorously; Mark Lemon, a bold, uneven hand. So much for the penmanship of men of genius.

to prevent the authorship being suspected, she played in it an indifferent part. It was received with the greatest approbation, and held the stage for many nights. We are told that her anxiety, both as actress and authoress, was so extreme, on the first night, that she completely lost her self-possession. Having to take up as her cue the words 'Hyde Park Corner,' she was so overcome with nervous timidity that she could hardly utter them, and her old habit of stuttering returning—as is customary in cases of excitement—she faltered out the words 'Ha-y-de P-p-pa-ark Co-co-co-corner!' in so doleful a tone and with so awful a visage as to convulse her audience with laughter—a circumstance which may have incidentally contributed to the success of the piece by predisposing her hearers to be amused.

The success of *The Mogul's Tale* emboldened Mrs. Inchbald to remind the manager that he held in his possession a comedy of hers which she had forwarded under the *nom de plume* of Woodby. He read, accepted, and produced it under the title of *I'll Tell you What.* She realized by its performance the sum of £100.

The clouds which had so long brooded over her adventurous career were now dissipated, and the sunshine of success gilded all her future path. The energy which had braved so many obstacles, the hopefulness which had survived so many defeats, were crowned with the good fortune they deserved. In rapid succession appeared the following dramas:—

Such Things Are, which brought her in	£410	12	0
The Married Man,	£100	0	0
The Wedding Day,	£200	0	0
The Midnight Hour,	£130	0	0

Every One has his Fault, ...	£700	0 0
Wives as they Were, and } *Maids as they Are,* ...... } ...	£427	10 0
Lovers' Vows, ...	£150	0 0

We may conjecture that she realized upwards of £3000 by her numerous dramatic ventures.

In 1791 she made her début as a novelist, producing the well-known romance in four volumes, 'A Simple Story.' Probably she called it 'simple' in allusion to her plainness of style, and because her characters were drawn from nature; but the plot is both intricate and complex, and many of the scenes smell of the stage rather than of real life. It is, however, a work of great interest and of remarkable ability, and may still be read with advantage. Some of the incidents are borrowed from her own wide and varied experience.

In 1796 she published her second novel, 'Nature and Art,' in two volumes. It is a work of merit, but inferior to the 'Simple Story' in conception and execution. Its design may be inferred from the moral which closes it: 'Let the poor be no more their own persecutors—no longer pay homage to wealth: instantaneously the whole idolatrous worship will cease—the idol will be broken.' In both her novels Mrs. Inchbald writes like a woman who has suffered much and struggled long, and she was one of the first of our novelists to express a deep and genuine sympathy with the poor. The following passage, which is often quoted, seems to us replete with simple pathos; it describes the miseries of a servant's life in London:—

' In romances, and in some plays, there are scenes of dark and unwholesome mines, wherein the labourer works

during the brightest day by the aid of artificial light.
There are, in London, kitchens equally dismal, though
not quite so much exposed to damp and noxious vapours.
In one of these underground abodes, hidden from the
cheerful light of the sun, poor Agnes was doomed to toil
from morning till night, subjected to the commands of
a dissatisfied mistress, who, not estimating as she ought
the misery incurred by serving her, constantly threatened
her servants with a dismission, at which the unthinking
wretches would tremble merely from the sound of the
words: for to have reflected—to have considered what
their purport was—to be released from a dungeon, relieved from continual upbraidings and vile drudgery, must
have been a subject of rejoicing; and yet, because these
good tidings were delivered as a menace, custom had
made her hearer fearful of the consequences. So, death
being described to children as a disaster, even poverty
and shame will start from it with affright; whereas, had
it been pictured with its benign aspect, it would have
been feared but by few, and many, many, would welcome
it with gladness.'

We have sketched the portrait of an admirable woman ;
but it must not be supposed she was without a defect of
character—that in any wise she could be compared to

'The faultless monster which the world ne'er saw.'

She was vain of her beauty to an extent scarcely to be
reconciled with her general good sense and the higher
qualities of her heart and mind. Thus, in her *Diary* we
find the following candid avowals:—

'1798. Rehearsing *Lovers' Vows:* happy, but for a

suspicion amounting to certainty—that of a rapid appearance of age in my face.'

'1799. Excessively happy, but for the still nearer approach of age.'

'1800. Still happy, but for my still increasing appearance of declining years.'

And it is said—though the anecdote is open to some doubt—that when John Kemble paid a leave-taking visit to her, on the occasion of his visiting the Continent, she received him with her face turned to the wall, and in that position continued throughout the interview, to conceal from him the ravages time had wrought on a once lovely countenance.

After all, her vanity was so open, so candid, so undisguised, that we may regard it as the eccentricity of a strong mind rather than the absurdity of a weak one.

Mrs. Inchbald was penurious in her habits—the natural consequence of the privations in which she had passed her early years; but her heart melted at a tale of pity, and her generosity towards her family was surpassingly beautiful. She allowed an invalid sister £100 per annum, cheerfully enduring the wants and necessities the sacrifice of so large a portion of her income brought upon her.

'Many a time this winter,' she records in her *Diary*, 'when I cried for cold, I said to myself, " But, thank God, my sister has not to stir from her room: she has her fire lighted every morning, all her provisions bought and brought ready cooked; she is now the less able to bear what I bear, and how much more should I suffer but for this reflection."' Well might she add, 'I trust I please God, though I may not please his creatures. I have always been aspiring, and now my sole ambition is to go to heaven when I die.'

But that she carried her parsimony to an extreme may be inferred from the following anecdote:—'When she was living at Kensington, Miss Wilkinson and Mrs. Siddons drove out in a pony-chaise to visit her. They were detained rather late at her house, and, to save time, wished to take a shorter route home than that by which they had come. But as this would involve paying a turnpike, and neither of them had any money, they asked her to lend them twopence. To their surprise they were steadfastly refused. "I'll lend you ten pounds," she said, "because you'll remember to p-p-pay; but I won't lend you twopence, because that you'll never pay again."'

During the latter part of her life Mrs. Inchbald lived in almost complete seclusion, preparing herself for that great change which the highest and the humblest, the wittiest and the least gifted, alike must undergo. Her last literary labour was writing biographical and critical prefaces to a 'Collection of Plays,' in twenty-five volumes. She also made a 'Collection of Farces,' in seven volumes, and edited 'The Modern Theatre,' in ten volumes. Her death took place at Kensington on the 1st of August 1821.

No great events or stirring incidents characterized her career; but as the life of a clever, persevering, noble-hearted woman, who was tried by many temptations but conquered all, who in her darkest hour never bated one jot of heart or hope, and who practised the largest charity and the noblest self-denial. it is neither without interest nor value.

VI

𝔉aithful to the 𝔈nd.

THE STORY OF LADY ARABELLA STUART.[*]

'Where London's Towere its turrets show,
  So stately by the Thames's side,
Faire Arabella, child of woe!
  For many a day had sat and sighed.

'And as shee heard the waves arise,
  And as shee heard the bleake windes roare,
As fast did heave her heartfelte sighes,
  And still so fast her teares did poure!'
               THE BALLAD OF ARABELLA STUART,
                     in Evans's Old Ballads.

THE ma erials of the life of Arabella Stuart, says D'Israeli, are so scanty that it cannot be written; and yet we have sufficient reason to believe that it would be as pathetic as it would be extraordinary, could we narrate its involved incidents, and paint forth her delirious feelings.

We must, therefore, sketch an outline, since we cannot paint a complete picture; and that outline will con-

[*] For the materials of this sketch we are indebted to the elder D'Israeli's Curiosities of Literature,' Miss Strickland's 'Queens of England,' Lodge's 'Illustrations of British History,' and Jesse's 'Memoirs of the Court of England.'

vince the reader how full of romantic interest must have been this royal lady's unhappy career. Her life was marked by the strangest antitheses and the most singular crosses. Thrice the crown of England seemed to hover above her head; yet she only felt 'the consciousness of royalty' when humbled in the poverty of dependence.

Many a well-born Cavalier aspired to her hand, yet when her heart at last responded to the magic touch of love, it was for ever deprived of all hope of domestic happiness. Authorities are not agreed upon the apparently easy question of her personal charms: some assert she was beautiful, others that she was plain; and her portrait, 'ambiguous as her life,' is neither the one nor the other. We are told that she was a poetess, but her claim to the laurel is not confirmed by a single couplet; and that she possessed no considerable acquirements, yet she could write an epistle in Latin. 'Acquainted rather with her conduct than with her character,' says D'Israeli, 'for as the Lady Arabella has no palpable historical existence, and we perceive rather her *shadow* than *herself*, a writer of romance might render her one of those interesting personages whose griefs have been deepened by their royalty, and whose adventures, touched with the warm hues of love and distraction, closed at the bars of her prison gate: a sad example of a female victim to the State!

> 'Through one dim lattice, fringed with ivy round,
> Successive suns a languid radiance threw,
> To paint how fierce her angry guardian frowned,
> To mark how fast her waning beauty flew!'

Sufficient, however, is known of her trials and sufferings to justify us in selecting her as an example of woman's constancy, of the truth and fervour of woman's affection. Heavy as was the burden laid upon her, and bitter as was the cup an adverse destiny held to her lips, she proved—Faithful to the End!

Arabella Stuart was the only child of Charles Stuart, fifth Earl of Lennox, by Elizabeth, daughter of Sir William Cavendish of Hardwick, in Derbyshire. Her father was of the royal blood both of England and Scotland, being a younger brother of Henry, Earl of Darnley, husband of Mary Queen of Scots, while through his mother, a daughter of Margaret, Queen of Scotland, he was the great-grandson of the Tudor sovereign, Henry VII.* She was probably born about 1577.

To an eye-witness of Arabella's birth, the new-born infant would doubtlessly have been a personage of extraordinary interest, and as he reflected that the blood of two royal dynasties ran in her veins, he would have been inclined to prognosticate for one so notably favoured a bright and dazzling career. But the accident of her birth made the misfortune of her life. By her descent from Margaret, the elder daughter of Henry VII., she was cousin to James I., and a kinswoman to Queen Elizabeth. To both she was, therefore, in after years, an object of jealousy; and they opposed her marriage, because secretly dreading the supposed danger of her having a legitimate offspring. Such, at least, is the common opinion of our historians, though it is difficult to reconcile it with the fact that James himself proposed for her husband Lord Esmé Stuart, whom he had created Duke of Lennox, and, being then unmarried, destined for his heir.

* Lodge, ' Illustrations of British History,' (3 vols., 1791.)

Of the early years of the Lady Arabella, of her education, of the influences to which she was exposed, or the qualities she displayed, we know nothing. We hear first of her in connection with a marriage; projects of marriage overshadowed all her later life; and a marriage was the immediate cause of her premature death.

The proposed match—to the young Lord Esmé—was in every respect unobjectionable. He was of illustrious descent and high birth; young, handsome, and energetic. It was approved of by the friends and kinsmen on both sides, and one might have supposed that, without let or hindrance, the marriage-bells would have been set a-ringing! Young, noble, well-favoured, wealthy—surely the Fates smiled auspiciously on this youthful pair. But one whose iron will was not to be brooked forbade the banns. Queen Elizabeth interposed; she cruelly flung the innocent lady into prison, and refused to release her at the Scotch King's solicitation, covering him with her royal contempt. This strange conduct is only explicable by its connection with Elizabeth's mysterious conduct respecting the succession to the English throne: so strong was her lust of power, so jealous was she lest her courtiers should turn their faces towards the rising sun, as her own orb declined in the shadow of old age and physical infirmity, that she neither thought herself nor would allow others to think of her successor.

But this jealousy was peculiarly impolitic, for it induced each party in the commonwealth to rally round its own particular claimant, and afforded the continental powers an admirable means of fomenting intestine disturbance. Thus, the Pope, opposed to James I. on account of his Protestantism, conceived the romantically wild idea of uniting Arabella to a prince of the House of Savoy, on the pretence that he was descended from a natural son of our Edward IV. The Duke of Parma, it is true, was married; but great is the power of the Head of the Roman Church! He selected the Duke's brother for his intended bridegroom, and as he was a Cardinal, proposed by the exercise of his infallibility to re-convert him into a layman. He had, then, only to marry the lady, and when she obtained the crown, he would become King of England in right of his wife. Was ever such a *Chateau d'Espagne* hatched by the teeming brain of a politician?

There seems no good reason to believe that Arabella was a Catholic, though the Catholic historians generally claim her as a member of their Church. And Winwood expressly states, writing in 1611, that 'the Lady Arabella hath not been found inclinable to Popery.' There is abundant evidence, on the other hand, that her supposed claims to the throne were espoused by a considerable faction. She appears to have been alarmed at the ambitious hopes which centred in her; and to withdraw herself from the wiles of political intriguers, designed to marry a son of the Earl of Northumberland. But Elizabeth was as jealous of an English Earl as she had been of a Scotch Duke, and the Lady Arabella's *third* marriage project fell to the ground.

Despite of her own unwillingness, she became the centre of a second conspiracy on the accession of James I. to the English throne. Full particulars of the plot, in which Sir Walter Raleigh was concerned, have not come

down to us, but its object was to set aside the Solomon
of Scotland, and crown Arabella. She made known to
the King all she herself knew of this 'state-riddle' (1603),
and the speculation vanished into thin air.

In the following year, 1604, a crown was offered to
the reluctant lady for the third time. This curious
circumstance was first brought to light by the elder
D'Israeli. The crown was a matrimonial one, the King
of Poland being a suitor for the Lady Arabella's hand.
We suspect that in this case the lady herself rejected the
proffered honour, and needed no instigation from James
or his ministers. In a contemporary letter quoted by
Lodge, we learn that yet another wooer had at this very
time presented himself. 'My Lady Arabella,' says the
writer, 'spends her time in lecture, reiding, &c., and she
will not hear of marriage. Indirectly there were speaches
used in the recommendation of Count Maurice, who
pretendeth to be Duke of Guildres.' Thus far, remarks
D'Israeli, crowns and husbands—to the Lady Arabella—
were like a fairy banquet seen at moonlight, opening on
her sight, impalpable and vanishing at the moment of
approach.

But we now approach the sad reality of her romantic
story. It was when her affections were first aroused
that her sorrows and sufferings began. Had she passed
through life,

'In maiden meditation, fancy free,

she would never, it is true, have tasted the luxury of
sympathy and the pleasures of a pure love, but she would
have escaped the slings and arrows of a malignant fortune,
and have lived to bear upon her brow the honours of a
ripe old age.

About Christmas 1608, or early in 1609, the Lady Arabella met with a playmate of her childhood, then grown into a handsome Cavalier, Mr. William Seymour, the second son of Lord Beauchamp, and grandson of the Earl of Hertford. He was a man of more than ordinary parts, of a graceful address, and a goodly person. Passionately addicted to study, he loved the seclusion of a lettered life; but when the Civil War broke out, he immediately drew his sword for his King, and displayed considerable military ability. Charles I. created him Earl of Hertford, and appointed him governor to the Prince of Wales—honours which his loyalty fully deserved. When the unfortunate Charles was doomed to death, he accused himself, in his capacity of Privy Councillor, of all the guilt and odium which were laid upon the King, and entreated that he might die in his stead. Afterwards, he was one of those who accompanied the dishonoured corse of the murdered King, when it was conveyed, in silence, and at the dead of night, to its last resting-place.

After the Restoration, this loyal nobleman received the blue ribbon of the Garter and the Dukedom of Somerset, which had previously been in his family, but was forfeited by the attainder of his grandfather, the great Protector, in the reign of Edward VI. Charles enhanced the value of these recompenses by the manner in which he conferred them. Addressing his Parliament, he said, 'If I have done an extraordinary act, it was done for an extraordinary person; one who has deserved so much both from my father and myself.' *

* 'Collins' Peerage,' i. 165

The love-passages between this faithful pair, and their contract of marriage, were discovered in February 1609, and the parties summoned before the Privy Council. Seymour was severely reprimanded for his presumption in seeking to ally himself with royal blood, although royal blood throbbed in his own veins. He addressed an humble apology to those most grave, potent, and reverend seniors :—'A younger brother,' said he, 'and sensible of mine own good, unknown to the world, of mean estate, not born to challenge anything by my birthright, and therefore my fortunes to be raised by mine own endeavour; and she a lady of great honour and virtue, and, as I thought, of great means; I did plainly and honestly endeavour lawfully to gain her in marriage.'

He proceeds to tell the story of his wooing :—*

'I boldly intruded myself into her ladyship's chamber in the court on Candlemas-day last; at what time I imparted my desire unto her, which was entertained, but with this caution on either part, that both of us resolved not to proceed to any final conclusion without his Majesty's most gracious favour first obtained. And this was our first meeting. After that we had a second meeting at Briggs's house in Fleet Street, and then a third at Mr. Baynton's; at both which we had the like conference and resolution as before.'

The lovers, while making these humble protestations, were nevertheless resolved to unite their fortunes in spite of King and Council—probably in the belief that when the irrevocable step was taken, they would patiently submit to a decision that could not be undone. They

* D'Israeli, 'Curiosities of Literature.' ii 500.

were accordingly married under circumstances of great
privacy; but as it is the nature of all such events to pro-
mulgate themselves, it was soon noised abroad, and
brought down the royal vengeance on the luckless pair.
The Lady Arabella was then committed to the custody
of Sir Thomas Parry, at Lambeth, while Seymour was
flung into the Tower, for 'his contempt in marrying a
lady of the royal family without the King's leave.'
Melvin, who was at the time a prisoner there on account
of his theological vagaries, addressed the unfortunate
bridegroom in the following couplet. It contains a
quibble on the Latin word *Ara*, an altar, which renders
translation difficult :—

> 'Communis tuum mihi causa est carceris : Ara-
> bella tui causa est,—Araque sacra mihi.'

[That is :—The cause is the same that has doomed you and me to suffer captivity; yours is *Ara-bella*,—a beautiful altar; and mine, *Ara sacra*,—a
holy altar.]

We are told that this, their first imprisonment, was
not marked by any rigorous circumstances; the lady
walked in a pleasant leafy garden, the husband in the
open area of the Tower. They contrived to carry on a
correspondence with each other, which being discovered,
the authorities determined to send Arabella to Durham, as an effectual means of preventing their future
intercourse.

But before we trace the story of their loves any further,
the reader may be willing to peruse a specimen or two of
Lady Arabella's epistolary powers.

The first letter which we quote was addressed to her
husband, and seems to us instinct with all the earnestness
of a fond and faithful heart.

'*The Lady Arabella to Mr. William Seymour.**

'Sir,—I am exceeding sorry to hear you have not been well. I pray you let me know truly how you do, and what was the cause of it. I am not satisfied with the reason Smith gives for it; but if it be a cold, I will impute it to some sympathy betwixt us, having myself gotten a swollen cheek at the same time with a cold. For God's sake, let not your grief of mind work upon your body. You may see by me what inconveniences it will bring one to; and no fortune, I assure you, daunts me so much as that weakness in body I find in myself; for *si nous vivons l'age d'un venu,* as Marot says, we may, by God's grace, be happier than we look for, in being suffered to enjoy ourself with his Majesty's favour.

'But if we be not able to live to it, I for my part shall think myself a pattern of misfortune in enjoying so great a blessing as you so little a while. No separation but that deprives me of the comfort of you. For wheresoever you be, or in what state soever you are, it sufficeth me you are mine! *Rachel wept, and would not be comforted, because her children were no more.* And that, indeed, is the remediless sorrow, and none else! And therefore God bless us from that, and I will hope well of the rest, though I see no apparent hope. But I am sure God's book mentioneth many of his children in as great distress, that have done well after, even in this world.

'I do assure you nothing the State can do with me can trouble me so much as this news of your being ill doth : and you see, when I am troubled, I trouble you too with tedious kindness; for so I think you will account so long a letter, yourself not having written to me this good

* Harleian MSS. 7003, cit. by D'Israeli, ii. 511

while so much as how you do. But, sweet sir, I speak not this to trouble you with writing, but when you please. Be well, and I shall account myself happy in being— Your faithful, loving wife,   ARB. S.'

About the same time must have been written the following letter to James I., in defence of her secret marriage. It is indorsed ' A copy of my Petition to the King's Majestie,' and runs as follows :—*

' *To the King.*

' May it please your Most Excellent Majesty,—I do most heartily lament my hard fortune that I should offend your Majesty the least, especially in that whereby I have long desired to merit of your Majesty, as appeared before your Majesty was my sovereign. And though your Majesty's neglect of me, my good liking of this gentleman that is my husband, and my fortune, drew me to a contract before I acquainted your Majesty, I humbly beseech your Majesty to consider how impossible it was for me to imagine it could be offensive to your Majesty, having few days before given me your royal consent to bestow myself on any subject of your Majesty's (which likewise your Majesty had done long since).

' Besides, neither having been prohibited any, or spoken to for any, in this land, by your Majesty, *these seven years* that I have lived in your Majesty's house, I could not conceive that your Majesty regarded my marriage at all ; whereas if your Majesty had vouchsafed to tell me your mind, and accept the free-will offering of my obedience, I would not have offended your Majesty, of whose

* Harleian MSS., *ut ante*.

gracious goodness I presume so much, that if it were now
as convenient in a worldly respect, as malice make it
seem, to separate us whom God hath joined, your
Majesty would not do evil that good might come thereof,
nor make me, that have the honour to be so near your
Majesty in blood, the first precedent that ever was.
though our princes may have left some as little imitable,
for so good and gracious a King as your Majesty, as
David's dealing with Uriah. But I assure myself, if it
please your Majesty in your own wisdom to consider
thoroughly of my cause, there will no solid reason appear
to debar me of justice and your princely favour, which I
will endeavour to deserve whilst I breathe.'

On the occasion of her contemplated removal to
Durham, Lady Arabella's firmness gave way, and her
mental anxiety acting on a frame not characterized by
any particular robustness, she fell so ill that she could
only travel in a litter, and accompanied by a physician.
Her illness increased apace. and the mournful cortège
was compelled to halt at Highgate.

The physician then returned to London to furnish the
King with a report of her condition. 'She was very weak,'
he said, 'her pulse slow and melancholy, her countenance
heavy and pale. She was wholly unfit to travel.' ' It is
enough,' said James, 'to make any sound man sick to be
carried in a bed in that manner she is: much more for her
whose impatient and unquiet spirit heapeth upon herself
far greater indisposition of body than otherwise she would
have.' His resolution, however, was taken : ' She should
proceed to Durham, if he were King.' ' We answered,'
says the doctor, 'that we made no doubt of her obedience.

'Obedience is that required,' replied the King; 'which being performed, I will do more for her than she expects.'

On the urgent representations of her physician, however, James consented that the Lady Arabella should remain for a month at Highgate, under the charge of Sir James Croft,* until she should have sufficiently recovered to continue her journey to Durham. A second month's delay was afterwards accorded, at the prayer of a letter penned by the lady herself, so forcibly and gracefully written that it received the applause of the King, Prince Henry, and the Privy Council.

The parted lovers took advantage of this delay to concert a plan of escape—as wild, as romantic, almost as impracticable, as any recorded in the annals of fiction.

The day preceding that which was appointed for the resumption of her journey to Durham, she won over a female attendant to consent to a last interview between her and her husband, and to wait for her return at an appointed hour. What woman but sympathizes with the sorrow of a distressed wife? This good attendant—this simple-hearted custodian—actually assisted the Lady Arabella to disguise herself in such a manner as to render detection almost impossible!

And now this daughter of a race of Kings drew a pair of large French-fashioned hose or trousers over her petticoats; put on a man's doublet or coat; a peruke, such as men wore, whose long locks covered her own ringlets; a black hat, a black cloak, russet boots with red tops, and a rapier by her side. Thus accoutred, the Lady Arabella set out, under the charge of a Mr. Markham, about three o'clock in the afternoon.

* 'Biographia Britannica,' L 175.

After walking about a mile and a half they stopped at a poor inn, where a confederate was in attendance with horses; but the Lady Arabella was already so sick and faint—with anxiety rather than fatigue, though the unaccustomed dress was probably wearisome—that the ostler who held her stirrup observed, the young gentleman would hardly hold out to London. But with the prospect of escape, and the invigorative effect of riding, she rapidly recovered, and at six o'clock reached Blackwall.

Here a boat was in waiting, and two female attendants with a change of apparel befitting the fugitive's sex. The watermen first dropped down to Woolwich; they were then desired to push on to Gravesend; and crossing to Tilbury, they landed and obtained refreshment. The promise of a heavy fee encouraged them to proceed to Leigh, where they discovered a French vessel lying to receive the lady.

Meanwhile Seymour had escaped from the Tower: he had left his servant watching at his door, with orders that no visitor should be suffered to disturb his master, who lay ill with a violent toothache. Disguising himself in a black wig and a pair of black whiskers, he then followed a cart that had brought some firewood to his apartments, and walked unmolested out of the western entrance to the Tower. At the Tower Wharf a boat was ready to row him to the part of the river where he expected to meet his bride. He reached Leigh in safety, but Arabella was gone; and as the danger of discovery was imminent, and a gale was rising, he got on board the first ship he fell in with, and was conveyed to Calais.

But why was Arabella gone?

Seymour did not arrive at the appointed hour, and the

Lady Arabella's attendants, apprehensive of being surprised by a king's ship, would not allow her to lie at
anchor as she desired, and hoisted sail—to the ruin of
all her hopes, and the fatal termination of her romantic
adventure. What her attendants feared really took place;
she was overtaken in the Calais roads, and compelled to
return to a dreary captivity.

As soon as the escape of Arabella became known, the
greatest consternation prevailed at court, though from
what causes it seems impossible for modern historians to
guess. The flight of an unhappy wife would appear a
trivial matter to a King firmly seated on his throne, and
with children to perpetuate his dynasty. The alarm,
however, was very great; couriers were despatched to
the sea-ports; and orders sent to the Tower to be doubly
vigilant over Seymour. On entering his apartment it was
found that the bird was flown—a circumstance which by
no means tended to diminish the King's jealous fears;
and at first he was bent upon issuing a proclamation, in
a style so wrathful and vindictive that it needed all the
astuteness of Cecil to preserve the dignity and conceal
the terror of his sovereign. Seymour, however, was safe,
and the royal indignation could only expend itself on a
miserable woman.

The Lady Arabella was immediately committed to the
Tower, where she lingered in wretchedness for only four
years. What passed in that dreadful captivity will never
be accurately known; but it is said that her deep and
unavailing sorrow impaired her reason, while it wore out
her feeble frame. Some loose effusions, says D'Israeli,
often begun and never ended, written and erased, inco-
herent and rational, yet remain in the fragments of her

papers. In a letter she proposed addressing to Viscount Felton, to entreat for her a renewal of the King's favour, she says : ' Good my lord, consider the fault cannot be uncommitted ; neither can any more be required of any earthly creature but confession and most humble submission. . . . Help will come too late ; and be assured that neither physician nor other, but whom I think good, shall come about me while I live, till I have his Majesty's favour, without which I desire not to live. And if you remember of old, I dare die, so I be not guilty of my own death ; and oppress others with my ruin, too, if there be no other way, as God forbid ! To whom I commit you ; and rest as earnestly as heretofore, if you be the same to me,—Your lordship's faithful friend, A. S.'

From the following passage, as well as the preceding letter, it would appear that thoughts of suicide had frequently crossed her distracted mind. ' I could not be so unchristian as to be the cause of my own death. Consider what the world would conceive if I should be violently enforced to do it.

Arabella Stuart died on the 27th of September 1615, in the 29th year of her age.* She was interred in Westminster Abbey.

An epitaph was written for her by Richard Corbet, Bishop of Norwich, which ran as follows :—

> ' How do I thank thee, Death, and bliss thy power,
> That I have passed the guard, and 'scaped the Tower !
> And now my pardon is my epitaph,
> And a small coffin my poor carcase hath :
> For, at thy charge, both soul and body were
> Enlarged at last, secured from hope and fear :
> *That* amongst saints, *this* amongst kings is laid,
> And what my birth did claim, my death hath paid '

* ' Biographia Britannica,' i. 176, 177.

We are told by Ballard that her coffin was at one time so broken and shattered, that her skull and body might be seen.* Seymour, in the chances of his after career, did not forget the unhappy lady whose constancy to him was so sorely tried and so severely punished. And he called one of his daughters by his second wife—Frances, daughter of Robert Devereux, Earl of Essex—by the well remembered name of Arabella Seymour.

* The following notice of the Lady Arabella's decease occurs in Camden's Annals:—'27th September 1615, Arabella Stuart, daughter of Charles, Earl of Lennox, cousin-german of Henry Darnley, father of King James, died in the Tower of London; was interred at Westminster, without any funeral pomp, in the night, in the same vault wherein Mary Queen of Scots and Prince Henry were buried. It is the saying of Charles the Fair, that those who die in the king's prison are deservedly deprived of funeral pomp, lest they should be thought to have been thrown into prison wrongfully.'—*Camden's Annals, in Kennet's 'History of England,'* ii. 644.

GENEALOGY OF LADY ARABELLA STUART,

SHOWING HER RELATIONSHIP TO THE ROYAL FAMILIES OF ENGLAND AND SCOTLAND.

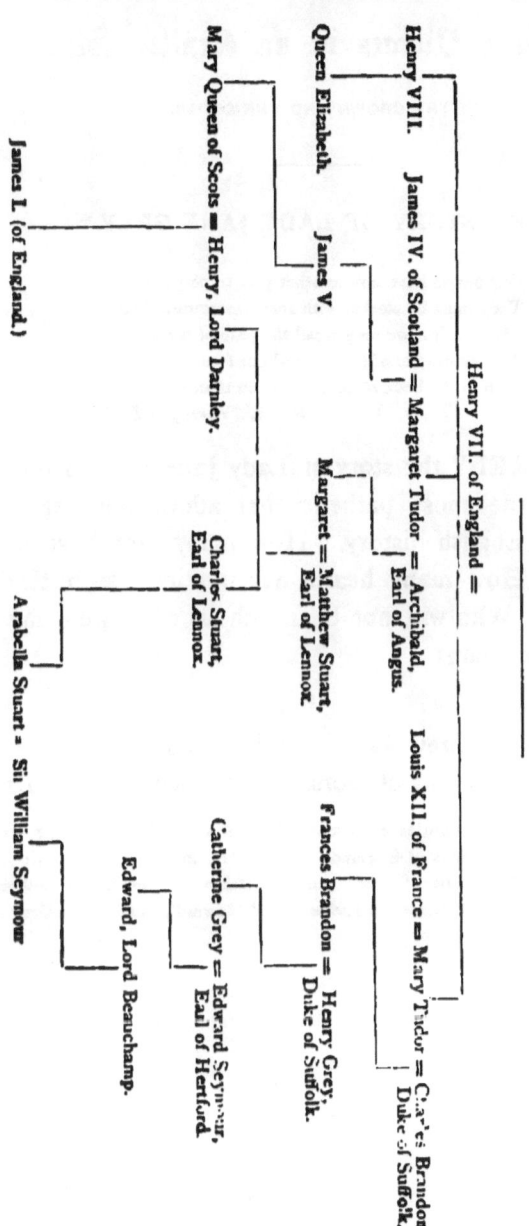

Henry VII. of England =

Henry VIII.   James IV. of Scotland = Margaret Tudor = Archibald,   Louis XII. of France = Mary Tudor = Charles Brandon,
                                                        Earl of Angus.   Duke of Suffolk.

Queen Elizabeth.   James V.   Margaret = Matthew Stuart,   Frances Brandon = Henry Grey,
                                          Earl of Lennox.   Duke of Suffolk.

Mary Queen of Scots = Henry, Lord Darnley.   Charles Stuart,   Catherine Grey = Edward Seymour,
                                             Earl of Lennox.   Earl of Hertford.

James I. (of England.)   Arabella Stuart = Sir William Seymour.   Edward, Lord Beauchamp.

VII

Womanly Virtues in an Exalted Station.

THE CROWN AND THE CROSS.

THE STORY OF LADY JANE GREY.*

'Our hearts have now another part to play;
They must be steeled with some uncommon fortitude,
That fearless we may tread the path of horror,
And, in despite of fortune and our foes,
Ev'n in the hour of death be more than conquerors.'

ROWE, *Tragedy of Lady Jane Grey*

SURELY the story of Lady Jane Grey is one of the most pathetic that adorn the pages of English history. How many eyes have wept over it! How many hearts has it stirred with tender emotion! Who will not bear with us while we essay to tell it once again?

I.

Lady Jane Grey was the eldest daughter of Henry Grey, third Marquis of Dorset, by his second wife, Lady

* The principal authorities consulted by us for the following sketch, are—Miss Strickland, ' Queens of England ;' Froude, ' History of England ;' Strype's ' Ecclesiastical Memorials ;' Stowe's ' Annals ;' Baker's ' Chronicle ;' Miss Wood's ' Letters of Royal and Illustrious Ladies ;' and Howard's ' Lady Jane Grey and Her Times.'

Frances Brandon. This Lady Frances was of royal blood, being the eldest daughter of Charles Brandon, Duke of Suffolk, by Mary Tudor, widow of Louis XII. of France, and second daughter of our English Henry VII. Lady Jane was also connected with the royal family on the father's side, her paternal great-great-grandmother, Elizabeth Woodville, having been the beautiful and cunning Queen-consort of the luxurious Edward IV. Her father, Henry Grey, when he succeeded to the Marquisate in 1530, stood forward among the first noblemen of his time. In 1547, the first year of Edward the Sixth's reign, he was appointed Lord High Constable to officiate at that monarch's coronation. Shortly afterwards he received the garter. In 1550, he was nominated Justice Itinerant of all the King's Forests; in 1551, Warden of the Border Marches; and finally, in October 15, in the same year, he was raised to the Dukedom of Suffolk.

This powerful noble was not, however, a man of commanding genius, and made no impress on his age. His virtuous character gave him a certain influence; he could appreciate genius in others, and rally learned men around him; and having been educated in Lutheran principles, he was a firm and consistent advocate of the reformation of religion.

When was Lady Jane born?

Distinguished as was her parentage, and illustrious as became her own career, it is difficult to answer this question positively; but taking quaint old Fuller as our authority, we may place the date of her birth in 1536.

Where was she born?

To this question we can reply with certainty. She

first saw the light at Bradgate, about five miles from Leicester, her father's stately mansion, of which some interesting remains are still extant. She was the eldest of three daughters—Jane, Katherinè, and Mary: her parents had no sons. At a very early age she gave abundant promise of a fair and noble womanhood; her disposition being gentle, her temper mild, her natural capacity very great, and her love of learning remarkable. That was an age in which women received as careful and elaborate an education as men; and for Lady Jane's tutors two learned divines were chosen—Thomas Harding and John Aylmer, her father's chaplains, and both professors of the Reformed doctrines. Aylmer appears to have had the more particular charge of her studies, and the teacher being as assiduous as the pupil was intelligent, Lady Jane soon acquired a mastery of the Latin and Greek languages, and also attained some degree of proficiency in Arabic, Chaldaic, French, Italian, and Hebrew. In these latter languages her progress could not have been very great, and yet enough remains to make us wonder how 'one little head contained it all!'

While worshipping with such intense devotion the grave-browed Minerva, she did not forget her duty to the Graces. Her voice was melodious, and she sang with great taste and pathos.: on various musical instruments she performed with more than ordinary skill. In needle-work and embroidery—important branches of female education in the days of the Tudors—her performances excited the wonder of her contemporaries; she knew something of the medical properties of herbs; be sure she could make preserves, and 'sweet waters,' and dainty household dishes; and she wrote with wonderful elegance and facility. In this latter art she received instructions from the learned Roger Ascham, who, unlike modern scholars, was no less distinguished for the beauty of his caligraphy than the extent of his erudition. Her acquirements, in fine, surpassed those of any of her equals in age and station, and she was frequently quoted as a model and an example for the benefit of the young Prince Edward—himself a ripe scholar, and a boy of extraordinary promise.

Her tutors, while so carefully educating and developing her intellectual powers, did not forget to train her up in a knowledge of the truths of Christianity, and while yet a child she learned the consoling and beautiful lessons of Hope and Faith inculcated by the Saviour's life, and hallowed by His death and resurrection.

After the death of Henry VIII., the youthful Lady Jane resided with the widowed Queen, Katherine Parr, at Chelsea; and, after her second marriage to Lord Seymour of Sudley, at Hanworth, in Middlesex, one of Henry the Eighth's favourite palaces, which he had bestowed upon her as a dowry. Queen Katherine did not long survive her second nuptials. She died at Sudley Castle, on September the 5th, 1548, in the thirty-sixth year of her age. We may estimate how deep was the affection subsisting between the widowed Queen and her protégé from the fact that Lady Jane officiated as chief mourner at her funeral.

It was soon after this sad event that Lady Jane addressed the following letter to the Lord High Admiral. It is noticeable as the first specimen extant of her epistolary powers:— *

* Wood, ' Letters of Royal and Illustrious Ladies,' iii. 197.

Lady Jane Grey to Lord Seymour of Sudley.

'*Oct. 1, 1548.*

'My duty to your lordship, in most humble wise remembered, with no less thanks for the gentle letters which I received from you. Thinking myself so much bound to your lordship for your great goodness towards me from time to time, that I cannot by any means be able to recompense the least part thereof, I purposed to write a few rude lines unto your lordship, rather as a token to show how much worthier I think your lordship's goodness than to give worthy thanks for the same; and these my letters shall be to testify unto you that, like as you have become towards me a loving and kind father, so I shall be always most ready to obey your godly monitions and good instructions, as becometh one upon whom you have heaped so many benefits. And thus, fearing lest I should trouble your lordship too much, I must humbly take my leave of your good lordship.— Your humble servant during my life,   JANE GREY.

'To the right honourable and my singular good lord, the Lord Admiral, give these.'

It cannot be said that such a letter is aught but a most creditable production on the part of a girl, only twelve years old.

Lord Seymour, a man of hasty temper and dissolute habits, was not exactly the guardian whom any fond parents would select for a young, personable, and accomplished daughter. The Marquis of Dorset and his wife, therefore, were naturally solicitous that Lady Jane should return to the safer asylum of her own home. Such a wish, one would think, could hardly be disputed, and yet it was with much reluctance, and only after an urgent correspondence, that the Lord Admiral could be prevailed upon to part with her. His ambition was unbounded, and as her parents would seem to have promised him the disposal of their daughter's hand—a prize in the great lottery of his fortunes, and one of the steps by which he hoped to climb to power—he was unwilling that she should be removed from his influence. And when he at length consented to her return, he used strenuous exertions to reclaim her; finally succeeding, by his promise that he would betroth her to King Edward, and by bribing the needy Marquis with a large sum of money.

There exists no evidence that he seriously contemplated her union with the youthful sovereign, and there is much greater reason to believe that he intended to marry her to his heir, the Lord Hertford, son of his brother, the Protector-Duke of Somerset. It has also been suggested that he may have designed to marry her himself, failing his designs upon the hand of the Princess Elizabeth. Her royal descent would have enabled him to make her the instrument of furthering his splendid schemes of personal aggrandizement.

We may conclude, at all events, that he was desirous to dispose of her, when she reached a marriageable age, in such a manner as would best advance his views or support his interests, without at any time being determined whether he should espouse her, or whether she should become the wife of his nephew, or of some other nobleman on whose fidelity he could rely.* Even at this early period of her life, the amiable and unfortunate girl seemed chosen by an evil destiny to be the victim of

* Sir Harris Nicolas, ' Memoirs of Lady Jane Grey.'

ambition, and her fine hopes and radiant promise to be rendered subservient to the dark intrigues of restless and aspiring spirits.

It is not impossible that Lady Jane at Bradgate may have regretted the indulgent ease and splendid hospitality of Sudley Castle. Her parents adopted in its fullest extent the maxim that to spare the rod is to spoil the child, and notwithstanding the amiability and industry of their daughter, subjected her to the most rigorous discipline. She was harshly punished for the slightest defect in her behaviour or the most trivial failure in her studies. She was taught to fear, rather than to love her parents; and reverence was insisted upon —rather than affection—as the duty of children towards those who gave them birth. It is no marvel, therefore, that from the brow ever stern, and the voice almost always harsh, she turned with increased delight towards that gentle Spirit of Knowledge, which has none but the serenest smiles for its assiduous votaries. In the pages of the wise she met with nothing but encouragement and consolation: they soothed her sorrows, they taught her the dignity of endurance, they inspired her with the nobility of thought, they lifted her into that glorious and cloudless sphere where ever dwell the Immortals! 'Thus,' says she, 'my book hath been so much my pleasure, and bringeth daily to me more and more pleasure, that in respect of it all other pleasures in very deed be but trifles and troubles unto me.'

'A good book,' says Milton, 'is the precious life-blood of a master-spirit, embalmed and treasured up on purpose for a life beyond life.' Of how many humble and unhappy souls does it become the joy, the solace, the inspiration ! What a brightness does it shed upon a dark and dreary time!—how sweet a music does it breathe into the hearts of the suffering and the weary ! Let the pitiless winds rage without ; let the clouds gather and the thunder roll ; let the mad waves spend their fury on a forsaken shore ; for in my books I find a brighter, a happier world, where neither storm, nor thunder, nor shipwreck perturbs the souls of men. They transport me into Fairy-land ; they make me the associate of stainless celestial spirits ; they fill me with a happiness which is unutterable and indestructible !

How great a proficiency the studious daughter of a royal race attained in the deathless literature and golden language of the Greeks, we know from an interesting record preserved by Roger Ascham, in the quaint and curious pages of ' The Schoolmaster.'

He visited Bradgate, he tells us, in the summer of 1550, when on his way to London to attend Sir Richard Morison, appointed ambassador to Charles V., the great Emperor of Germany.

On his arrival, he found the stately mansion deserted ; its lord and lady, with all their household, were hunting merrily in the park to the music of horn and hound; and making his way through the silent chambers, he at length came upon a retired apartment, where the fair daughter of the house was calmly perusing the divine pages of Plato's immortal ' Phædon ' in the original Greek.*

---

* Another learned lady was the Princess Elizabeth, afterwards the great Queen, who so worthily ruled the realm of England. Her education was severely classical; she spoke Latin fluently, and was well versed in Greek. In those days women were taught something more than to 'chronicle small beer,' embroider flower-baskets, and play 'a little' upon the piano.

So unusual a spectacle surprised and delighted the worthy scholar, and after the usual compliments, he inquired why she had not accompanied the gay lords and ladies in the park, to enjoy the brisk pastime of the chase.

'I wis,' she replied, with a calm sunny smile, 'that all their sport in the park is but a shadow to the pleasure which I derive from Plato. Alas! good folk, they never felt what true pleasure means.'

'And how came you, madam,' inquired Ascham, in his astonishment that a girl of fourteen could not only *read* but *enjoy* Plato, 'to this deep knowledge of pleasure ! And what did chiefly allure you into it, since not only few women, but even very few men, have attained thereunto ?'

'I will tell you, and tell you a truth which, perchance, you will marvel at.'

She then spoke of the rigorous discipline practised by her parents, and the solace which, under such circumstances, she found in the pursuit of letters ;—how, in the retirement of her chamber, she conversed with Demosthenes and Plato as with old and trusty friends ; or listened to the wise precepts of her instructor, Aylmer, always couched in gentle language, and given with a delightful mildness of manner.

Ascham does not appear to have seen her again after this memorable interview, but they occasionally corresponded ; and in his letters to his learned friends he was never weary of extolling the depth of her acquirements and the amiability of her character. He spoke of Lady Mildred Cooke, the wife of Sir William Cecil, and of the Lady Jane Grey as the two most learned women

in England ; and summed up his praises of the latter in
the panegyric that, 'however illustrious she was by her
fortune and royal extraction, this bore no proportion to
the accomplishments of her mind, adorned with the
doctrine of Plato and the eloquence of Demosthenes.'

Both on account of her piety, her erudition, and her
illustrious rank, the Lady Jane was necessarily an object
of eager interest to the leaders of the Reformed Church
in England and on the Continent. The learned Martin
Bucer, one of the Fathers of Protestantism, whom Edward
VI. appointed Professor of Divinity at the University of
Cambridge, watched over her early life with fervent
anxiety. Bullinger, a minister of Zurich, and another of
the lights of the Reformed Church, corresponded with
her frequently, and encouraged her in the practice of
every Christian virtue. Under the advice and direction
of these, and other eminent divines, she pursued her
theological studies with assiduity and success, so as to
be able to justify the creed she had adopted, and give
abundant reason for the faith that was in her.

The Marquis of Dorset was elevated to the Dukedom
of Suffolk in October 1551, on the death of his wife's
brother, Henry Brandon. It should be noted that on
the same day the dark, ambitious, intriguing man, who
afterwards exercised so evil an influence on her destiny,
John Dudley, Earl of Warwick, was created Duke of
Northumberland.

The Lady Jane was now removed to the metropolis,
residing with her family at her father's ' inn,' or town
house, in Suffolk Place. She necessarily moved in the
brightest social circles, and shared in the festivities of
the Court ; but we find, upon good evidence, that she

was invariably distinguished by a peculiar plainness of apparel—in this respect conforming to the injunctions laid upon her by Bullinger and Aylmer, as well as following the dictates of her own simplicity of spirit. On one occasion a sumptuous robe was presented to her by the Princess Mary, and she was desired to wear it out of compliment to the donor.

'Nay,' she replied, 'that were a shame, to follow my Lady Mary, who leaveth God's word, and leave my Lady Elizabeth, who followeth God's word.' For the Princess Elizabeth was then addicted to a Puritanic decorousness of attire, very unlike the pomp of dress in which, at a later period, she loved to array herself.

To the Princess Mary she paid a visit in June 1552, at her mansion of New Hall in Essex ; and while residing under her roof, displayed her Protestant principles in a manner which gave no small offence to her bigoted cousin.

She was walking, one afternoon, with the Lady Anne Wharton, when the latter lady, on their passing the Popish chapel, made a low obeisance, intended for the honour of the host or wafer suspended, as was the custom, over the holy altar. The Lady Jane was at a loss to conceive for whom the homage was intended, and inquired if the Princess Mary was worshipping in the chapel. 'No,' said her companion, 'but I make obeisance to Him who made us all.'—'Why,' rejoined Lady Jane, with a touch of that piquant satire in which the Princess Elizabeth excelled, 'why, how can that which the baker made be He who made us all ?'

The retort was conveyed to the Princess Mary, and it wrapped up a truth too pungent to be forgiven. Thence-

forth the Princess hated her with all the malice of her
sullen and resentful nature. She was no longer her
cousin, and of the royal blood, but a heretic—a member
of a false and damnable church ; and Mary proved the
fervour of her piety by the fervour of her antipathy to
heretics.

II.

The life of Lady Jane Grey may be compared to a
Shakspearian tragedy, which opening with scenes of pomp
and sunshine, is soon overspread with darker hues, and
closes at length in some lurid and terrible catastrophe.
Hitherto the stream has rippled onwards under a screen
of leaf and blossom ; now it begins to seethe and fret ;
and from the ominous voices that come up on the wind,
we know that an angry sea and a wreck-strewn shore are
near at hand.

Early in the year 1553 it became evident that the brief
reign of Edward VI. was drawing to an abrupt termination. Attacks of measles and small-pox, aggravated by
injudicious treatment, and followed by a severe cold,
had sown the seeds of death in a frame that was never
robust, and which a studious disposition and over-wrought
brain had sorely weakened. His successor was Mary,
whose bigoted character and morose disposition had
already filled the minds of the Reformers with just
apprehension. Her unpopularity, and the terrible consequences to the Reformed Church which would assuredly follow her accession, inspired the ambitious
spirit of Dudley, Duke of Northumberland, the Protector
of the kingdom, with a bold and daring project. He
could not hope to wear the crown himself, but, at least,
he might place it on his son's brow, and while leaving to

him the symbol, concentrate in his own person the reality, of sovereign power. To carry out his scheme, it was necessary this son should be allied to the blood-royal. Looking around him, he found among the nearest heirs to the throne a comely lady, of spotless virtue and un-equalled erudition—the daughter of the Duke of Suffolk. He immediately proposed a marriage between her and his fourth son, Lord Guildford Dudley, his three other sons being already provided with wives. The match was so suitable, that the Lady Jane's parents willingly sanc-tioned it; and the young Lord Guildford being a tall and handsome gentleman, of amiable disposition and agreeable manners, the lady herself said never a word of objection. On the contrary, a sincere and devoted attachment speedily sprang up between the well-assorted pair.

Under the happiest auspices, apparently, their marriage was solemnized early in June 1553, at the Duke of Northumberland's mansion in the Strand, the costliest bridal dresses being supplied by order of King Edward from the royal wardrobe, and the proudest peers of England gracing the splendid ceremony with their presence.

> ' Fair laughs the morn, and soft the zephyr blows,
>   While proudly riding o'er the azure realm
> In gallant trim the gilded vessel goes;
>   Youth on the prow and Pleasure at the helm;
> Regardless of the sweeping whirlwind's sway,
> That, hushed in grim repose, expects his evening prey.'
>
> GRAY, *The Bard.*

Thus far, Northumberland's scheme of ambition had prospered. He had provided his son with a gentle and lovely wife—it now remained to invest him with the

purple of royalty.   In carrying out this bolder portion of
his project the difficulties which confronted him were of
the gravest character.

The Lady Jane was but a distant heir to the throne.
Others, with more tangible claims, stood before her.

It was true that Henry VIII. had declared his daughters by Catherine of Arragon and Anne Boleyn—the
Princesses Mary and Elizabeth—illegitimate, and that
his declaration had been confirmed by a subservient
Parliament.   But later in his reign, the astute monarch
perceived the delicacy of the Prince Edward's constitution, and the necessity of strengthening the succession
to the crown by including his daughters in it.   Their
illegitimacy, therefore, was reversed by an Act of Parliament in 1544, which enacted: 'That, should his Majesty's
only son and nearest heir, Edward, Prince of Wales, die
without issue, and his Majesty himself die without issue
by his beloved wife Queen Katherine, or any other wife
he might afterwards marry, the crown should devolve
upon his eldest daughter, the Princess Mary, and the
issue lawfully begotten of her body ; and in the event of
her dying childless, it should descend to his daughter
the Princess Elizabeth, and her legitimate children ;
failing all which, Henry VIII. was invested with full
power to dispose of it as he pleased by his letters-patent
or by his last will.   He was also authorized to impose
certain conditions upon the Princesses Mary and Elizabeth as his presumptive successors' (35 Henry VIII. c. 1).

The King's last will,—dated December 20, 1546,—repeated the provisions of the Act of Parliament, but
added two conditions:—

First, That the Princess Mary and Elizabeth should

inherit the crown only on the understanding that neither was to marry without the approval of the majority of the Privy Councillors; and,—

Second, That next to the Princess Elizabeth, if she died without issue, should rank the heirs of the body of Lady Frances Brandon, Duchess of Suffolk, eldest daughter of Henry the Eighth's sister, Mary Tudor, by Duke Charles of Suffolk; and failing them, the legitimate children of Lady Eleanor, second daughter of Mary Tudor, and wife of Henry Clifford, Earl of Cumberland.[*]

Such was the state of the succession to the English crown at the epoch when Dudley conceived his darkly ambitious designs, whose success, it is evident, depended upon the absolute exclusion of the two nearest heirs, the Princesses Mary and Elizabeth.

Northumberland was not a man whom obstacles could daunt. They seemed only to stimulate his impetuous temper and strengthen his iron will. His influence over Edward VI. was unbounded, and he proceeded to extort from the feeble King letters-patent, appointing Lady Jane heir to the throne he was so soon to vacate. He wrought upon the young King's affection for the Reformed Church, and alarmed him with glowing pictures of the dangers to religion which would result from Mary's succession. And when Edward showed himself unwilling to pass over the claims of his sister Elizabeth, who, at least, was neither a bigot nor a Papist, he pointed out that if the one sister was illegitimate, so must be the other, and that Mary could not be set aside unless the pretensions of Elizabeth were also invalidated.

[*] Rymer's ' Fœdera,' vi. pt. 3. See also Froude, ' History of England,' iv. 50.

The King's signature was at length obtained.   Northumberland next addressed himself to the judges, and,
by bribes or menaces, secured the subscription of all
except Sir John Hales, a Protestant.   The Lords of the
Privy Council signed unanimously, as well as several
other persons of influence and distinction, and the letters-
patent, with this formidable array of names, were issued
on the 21st day of June 1553: but owing to Edward's
death a fortnight later (July 6th), they were never
formally ratified, either by his personal will and testament
or by Act of Parliament.

The development of this crafty project was carefully
concealed from the one whom it most nearly concerned,
the Lady Jane, until a day or two before the King's
decease, when the unwelcome intelligence was communicated by her mother-in-law, the Duchess of Northumberland.   'Which,' says the unfortunate lady, 'being
spoken to me most unexpectedly, put me in great per-
turbation, and greatly disturbed my mind at first, and
soon afterwards oppressed me much more.'*   Fain would
she have cast off the burden laid upon her, and turned
to the innocent pleasures of lettered ease, and a home
brightened by conjugal affection.

It was on the evening of the 9th of July 1553 that
the Duke of Northumberland, accompanied by his
principal confederates, the Marquis of Northampton, the
Earl of Arundel, the Earl of Huntingdon, and the Earl
of Pembroke, presented himself before the gentle lady,
in her quiet chamber at Northumberland House, and
pressed upon her the acceptance of a crown which to
her was destined to be 'a crown of thorns.'   Troubling

* Miss Wood, 'Letters of Royal and Illustrious Ladies,' iii 472-279.

herself little about abstract right, or the legitimacy or illegitimacy of King Henry's daughters, she meekly complained that she was unfit to govern a great kingdom, and that the sceptre would assuredly fall from hands so feeble as hers. 'How I was beside myself,' she afterwards wrote, in her touching and eloquent pathetic letter to Queen Mary—'how I was beside myself, stupified and troubled, I will leave it to those lords who were present to testify, who saw me overcome by sudden and unexpected grief, fall on the ground, weeping very bitterly; and then declaring to them my insufficiency, I greatly bewailed myself for the death of so noble a prince, and at the same time turned myself to God, humbly praying and beseeching him, that if what was given to me was *rightly and lawfully* mine, his Divine Majesty would grant *me* such grace and spirit that I might govern it to his glory and service, and to the advantage of this realm. With what house,' she continues, 'does Fortune present me? A crown which hath been violently and shamefully wrested from Katharine of Arragon; made more unfortunate by the punishment of Anne Boleyn, and others that wore it after her.'

Turning to the ambitious Duke and his abettors, she exclaimed, in reproachful accents that might have melted, one would think, even their stern hearts, 'Why will you have me add my blood to theirs? Why must I be the third victim from whom this fatal crown may be ravished with the head that wears it? And even in case it should not prove thus fatal, even if all its venom be consumed, even if Fortune should give me assurance of her constancy, shall I be well advised to take upon me these thorns, which would lacerate though not kill me outright?

My liberty is better than the chain you proffer me, with
what precious stones soever it be adorned, or of what
gold soever framed.'

To this the lords replied with protestations of devoted
service, and endeavoured to excite her ambition by pictures of the great glory to be gained by the ruler of so
powerful a kingdom. Such pictures, however glowingly
coloured, had no charm for her studious and contented
disposition, and she exclaimed,—

' I will not exchange my peace for honourable and
precious jealousies, for magnificent and glorious fetters.
Oh, my lords,' said the unfortunate lady, ' if you love me
sincerely, and in good earnest, you will rather wish me
a secure and quiet fortune, though mean, than an exalted condition, exposed to the wind, and followed by
some dismal fall.'

But her remonstrances and appeals could not prevail
over the entreaties of her father, the solicitations of her
husband—who was not proof against the golden dream
of royal power—and the continuous pressure put upon
her by Northumberland. Her loving and gentle nature
also urged her to her own ruin, for she saw not how she
could save her father and father-in-law from certain
destruction but by accepting the crown. If Mary became Queen, it was obvious that their heads would fall
upon the scaffold.

Swayed by conflicting emotions, she yielded; but never
was a crown accepted with greater reluctance, or with a
surer presentiment of the evils it would inflict upon its
possessor.

The accession of Lady Jane Grey to the throne evoked
no tumult of popular exultation. On the 9th of July,

the chief officers of state and the guard took their oaths of allegiance to the new Queen at Greenwich, and on the following day she was conveyed—in great pomp, and with all the luxury of regal show—to the Tower of London. She arrived at that famous pile—which was then a palace, a fortress, and a prison— between four and five o'clock in the afternoon, attended by her father-in-law and a glittering train of lords and ladies, and received by the blare of trumpets and the clash of ordnance. But it was observed that, as she passed through the city, and moved along the crowded streets, she was received with none of those plaudits which generally welcome a new ruler. The curious multitude looked on in silence as the bright pageant passed by, and seemed to regard it, not as the solemn reality of a great public ceremonial, but as the unsubstantial show of a stage-spectacle.

At six o'clock the usual proclamation was made of her accession to the throne, under the name and title of Jane, Queen of England, France, and Ireland, first at Cheapside, and next in Fleet Street. The proclamation duly set forth her claims to the crown as based upon the letters-patent signed by the late King, Edward VI., and the illegitimacy of the Princesses Mary and Elizabeth, publicly declared by Acts of Parliament passed in the 25th and 28th years of the reign of Henry VIII. No jubilant voices shouted approval, however, of this first act of the new sovereign ; it was heard in silence ; save that a London 'prentice loudly affirmed the title of the Princess Mary to the throne. The young man was straightway arrested, and on the following day, at eight o'clock, was set in the pillory. Both his ears were nailed, and cut off; whereupon a herald blew his trumpet, and read the culprit's offence in the presence of one of the sheriffs of London. He was then flung into prison.

With this cruel and impolitic deed opened the brief reign of Lady Jane Grey. To understand why it *was* so brief, the reader has only to remember that the English have always displayed a strong preference for hereditary claims and prescriptive rights. A popular historian justly remarks, moreover, that at this time Protestantism was not understood among the body of the people; the new proprietors of the church-estates had alienated their neighbours by abridging their ancient privileges; parishes lay at such a distance from each other, and even towns had so little communication, that there must have been large tracts of country where the late proceedings had never been heard of; and therefore it was impossible to get up any enthusiasm on behalf of a Protestant defender of the faith, without an hereditary right to the throne, amidst such a mass of ignorance, apathy, and discontent. Honest English sense of justice also, and the regard for lofty birth which has always distinguished our countrymen, were revolted by an attempt to exclude the eldest sister of Edward, and the daughter of a royal pair, in favour of the nominee of a youthful sovereign on his death-bed, and wife of the grandson of Dudley, the unpopular minion of Henry VII.

Northumberland had made an attempt to get possession of the persons of Elizabeth and Mary, but information of his designs was conveyed to them, and they effected their escape. Mary retired to her castle at Framlingham, in Suffolk. There, on the 8th of July, two days after Edward's death, she first received the intelligence of that event, and of Northumberland's schemes to ensure the accession of the Lady Jane. She immediately asserted her claims, and assumed the royal title. ' On the same day she wrote to several of her supporters, claiming the crown as her lawful birthright, and commanding them to repair to her as their sovereign, at her manor of Kenninghall in Norfolk.

On the following day she addressed herself to the Council, vehemently expostulating with them on the disloyal course they had adopted, and claiming the crown as hers, both by birthright and the laws of the kingdom. In reply, the Council stated that their sovereign lady, Queen Jane, was invested with the imperial crown, by their late sovereign lord's letters-patent, signed with his own hand, and sealed with the Great Seal of England, in presence of the most part of the nobles, councillors, judges, with divers other grave and sage personages assenting and subscribing to the same. They added that, in consequence of the divorce effected between Henry VIII. and Katharine of Arragon, a divorce demanded by the everlasting laws of God, and also by ecclesiastical laws, and confirmed by the judgment of the most part of the noble and learned universities of Christendom, as well as by sundry acts of Parliament, remaining yet in their force, she was justly made illegitimate, and uninheritable to the crown imperial. And they bade her take heed lest, under any pretence whatsoever, ' she should vex and molest any of their sovereign lady Queen Jane's subjects from their true faith and allegiance due unto her grace. Given at the Tower of London, on the ninth day of July, in the year of our Lord 1553.' *

* Holinshed, 'Chronicles, iii. 1066. et seq.

III.

It is not in our province in these pages to narrate events which are purely historical. ' Queen Jane's' sway was a nine days' wonder. The great body of the Protestants supported the hereditary claims of the Princess Mary. The clergy denounced her gentle rival from the pulpit; all except Ridley, Bishop of London, who exerted his eloquence in vain. The gentry and the lower orders were unanimous in her favour. By slow stages she advanced from Norfolk towards the metropolis, her forces rapidly increasing as she went; and everywhere the most powerful leaders rallied to her standard, and gave in their adhesion to her cause. The Council, on receiving this alarming intelligence, ordered a large body of troops to be despatched against her, to whose command it was designed to appoint the Duke of Suffolk; but Jane would not consent to her father's departure. Northumberland, therefore, placed himself at their head, and marched out of London on the 13th of July, at the head of 6000 men. He went under sore discouragement, for of the multitudes that gathered to witness his departure, not one said, ' God speed you.' *

On reaching Edmondsbury, he found Mary with an army of 20,000 well-appointed troops; and unable to withstand such a preponderance of numbers, he sent pressing solicitations to the Council for the immediate despatch of reinforcements.

But the Council, meanwhile, distrustful of Northumberland's success, and alarmed at the hourly evidence they received of Mary's popularity, were bethinking them

* Stowe's ' Annals,' pp. 610 612

selves of securing their own safety. One after another deserted the unhappy Jane, and made haste to salute the rising sun. At a meeting held on the 19th of July, in the Earl of Pembroke's mansion of Baynard's Castle, the majority of the Council, and others of the nobility, resolved upon acknowledging Mary's title to the crown. Accompanied by the Lord Mayor and Aldermen of London, they accordingly proceeded to Cheapside, and solemnly proclaimed her Queen, in the presence of an excited throng and press of people, who testified their glad loyalty by loud and enthusiastic shouts. Afterwards they repaired to St. Paul's Cathedral, when the *Te Deum Laudamus* was chanted, the congregation swelling its triumphant strain, and the organ bearing the burthen of its glorious music.

Great was the rejoicing, says a contemporary—so great, that the like of it had never been seen by any living. The number of caps that were flung into the air at the proclamation could not be told. The Earl of Pembroke cast among the crowd a liberal largess. Bonfires blazed in every street; and what with shouting and crying of the people, and ringing of bells, there could no one man hear what another said; besides banqueting, and skipping the streets for joy ! *

Lady Jane's father, the Duke of Suffolk, now abandoned his daughter's cause, and openly proclaimed Queen Mary on Tower Hill. The dream of ambition had vanished like other dreams, and there were none now who bethought themselves of the ill-fated lady, sorrowing in sad retirement, and gazing through her tears at a cloudy future.

Northumberland, deserted by all his adherents, retired

* Howard, 'Lady Jane Grey and Her Times,' pp. 269, 270.

to Cambridge with a handful of troops; and hastened to the market-place, where he, too, flung his bonnet into the air, and shouted, ' God save Queen Mary,' with lusty, but newborn loyalty.   He was soon afterwards arrested, and carried a prisoner to the Tower of London (July 25, 1553).

On approaching the metropolis, Mary was received by the Princess Elizabeth, who rode out to meet her at the head of a thousand horse.   Whatever her feelings, the Queen could not refuse an acknowledgment of her sister's fealty and affection.   The two entered the tumultuous excited city side by side, amidst the most enthusiastic demonstrations of popular delight, and, crowned with the glory of success, Mary entered the Tower.

Meanwhile, Lady Jane had divested herself of the trappings of royalty with more pleasure than she had assumed them.   Her only desire was to return to the private station from which she had been most unwillingly elevated.   Nor was Mary wholly a stranger to all generous emotions; but influenced by the counsels of Renard, the Spanish ambassador, she ordered that Jane and her husband, and the Duke and Duchess of Suffolk, should be strictly guarded as prisoners of state.   To increase the bitterness of the poor lady's sorrows, she was separated from her husband, and deprived of the solace his affection might have afforded.   Yet even in this hour of trial she displayed a matchless constancy and a serene fortitude worthy of happier fortunes.

The Duke and Duchess were released after a few days' confinement; but Renard insisted that no such indulgence should be extended to Lady Jane and her husband, who were far less culpable, and whose youth and inexperience powerfully pleaded for mercy.

The Duke of Northumberland perished on the scaffold on the 22d of August. In his last hours he declared himself a Catholic, and loaded with opprobrium the professors of that new religion of which he had recently been a disciple. He fell unlamented, as he had lived unloved.

His apostasy amazed and disgusted his victim, Lady Jane, who had hitherto been unable to penetrate all the intricacies of his dark and subtle character. She had thought him animated by zeal for the Reformed Church; she now discovered that grasping ambition had been his motive principle. Her opinions on his conduct have been preserved by a contemporary chronicler,* who dined with her at the house where she was confined— the house of one Partridge, a warder of the Tower. His narrative seems to us full of interest :—

How Rowland Lea dined with the Lady Jane Grey, and what the Lady Jane spoke concerning the Duke of Northumberland.

'On Tuesday, the 29th of August, I dined at Partridge's house with my Lady Jane, she sitting at the board's end, and there being present Partridge, his wife, Jacob, my lady's gentlewoman, and her man. She commanding Partridge and me to put on our caps, amongst our communication at the dinner this was to be noted : after she had once or twice drunk to me, and bade me heartily welcome, saith she,—

'"The Queen's Majesty is a merciful princess; I beseech God she may long continue, and may he send his bountiful grace upon her."

* This is supposed to have been Rowland Lea, an officer of the Mint. His 'Chronicle of Queen Jane and Queen Mary' was published by the Camden Society.

' After that we fell in discourse of matters of religion ; and she asked who he was that preached at Paul's on Sunday before ; and so it was told her to be one ——

'" I pray you," quoth she, "have they mass in London ?"

'" Yea, forsooth," quoth I, " in some places."

'" It may so be," quoth she ; " it is not so strange as the sudden conversion of the late Duke ; for who would have thought he would have so done?"

' It was answered her, " Perchance he thereby hoped to have had his pardon."

'" Pardon !" quoth she, "wo worth him ! he hath brought me and our stock in most miserable calamity and misery by his exceeding ambition ; but for the answering that he hoped for life by his turning, though other men be of that opinion, I utterly am not. For what man is there living, I pray you, although he had been innocent, that would hope of life in that case ; being in the field against the Queen in person as general, and after his taking so hated and evil-spoken of by the commons ; and at his coming into prison, so wondered at (gazed at, as if he had been a wild beast—a show of wonder) as the like was never heard by any man's time? Who can judge that he should hope for pardon, whose life was odious to all men? But what will ye more? Like as his life was wicked and full of dissimulation, so was his end thereafter. I pray God, I, nor no friend of mine, die so ! Should I, who am young and in the flower of my years, forsake my faith for the love of life? Nay, God forbid ! Much more he should not, whose fatal course, although he had lived his just number of years, could not have long continued. But life was sweet, it appeared; so he might have lived (you will say) he cared not how. Indeed, the reason is good; for he that would have lived in chains to have had his life, by like would leave no other means unattempted. But God be merciful to us, for he saith, 'Whoso denieth him before men, he will not know him in his Father's kingdom.'" With this, and much like talk, the dinner passed away; which ended, I thanked her ladyship that she would vouchsafe to accept me in her company; and she thanked me likewise, and said I was welcome. She thanked Partridge also for bringing me to dinner. "Madam," said he, "we were somewhat bold, not knowing that your ladyship dined below, until we found your ladyship there." And so Partridge and I departed.'

On the 13th of November, Lady Jane and her husband, with his two brothers, Lords Ambrose and Henry Dudley, were brought to trial at the Guildhall. As no defence could be successfully attempted, they all pleaded guilty to the charges of the indictment, and the terrible sentence of death was passed upon them. They were then removed to the Tower under a strong guard; the populace, as Lady Jane passed by, testifying their sympathy for her in a very marked and evident manner. They had refused to acknowledge her as Queen, but they respected her misfortunes and admired her. virtues. On this occasion Lady Jane and her husband met for the first time since their imprisonment—met under the shadow of death, and on the margin of a premature grave! They were conveyed into separate apartments on their return to the Tower, and spoke to each other no more in this work-day world. Alas, how brief their dream of happiness! How quickly had the promise of their young lives faded into the sere and yellow leaf! Youth was still at the prow, but Death had taken possession of the helm; and the bark drove rapidly down the tide to a storm-tossed sea!

Great efforts were made by Lady Jane's friends and kinsmen to obtain for her the royal clemency, and some authorities—Foxe, the martyrologist, among others—assert that it was solemnly promised if she would abjure the Protestant faith. Jane, however, was made of sterner stuff than to abandon what she believed to be God's truth for the sake of a shameful life. Had she apostatized, she would have felt herself dishonoured; and she calmly rejected all the promises held out to her by Mary's subtle myrmidons. Whether she would eventually have been brought to the scaffold may, however, be considered doubtful, had not the Queen's jealous fears been aroused by Sir Thomas Wyatt's inopportune and abortive insurrection.

It is necessary to remind the reader that early in 1534 Mary contracted a marriage with Philip II. of Spain—that obstinate fanatic whose character has been so vividly portrayed by Mr. Lothrop Motley's merciless pen. The alliance was hateful to the great majority of the English people, who have no stomach for foreign rulers, and who, alarmed at the preponderating power of Spain—in those days the leading European nation—not unnaturally feared that England might sink into a mere dependency of the Peninsular kingdom.

An insurrection broke out, headed by Sir Thomas Wyatt, who raised the men of Kent by his vigorous and stirring appeals. Sir Peter Carew, at the same time, roused the sturdy spirit of the Devonshire peasants, and the flames of revolt spread so rapidly as soon to threaten a conflagration of the entire kingdom. Unhappily for the movement, and unhappily for himself and daughter, it was joined by the old Duke of Suffolk, who attempted to divert it in favour of the Lady Jane.* But the insurgents were rebelling, not against the Queen, but against the Queen's proposed husband; and many of the most powerful leaders immediately abandoned the scheme, when it was sought to convert it into a design against the throne. Wyatt, however, rapidly and successfully advanced upon the metropolis; and had he pushed on to London, where the spirit of Protestantism and independence was notably strong, he would probably have brought Mary to terms. But the man who pauses when halfway across a dangerous torrent, is surely lost. Wyatt lost courage; retired from the Surrey side of the river, and fell back upon Kingston (February 7, 1554). His hesitation gave Mary's councillors the time they needed to complete their preparations; and when, crossing the river by Kingston Bridge, he returned on London, he was intercepted at Knightsbridge by an overpowering force. His followers deserted him; and after a brief, fierce struggle he was taken prisoner. Carew and Suffolk were equally unsuccessful, and the insurrection was promptly quelled. A *Te Deum* was sung and the bells were rung in every parish-church in London; and the leaders of the revolt expiated their errors on the scaffold.

'The fathers have eaten sour grapes,' says an old historian, 'and the children's teeth are set on edge.' Neither Lady Jane Grey nor her husband had taken the

* Froude, 'History of England,' vi. 169-180.

smallest share in this insurrection, or had given its leaders their sympathy or encouragement. But the Queen, in her alarm, determined that they should be removed from her path. ''The innocent lady must suffer for her father's fault: had not the Duke of Suffolk this second time made shipwreck of his loyalty, his daughter, perhaps, had never tasted the salt water of the Queen's displeasure, but now, as a Rock of Offence, she is the first that must be removed.' Her youth, her innocence, her gentleness, her erudition, rendered her all the more hateful in Mary's eyes, who probably regretted that so many virtues should adorn a hopeless heretic.

On the 8th of February, the Queen's confessor, John of Feckenham, informed the ill-fated prisoner—the unhappy victim of the ambition of others—that she was to die on the following day. She listened to the terrible intelligence with serene composure, with all the tranquillity of a spirit that had learned to place its hopes of happiness in a future world. Feckenham endeavoured to engage her in a theological disputation, but she replied that she had now no time to think of aught but her preparation for eternity. In his zeal to reclaim so gentle a lamb within the folds of his Church, Feckenham obtained from Mary a respite for three days, but Lady Jane had no desire to linger so long in the Valley of the Shadow of Death. 'You are much deceived,' she said to him, 'if you think I had any desire of longer life: for I assure you since the time you went from me, my life has been so tedious to me, that I long for nothing so much as death, and since it is the Queen's pleasure, I am most willing to undergo it.'

If Feckenham supposed that in these three days he

would induce Lady Jane to swerve from a faith which she had embraced with her whole heart, her whole mind, and her whole soul, he soon found how greatly he had deceived himself. And subtle disputant as he was, he was effectually baffled by the force and simplicity of the heretic's arguments. He behaved towards her, however, with a courtesy and a reverence which did him no small honour.

These theological discussions would have no interest for our younger readers, but they will peruse with sympathy the touching letters which the doomed lady, on the very threshold of death, addressed to her father and her sister, and which will be found subjoined to this brief narrative.

· During her captivity she occasionally beguiled her time by engraving some sentences expressive of her resignation and her hopefulness on the walls of her prison with a pin. Thus, she wrote:—

> ' Non aliena putes homini quæ obtingere possunt:
> Sors hodierna mihi cras erat illa tibi.'

> *Translated:*

> ' Believe not, man, in care's despite,
>   That thou from others' ills art free,
> The *cross* that now *I* suffer might
>   To-morrow, haply, fall on *thee*.

And again:—

> ' Deo juvante nil nocet livor malus,
>   Et non juvante, nil juvat labor gravis,
>   Post tenebras spero lucem.'

Of which the following translation is usually given:—

> ' Endless all malice, if our God is nigh;
>   Fruitless all pains, if he his help deny.
>   Patient I pass these gloomy hours away,
>   And wait the morning of eternal day.'

A manual of prayers, in manuscript and on vellum, was ever in her hand during her last hours. It contained thirty-five prayers, but by whom written historians have not been able to ascertain. It is generally supposed that they were compiled for the use of the Duke of Somerset, the Protector, during his imprisonment in the Tower, and from thence descended to Lord Guildford Dudley. After the Duke of Suffolk was captured, leave was granted to him, his daughter, and her husband, to borrow this book from one another, and it accordingly furnished them with a channel for the communication of mutual assurances of love and tenderness. We find the following brief but pathetic note from Lady Jane to her father:—

'The Lord comfort your grace, and that in his Word, wherein all creatures only are to be comforted; and though it hath pleased God to take away two of your children, yet think not, I most humbly beseech your grace, that you have lost them; but trust that we, by leaving this mortal life, have won an immortal life. And I, for my part, as I have honoured your grace in this life, will pray for you in another life.—Your grace's humble daughter, JANE DUDLEY.'

She appears to have bequeathed this book, as a souvenir, to Sir John Brydges, the Lieutenant of the Tower, and inscribed on a leaf the following sentences of farewell:—

'Forasmuch as you have desired so simple a woman to write in so worthy a book, good Master Lieutenant, therefore I shall, as a friend, desire you, and, as a Christian, require you, to call upon God to incline your heart to his laws, to quicken you in his way, and not to take the word of truth utterly out of your mouth.

'*Live still to die*,* that by death you may purchase eternal life; and remember how Methuselah, though, as we read in the Scriptures, he was the longest liver that was of a man, died at the last: for, as the preacher saith, "There is a time to be born, and a time to die; and the day of death is better than the day of our birth."—Yours, as the Lord knoweth, as a friend,   JANE DUDLEY.' †

IV.

The supreme hour at length arrived. It was the 12th of February 1554, and the place where the last scene of a mournful tragedy was to be played out, the Tower —so fatally memorable in the annals of the Tudor reigns. The Government had originally designed that both Lady Jane and her husband should be executed together on Tower Hill; but it was rightly judged that the spectacle of so youthful and comely a pair, suffering for what was rather the crime of others than their own, might too powerfully arouse the generous sympathies

---

* A sentiment finely expressed by the American poet, Bryant :—

> ' So live, that, when thy summons comes to join
> The innumerable caravan, that moves
> To the pale realm of shade, where each shall take
> His chamber in the silent halls of death,
> Thou go not like the quarry slave at night,
> Scourged to his dungeon; but, sustained and soothed
> By an unfaltering trust, approach thy grave,
> Like one who wraps the drapery of his couch
> About him, and lies down to pleasant dreams.'

† ' Chronicle of Queen Jane and Queen Mary,' p. 57, note.

of the multitude.. The Council therefore ordered that
Lady Jane should be put to death within the Tower
walls.

Guildford, on the morning of his execution, had obtained permission to take a last farewell of his beloved
wife, but she perceived that so bitter a parting might
overwhelm them both, and deprive them of the courage
needful for a calm endurance of the last great trial.
She sent him, therefore, many loving messages, remind-
ing him how brief would be their separation, and how
quickly they would rejoin each other 'where the wicked
cease from troubling, and the weary are at rest,' but
affectionately declined to see him. In going to the
place of execution, however, he passed beneath the
window of her cell, so that they had an opportunity of
exchanging a farewell look, and mutely expressing the
depth and sincerity of their love.

On the scaffold Guildford behaved with great intrepidity. After spending a brief space in silent devotion,
he requested the prayers of the spectators, and laying
his head upon the block, gave the fatal signal. At one
blow his head was severed from his body.

The scaffold on which Lady Jane was doomed to
suffer stood on the green opposite the White Tower. As
soon as her husband was dead, the officers announced
that the sheriffs waited to attend her thither. And being
come down and delivered into their hands, the bystanders
noted in her 'a countenance so gravely settled with all
modest and comely resolution, that not the least symptom
either of fear or grief could be perceived either in her
speech or motions; she was like one going to be united
to her heart's best and longest beloved.'

So, like a martyr, crowned with everlasting glory, she went unto her death. Only for one moment was her serene composure shaken, when, through an unfortunate accident, for 'it was not wilful cruelty,' she met on her way her husband's headless corpse being carried to its last resting-place. At so pitiful a sight she was a little startled, and many tears were seen to descend upon her cheeks. 'O Guildford! Guildford!' she exclaimed; 'the ante-past is not so bitter that you have tasted, and that I shall soon taste, as to make my flesh tremble; it is nothing compared to the feast that you and I shall this day partake of in heaven.' With this thought she consoled her stricken heart, and, surely comforted and supported by invisible spirits, proceeded to the scaffold as if bidden to a wedding-banquet.

She was conducted thither by Sir John Brydges, the Lieutenant of the Tower, and attended by her two waiting-women, Mrs. Elizabeth Tylncy and Mrs. Ellen. While these were sobbing bitterly, she shed not a tear, and the sunshine of assured hope brightened her youthful countenance. She read earnestly her Manual of Devotion. On reaching the place of execution she saluted the lords and gentlemen present with unshaken composure and infinite grace. No Protestant minister was allowed to attend her; and to the benevolent exhortations of Feckenham, the Queen's confessor, she gave but little heed. Yet was she not indifferent to his respectful sympathy, and when bidding him farewell, she said: 'Go now; God grant you all your desires, and accept my own warm thanks for your attentions to me; although, indeed, those attentions have tried me more than death could now terrify me.'

She then addressed a few words to the spectators. They breathed a gentle and forgiving spirit. She declared that she had accepted the crown contrary to her own judgment and against her own desire, but vindicated the justice of God in her premature death, which did but rightly punish her for the many sins she had committed. 'Good people,' she exclaimed, 'I am come hither to die, and by law I am condemned to the same. My offence against the Queen's highness was only in consent to the device of others, which now is deemed treason; but it was never my seeking, but by counsel of those who should seem to have further understanding of things than I, who knew little of the law, and much less of the titles to the crown. I pray you all, good Christian people, to bear me witness that I die a true Christian woman, and that I look to be saved by none other means but only by the mercy of God, in the merits of the blood of his only Son, Jesus Christ: and I confess, when I did know the Word of God I neglected the same, loved myself and the world, and therefore this plague or punishment is happily and worthily happened unto me for my sins; and yet I thank God of his goodness, that he hath thus given me a time and respite to repent. And now, good people, while I am alive, I pray you to assist me with your prayers.'

She then knelt down to perform her devotions, and turning to Feckenham, inquired, whether she should repeat the fifty-first Psalm, 'Miserere mei, Deus,'— 'Have mercy upon me, O Lord?' He replied in the affirmative, and she said it with great earnestness, from beginning to end. Rising from her knees, she next began to make ready for the headsman, and pulling off her gloves, gave them and her handkerchief to Mistress Tylney. The manual of prayers which had afforded her so much comfort, she handed to Master Thomas Brydges, the Lieutenant's brother. When she began to undo her robe, the executioner would have assisted her, but she put him aside, and accepted the last offices of her waiting-women, who then gave her a white handkerchief to bandage her eyes.

The headsman now threw himself at her feet and craved her forgiveness, which she willingly granted. He next requested her to stand upon the straw. In taking up this position, she for the first time saw the block, but it did not disturb her composure, and she simply entreated the executioner to despatch her quickly. Again kneeling, she asked him, 'Will you take it off before I lay me down?' 'No, madam,' he replied. She bound the . handkerchief round her eyes, and feeling for the block, exclaimed, 'What shall I do? Where is it?' She was guided to it by one of the bystanders, and laying her head upon it, exclaimed, in an audible voice, 'Lord, into thy hands I commend my spirit.'

In an instant the axe fell, and all was over. A groan from the assembled multitude proclaimed that vengeance, rather than justice, had been satisfied. *

So was this gentle lady summoned in mercy to a heavenly crown, lest, haply, a longer pilgrimage through a busy world should have sullied the pure spirit which no circumstances could have rendered more fit for heaven.

* 'Chronicle of Queen Jane and Queen Mary,' pp. 58, 59.

Lady Jane Grey was eighteen years old when she died. History has preserved with satisfactory fulness the events of her life, and the incidents of its final scene, but has neglected to record the place where her body was interred. Probably both she and her husband were buried in that Chapel within the Tower where reposes so much illustrious and ill-fated dust.*

Letter of Lady Jane Grey to her Father, the Duke of Suffolk: Written Three Days before her Execution.†

'FATHER,—Although it hath pleased God to hasten my death by you, by whom my life should rather have

---

* Of this chapel Macaulay finely says:—' In truth there is no sadder spot on the earth than that little cemetery. Death is there associated, not, as in West-minster Abbey and St. Paul's, with genius and virtue, with public veneration and imperishable renown; not, as in our humblest churches and churchyards, with everything that is most endearing in social and domestic charities: but with whatever is darkest in human nature and human destiny, with the savage triumph of impla-cable enemies, with the inconstancy, the ingratitude, the cowardice of friends, with all the miseries of fallen greatness and of blighted fame. Thither have been carried, through successive ages, by the rude hands of jailers, without one mourner following, the bleeding relics of men who had been the captains of armies, the leaders of parties, the oracles of senates, and the ornaments of courts. Ed-ward Seymour, Duke of Somerset, and Protector of the realm, reposes there by the brother whom he murdered. There has mouldered away the headless trunk of John Fisher, Bishop of Rochester and Cardinal of St. Vitalis, a man worthy to have lived in a better age, and to have died in a better cause. There are laid John Dudley, Duke of Northumberland, Lord High Admiral, and Thomas Cromwell, Earl of Essex, Lord High Treasurer. There, too, is an-other Essex, on whom nature and fortune had lavished all their bounties in vain, and whom valour, grace, genius, royal favour, popular applause, conducted to an early and ignominious doom. Not far off sleep two chiefs of the great House of Howard, Thomas, fourth Duke of Norfolk, and Philip, eleventh Earl of Arundel. Here and there, among the thick graves of unquiet and aspiring statesmen, lie more delicate sufferers: Margaret of Salisbury, the last of the proud name of Plantagenet, and those two fair queens who perished by the jealous rage of Henry.'—*History of England*, ch. v.

† Sir Harris Nicolas. ' Literary Remains of Lady Jane Grey.' ed. 1832.

been lengthened, yet can I so patiently take it, that I yield God more hearty thanks for shortening my woful days than if all the world had been given into my possession, with life lengthened at my own will. And, albeit I am well assured of your impatient dolours, redoubled many ways, both in bewailing your own woe, and especially, as I am informed, my woful estate; yet, my dear father (if I may, without offence, rejoice in my own mishaps), meseems in this I may account myself blessed, that washing my hands with the innocency of my fact, my guiltless blood may cry before the Lord, Mercy to the innocent! And though I must needs acknowledge that, being constrained, and, as you know well enough, continually assayed, in taking [the royal authority] upon me, I seemed to consent, and therein grievously offended the Queen and her laws; yet do I assuredly trust, that this my offence towards God is so much the less, in that, being in so royal state as I was, my enforced honour never blended with mine innocent heart. And thus, good father, I have opened unto you the state wherein I presently stand. My death at hand, although to you, perhaps, it may seem right woful, yet to me there is nothing that can be more welcoming, than from this vale of misery to aspire to that heavenly of all joy and pleasure, with Christ our Saviour, in whose steadfast faith (if it may be lawful for the daughter so to write to the father) may the Lord, that hath hitherto strengthened you, so continue to keep you, that at the last we may meet in heaven with the Father, the Son, and the Holy Ghost.—I am, your obedient daughter unto death,

'JANE DUDLEY.'

Letter of Lady Jane Grey to her Sister, the Lady Katherine. Written, on the Eve of her Execution, at the end of a New Testament (in Greek) which she sent to her as a farewell token.*

'I have here sent you, my dear sister Katherine, a book, which, although it be not outwardly trimmed in gold, or the curious embroidery of the artfullest needles, yet inwardly is more worth than all the precious mines which the vast world can boast of. It is the book, my only best and best beloved sister, of the law of the Lord; it is the testament and last will which he bequeathed unto us wretches and wretched sinners, which shall lead you to the path of eternal joy. And, if you with a good mind read it, and with an earnest desire follow it, no doubt it shall bring you to an immortal and everlasting life. It will teach you to live, and learn you to die; it shall win you more, and endow you with greater felicity, than you should have gained by the possession of your woful father's lands; for as, if God had prospered him, you should have inherited his honours and manors; so, if you apply diligently to this book, seeking to direct your life according to the rule of the same, you shall be an inheritor of such riches as neither the covetous shall withdraw from you, neither the thief shall steal, neither yet the moths corrupt. Desire, with David, my best sister, to understand the law of the Lord your God; live still to die, that you by death may purchase eternal life, and trust not that the tenderness of your age shall lengthen your life; for unto God, when he calleth, all hours, times, and seasons are alike, and blessed

* Sir Harris Nicolas, 'Literary Remains of Lady Jane Grey,' ed. 1832.

are they whose lamps are furnished when he cometh, for as soon will the Lord be glorified in the young as in the old.

' My good sister, once more again let me entreat you to learn to die; deny the world, defy the devil, and despise the flesh, and delight yourself only in the Lord; be penitent for your sins, and yet despair not; be strong in faith, yet presume not; and desire, with Saint Paul, to be dissolved and to be with Christ, with whom even in death there is life.

' Be like the good servant, and even at midnight be waking, lest, when death cometh and stealeth upon you like a thief in the night, you be, with the servants of darkness, found sleeping; and lest, for lack of oil, you be found like the five foolish virgins, or like him that had not on the wedding-garment, and then you be cast into darkness or banished from the marriage. Rejoice in Christ, as I trust you do; and, seeing you have the name of a Christian, as near as you can, follow the steps, and be a true imitator of your Master, Christ Jesus, and take up your cross, lay your sins on his back, and always embrace him.

' Now, as touching my death, rejoice, as I do, my dearest sister, that I shall be delivered of this corruption, and put on incorruption; for I am assured that I shall, for losing a mortal life, win one that is immortal, ever-lasting, and joyful; the which I pray God grant in his most blessed hour, and send you his all-saving grace to live in his fear, and to die in true Christian faith, from which, in God's name, I exhort you never swerve, neither for hope of life nor fear of death; for if you will deny his truth, to give length to a weary and corrupt breath,

God himself will deny you, and by vengeance make short what you, by your soul's loss, would prolong; but if you will cleave to him he will stretch forth your days to an uncircumscribed comfort, and to his own glory, to the which glory God bring me now, and you hereafter, when it shall please him to call you. Farewell, once again, my beloved sister, and put your only trust in God, who only must help you. Amen.—Your loving sister,

'JANE DUDLEY.'

VIII

A Noble English Mother.

THE STORY OF MARY, COUNTESS OF PEMBROKE.

'But still the better part of me will live,
And in that part will live thy reverend name,
Although thyself dost far more glory give
Unto thyself, than I can by the same.'

GEORGE DANIEL.

THIS was the wise and amiable sister of Sir Philip Sidney—of him whose life was poetry put into action—of him whom all men have agreed to admire as the English Bayard, *sans peur et sans reproche* —and it is no slight praise when we say that she was the worthy sister of such a brother.

She came of a good stock. Her father, Sir Henry Sidney, of Penshurst Place, in the county of Kent, was one of Elizabeth's most trusty councillors: a far-seeing legislator and a skilful captain, he administered the government of Ireland with singular success, and conciliated the affections of the Irish, while sternly repressing every rebellious outbreak. As a man, his life was eminently noble: his soul was free from every sordid thought or debasing passion; his charity was open as the day; his sense of duty governed every action; as a husband and a father he mingled love with firmness, decision of will with the utmost sweetness of disposition.*

Her mother was Mary Dudley, daughter of John, Duke of Northumberland. As she was by descent of great nobility, so was she by nature of a noble and congenial spirit. She possessed the ability without the darker qualities of her race, and had the remarkable fortune of giving to English history Sir Philip Sidney, and to English society Mary, Countess of Pembroke. How can one judge better of a tree than by the fruits it brings forth?

Mary was born at Penshurst Place, and spent her childhood in that fair demesne which Spenser's memory and Ben Jonson's verse have immortalized. Her parents superintended her studies with peculiar care, and had the satisfaction of seeing their labours recompensed by the rapid development of more than ordinary powers of mind. In after-years her acquirements extorted a warm eulogium from no incompetent a judge, Osborn, the historian of the reign of James I.—'She was that sister of Sir Philip Sidney,' he says, 'to whom he addressed his "Arcadia," and of whom he had no other advantage than what he received from the partial benevolence of fortune in making him a man (which yet she did, in some judgments, recompense in beauty), her pen being nothing short of his, as I am ready to attest, having seen some incomparable letters of hers.' And Spenser refers to her as

> 'Clorinda bright
> The gentlest shepherdess that lives this day,
> And most resembling both in shape and spirit
> Her brother dear.'†

* Froude, 'History of England,' vol. vii. p. 466.
† Spenser, 'Astrophel,' last stanza.

Of the domestic life of Penshurst, and the happy household that flourished under its ancient roof, Ben Jonson furnishes a pleasant picture, too long for quotation in these pages, though we may extract his allusion to the care with which Sir Henry and Lady Mary watched over the ripening promise of their children * :—

> ' They are, and have been taught religion; thence
> Their gentler spirits have suck'd innocence.
> Each morn, and even, they are taught to pray,
> With the whole household, and may, every day,
> Read in their virtuous parents' noble parts,
> The mysteries of manners, arms, and arts.
> Now, Penshurst, they that will proportion thee
> With other edifices, when they see
> Those proud ambitious heaps, and nothing else,
> May say, Their lords have built, but thy lord dwells.'

A sweet affection subsisted between Mary Sidney and her accomplished brother. Their dispositions presented many points of resemblance, and they delighted in the same studies. To each poetry was an exceeding great good, and they loved to cultivate the muse in the retirement of Penshurst. It is to Mary Sidney's appreciation of the beautiful that we owe the ' Arcadia,' which but for her gentle admonitions and her loving care would never have been preserved for the world. She did not possess the inventive faculty of genius, and could essay no lofty flights of song. But, warmed by the example of her brother, and stimulated, perhaps, by her brother's friend, the poet of ' The Faery Queen,' she occasionally thought in numbers, and ' the numbers came.' Either at Penshurst, or in later life, at Wilton, she composed that version of the Psalms known as the Sydnean Psalms, whose sweetness and tender grace have induced Hartley

* Ben Jonson, ' The Forest;' ii. Penshurst.

Coleridge to remark that 'it was a pity they were not
authorized to be sung in churches, for the present
versions are a disgrace and a mischief to the Establishment.' And quaint old Daniel, the Elizabethan poet,
eulogizes,——

> 'These hymns which thou didst consecrate to heaven,
> Which Israel's singer to his God did frame;'

and which, he says,

> 'Unto thy voyage eternity have given,
> And make thee dear to him from whence they came.'*

Mary Sidney was also the authoress of a 'Pastoral
Dialogue in praise of Astræa'—that is, of Queen Elizabeth—which abounds in the flowery conceits of the time.
It is not without a certain ease of versification, as the
following stanzas evidence:—

> *Thenot* 'Astræa may be justly said,
> A field in flowery robe arrayed,
> In seasons freshly springing.
>
> *Piers* 'That Spring endures but shortest time,
> This never leaves Astræa's clime;
> Thou nest instead of singing.'
>
> *Thenot* They Piers of friendship tell me why,
> Thy meaning true, my words should lie,
> As I strive in vain to raise her?'
>
> *Piers* Words from conceit do onely rise,
> Above conceit her honour flies,
> But silence nought can praise her.

In the same connection we may refer to her elegy on
the death of her illustrious brother, which contains some
passages of exquisite beauty, and the 'sweetness of
whose verse' has been commended by Spenser. It is
entitled the 'Doleful Lay of Clorinda,' and among the
more pathetic stanzas are the following :—

* George Daniel, Dedication of 'Cleopatra, a Tragedy,' A.D. 1591.

'The fairest flower in field that ever grew,
  Was Astrophel; that was, we all may rue.

'Oh, death! that hast us of such riches reft,
  Tell us at least what hast thou with it done
What is become of him whose flower here left
  Is but the shadow of his likeness gone?
Scarce like the shadow of that which he was,
Nought like, but that he like a shade did pass.

'But that immortal spirit, which was deckt
  With all the dowries of celestial grace,
By sovran choice from th' heavenly quires select,
  And lineally derived from angels' race,
Oh, what is now of it become aread,
Ay, me, can so divine a thing be dead?

'Ah, no; it is not dead, nor can it die,
  But lives for aye in blissful Paradise:
Where like a new-born babe it soft doth lie,
  In bed of lilies wrapt in tender wise;
And compassed all about with roses sweet,
And dainty violets from head to feet.

'There thousand birds, all of celestial brood,
  To him do sweetly carol day and night;
And with strange notes, of him well understood,
  Lull him asleep in angelic delight;
Whilst in sweet dream to him presented be
Immortal beauties, which no eye may see.

'But *he* them sees, and takes exceeding pleasure
  Of their divine aspécts, appearing plain,
And kindling love in him above all measure,
  Sweet love still joyous, never feeling pain.
For what so goodly form he there doth see,
He may enjoy from jealous rancour free.

'There liveth he in everlasting bliss,
  Sweet spirit, never fearing more to die;
No dreading harm from any foes of his,
  No fearing savage beasts more cruelty.
Whilst we here, wretches, wail his private lack,*
And with vain vows do often call him back.

          * That is, lament his individual loss.

'But live thou there, still happy, happy spirit,
  And give us leave thee here thus to lament !
Not thee that dost thy heaven's joy inherit,
  But our own selves that here in dole are drent.*
Thus do we weep and wail and wear our eyes,
Mourning, in other, our own miseries !'

It may be objected that the grief for a brother's loss
which could find expression in a 'copy of verses' could
not have been very sincere or lasting. But the reader
must remember the character of the age in which Sir
Philip and Mary Sidney flourished. A virgin queen was
on the throne, surrounded by an atmosphere of poetry
which interpenetrated every social relation. Queen and
courtiers, statesmen, warriors, nobles, all played their
parts, as it were, in a gorgeous masquerade, as if England were the Arcady of the old myths, and the days of
gods and goddesses had come back again. Passion was
real, and thought and feeling were real, but they sought
expression in a revivification of the old forms. The
English gentleman wooed the English maiden under the
sweet guise of Strephon and Thyrsis, and when Strephon
and Thyrsis were married, poets chanted their bridal
hymn, or Epathalamion, as in the palmy time of Grecian
splendour. When they died, flowers were cast upon
their graves, monodies, and elegies, and rhymed laments,
which seem to a more prosaic age the excess of artifice,
but were the true utterances of a genuine sorrow. This
stage-play, acted in so large a theatre, and in which the
performers were the leading spirits of the nation, was not
without a beneficial influence. It encouraged a poetical
and enthusiastic spirit; it stimulated a love of art; it
refined the manners and tastes of an age which retained

* ' In dole are drent '—that is, in grief are drowned, or overwhelmed !

much of the grossness of the past ; it fostered the genius
of men like Spenser, and Ben Jonson, and Shakspeare ;
and it inspired the heroic to deeds of daring, like those
of Drake and Raleigh ; or of noble self-denial, like
Sidney's on the field of Zutphen.

Let not the reader, therefore, conclude that Mary
Sidney's sorrow was unreal, when it found utterance in
the ' Doleful Lay of Clorinda.'

Happy must have been the young lives of the brother
and sister in the shadow of the stately halls of Penshurst,
enjoying sweet communion over the immortal page of
poet, moralist, and divine, contemplating the fair Kent-
ish landscapes that smiled around their ancient home,
and occasionally essaying a gentle flight of song.   Sidney
himself in his ' Arcadia ' has described the pleasant
scenes among which he and his fair sister thus passed
their early years :—

'There were hills,' he says, ' which garnished their
proud heights with stately trees ; humble valleys whose
base estate seemed comforted with the refreshing of silver
rivers ; meadows enamelled with all sorts of eye-pleasing
flowers ; thickets which, being lined with most pleasant
shade, were witnessed so too, by the cheerful disposition
of many well-tuned birds ; each pasture stored with sheep
feeding with sober security, while the pretty lambs' with
bleating oratory craved the dam's comfort ; here a shepherd's boy piping as though he should never be old,
there a young shepherdess knitting, and withal singing,
and it seemed that her voice comforted her hands to
work, and her hands kept time to her voice-music.   As
for the houses of the country (for many houses came

under their eye), they were all scattered, no two being
one by the other, and yet not so far off as that it barred
mutual succour; a show, as it were, of an accompanion-
able solitariness and of a civil wilderness.'

Penshurst—we have said elsewhere [*]—is one of the
fairest of the many fair halls of Kent, and brings, as it
were, the splendour and *poetical materialism*—that day-
light masquerade of which we have already spoken—
visibly before the eyes of the present. The park is now-
a-days somewhat deficient in timber, but has, nevertheless, an excellent sprinkling of fine old trees, and many
sunny spots of greenery for poets made. From several
points the views are extremely beautiful : the park
ascends from the house in a northerly direction, and
sends out on either hand a number of small dells to lose
themselves in the green depths of the distant hills. Hop-
clusters hang upon the slopes, save where the green-
sward teems with sheep 'feeding in sober security,' or
lies enamelled 'with all sorts of eye-pleasing flowers.'
Besides these general beauties, the scene has special
attractions for artist, poet, and scholar in its memorials
of genius and virtue, love and loveliness. Assuredly, the
pilgrim will not forget the *Sidney Oak*—

> "That taller tree, which of a nut was set
> At his great birth, where all the muses met [†]

or the famous grove of beeches, named *Saccharissa's
Walk*, from the Lady Dorothy Sidney, immortalized as
Saccharissa by the poet Waller :—

> 'Ye lofty beeches! tell this matchless dame,
> That if together ye fed all one flame,

---

[*] London Society,' i. 44-48 : 'The Story of an Old English Mansion.'
[†] Ben Jonson 'Penshurst, ut supra

It could not equalize the hundredth part
Of what her eyes have kindled in my heart.
. . . . The plants admire,
No less than those of old did Orpheus' lyre:
If she sit down, with tops all tow'rds her bowed,
They round about her into arbours crowd:
Or if she walks, in even ranks they stand,
Like some well-marshalled and obsequious band.'*

But, perhaps, the finest thing in the park is a noble
avenue of limes, extending from the terrace eastward,
which has often inspired our landscape painters, and in
whose cool shade the Lady Mary may have often
meditated—·

'Are days of old familiar to thy mind,
O reader? Hast thou let the midnight hour
Pass unperceived, whilst there in fancy lived
With high-born beauties and enamoured chiefs,
Sharing their hopes, and with a breathless joy
Whose expectation touched the verge of pain,
Following their dangerous fortunes?

'If *such* love
Hath ever thrilled thy bosom, thou wilt tread,
As with a pilgrim's reverential thoughts,
The groves of Penshurst.' †

Among such scenes, we say, was Lady Mary nurtured,
and their influence coloured all her later life, cherishing
that love of the beautiful which she preserved to her
last hour, and favouring a simplicity and purity of taste
somewhat rare in the days of the Tudors and the Stuarts.

In 1576, the Lady Mary was married to Henry Herbert, Earl of Pembroke; and thus brought to the noble
stock of the Herberts the high acquirements and chivalrous spirit of the Sidneys. The best blood of both these
famous races was recently seen in the lamented Sidney

* Waller, 'Poems:' Miscellanies, xii.   † Southey, 'Poems:' Inscriptions.

Herbert, Lord Herbert of Lea. She was the earl's third wife, and much his junior, but the match was crowned by no ordinary felicity. The issue was two sons—one of whom, William, became a distinguished cavalier in the days of Charles Stuart; the younger, Philip, espoused the cause of the Parliament.

At Wilton, the seat of the Earl of Pembroke, a magnificent hospitality was maintained, and the Countess loved to surround herself with the wits and poets of the day—Raleigh, and Spenser, and Ben Jonson, Philip Massinger, and the poet and divine, Dr. John Donne. She possessed that social tact which puts the stranger immediately at his ease, and insensibly draws him forth to contribute his due quota to the instruction and entertainment of the company. A woman of varied acquirements, she could take her share in the gravest conversation or the lightest talk, and while she appreciated the jests of Ben Jonson, could relish the grave sententiousness of Dr. Donne. Her portrait gives one at first the impression of a plain, long face, with somewhat heavy features; but examine it more closely, and you see that the eyebrows are finely arched, and that the eyes are full of thoughtfulness. The abundant hair is lifted off a low, broad, firm-set forehead, and dressed in a cluster of tiny curls. A smile plays around the well-chiselled lips, which indicate considerable firmness of character. The dress is sumptuous, but betrays the rigid stateliness of the Elizabethan style. An enormous ruff of rich lace, vandycked at the edges in a double row, encloses a fair round throat and neck, which two rows of immense pearls closely embrace. A velvet mantle, bordered with miniver, falls over the long tight sleeves of the close-

fitting bodice. Two pear-shaped pearls glitter beneath
the hair, and a Psalter is clasped in the long, thin,
aristocratic hand.

The deep affection which prevailed between Sir Philip
and his noble sister was not diminished by her marriage, ·
and glowed undimmed until his bright career was prematurely ended on the field of Zutphen. We have
already shown how deeply she mourned him, and how
her love reared an enduring monument to his memory.
He had left his ' Arcadia '—the great prose-poem whose
composition had been encouraged by her approval—in
scattered fragments. These she collected and threaded
together, giving them to the world after a careful revision.
Though little read at the present day, there are many
books which the world could have better spared.

The life of a noble English gentlewoman presents but
few incidents of interest, and is seldom lit up with any
gleams of startling romance. We must, therefore, pass
to the close of Mary Sidney's blameless career,—chiefly
valuable to us because adorned with all those graces and
gentle virtues which make up the Sunshine of Domestic
Life. She survived her husband twenty years, and then
descended to the grave, rich in the golden opinions of all
good men : ' Happy,' says Hartley Coleridge, ' as the
praises of grateful poets could make her—happy in her
fair reputation, and, it is to be hoped, in the duteous
attendance of her elder son, and happy in dying too soon
to see her younger offspring—

" . . . . Hold a wing
Quite from the flight of all his ancestors ! " '

She died at her town mansion in Aldersgate Street—
then one of the most picturesque localities in London—

in 1621, and having been fortunate in her life was fortunate in her death, for Ben Jonson transmitted her fame to posterity in an immortal stanza :—

BEN JONSON'S EPITAPH ON THE COUNTESS OF PEMBROKE.

'Underneath this marble hearse
Lies the subject of all verse—
Sidney's sister, Pembroke's mother:
Death, ere thou hast slain another,
Learned, and fair, and good as she,
Time shall throw a dart at thee.' *

Such a woman in her time plays many parts; and as daughter, sister, wife, and mother, as a patron of letters and a friend of the lettered, as the mistress of a splendid household, the dispenser of a stately hospitality, the star of a glittering social circle, and the ornament of a magnificent court—Mary, Countess of Pembroke, was worthy of all the praises which her contemporaries delighted to heap upon her.

* See Ben Jonson's Poetical Works: Underwoods. xv.

IX

A Heroic Life.

THE STORY OF JEANNE D'ALBRET.*

Pax certa, Victoria integra, Mors honesta.
Legende de Jeanne D'Albret.

I.

EANNE D'ALBRET was the eldest child of Henry II., King of Navarre, and his wife, Marguerite d'Angoulême, sister of Francis I., King of France. She was born at the Palace of Fontainebleau, on Tuesday, the 7th of January 1528. The witnesses of her birth were loud in their praises of her comely countenance and vigorous frame, and she gave early proof of a very active and energetic temperament. When about ten days old, she was privately christened in the palace-chapel; her sponsors being King Francis, who was represented by proxy; the Duchess d'Angoulême; and one of her aunts, probably Madame Isabel D'Albret. Under such distinguished auspices did she enter upon what proved to be a stormy and stirring career.

* This sketch is founded upon Sismondi, 'Histoire de France;' Brantome, 'Les Dames Illustres;' and M. W. Freer, 'Life of Jeanne D'Albret.'

Her infancy was passed at Lonray, near Alençon, the residence of her gouvernante, Madame de Silly. Here she throve apace, and developed a strong and healthy constitution. She joined Madame de Silly's children in their pastimes, evincing a singular contempt of danger, and a lively and mirthful disposition, and deriving much advantage from the excellent principles instilled into her youthful mind by her exemplary guardian. She occasionally visited the royal court at St. Germain, and so won the heart of her royal uncle, that he loaded her with indulgences which would assuredly have spoiled a less noble character. Her father loved her and was proud of her, so that at court she received the pet appellation of 'La Mignonne des Rois'—the Darling of the Kings—and the greatest nobles of the kingdom solicited, as a special grace, that their own daughters might be selected as companions for the youthful Princess.

In 1531, Marguerite and her husband retired to his own capital of Pau in Navarre, where they contemplated a residence of eighteen months. It was their desire to take with them the Princess Jeanne, and present her to her future subjects; but Francis insisted on detaining her, and declared that her education should be completed in France under his own direction. He at the same time intimated his design of bestowing her in marriage on his second son, Henry, Duke of Orleans, who was then in his thirteenth year, and had already given evidence of great good sense and judgment. The alliance was highly acceptable both to Marguerite and the King of Navarre, and might have proved of good omen for the two kingdoms; but it was destined never to be accomplished.

The royal castle of Plessis-les-Tours was now allotted
to the Princess Jeanne for her permanent residence, and
her household established on a scale commensurate with
her rank and future fortunes. Madame de Silly was
appointed chief lady of honour and governess to the
Princess ; the poet, Nicholas de Bourbon, her preceptor
in languages, belles-lettres, and poetry. While her mind
was thus provided for, due care was bestowed on her
spiritual education; two chaplains were engaged to in-
struct her in theology and her religious duties, under the
superintendence of Pierre du Châtel, Bishop of Tulle and
Maçon. The head-steward of her household was M.
d'Izernay. She was furnished with companions of her
own age to amuse her leisure, and numerous subordinate
officials and attendants ministered to her comforts.

In this somewhat pompous solitude—away from her
beloved parents, shut out from the external world—
Jeanne D'Albret spent five years, 1532 to 1537, with a
moderate degree of happiness. Having formed but few
desires, she had few disappointments to regret. The
bird had hardly learned to plume her wings, and therefore had not yet felt the bitterness of her gilded captivity.
But in the spring of 1538 Plessis was visited by Jeanne's
paternal aunt and godmother, the Princess Isabel
D'Albret, and her children, who made 'a sunshine in
the shady place' by their vivacity and glee. Their companionship awakened new desires in Jeanne's childish
breast. She became conscious of new wants, of aspirations before unheeded, of sorrows hitherto unfelt. Her
education had been elaborate, and her character, accordingly, was prematurely developed. It was marked by
extraordinary firmness of will and clearness of judgment.

She soon perceived that the Palace of Plessis was really a prison, and her royal uncle little better than a gaoler. She longed for liberty. A fit of melancholy seized her ; she neglected her studies ; she refused to answer the King's letters ; her eagerness concentrated itself upon one of two alternatives—either that she might rejoin her parents, or reside at the court of France.

'For hours together,' says Miss Freer,* 'the Princess wept in her lonely chamber at Plessis, listening to the wailing of the wind as it swept through the dense forests which, at this period, encircled the fortress-palace of Louis XI. The gloomy courts of Plessis, bristling still with the terrible defences and iron cages in which that stern despot immured the helpless victims of his tyranny, filled the sensitive mind of the Princess with dismay. Nor could the internal splendour of the palace, assigned for her home by her uncle, reconcile her to its gloom. Jeanne eagerly listened to every fearful legend connected with the past history of the castle. The magnificent hall of Plessis, in which the ceremonies of betrothment of Francis I., when Duke de Valois, with the Princess Claude of France had been performed, brought reminiscences only, to the excited mind of Jeanne, of the terrible interviews which King Louis had there granted to the famed provost of his archers, Tristan l'Hermite ; whose victims had often knelt in mute agony on the marble pavement at the feet of the inexorable monarch. When she walked abroad, yawning chasms marked the spots where Louis had caused pitfalls to be constructed to defend the approaches of his fortress-palace against unauthorized intruders. Even the rushing waters of the

* Miss Freer, 'Life of Jeanne D'Albret,' pp. 12, 13.

her father should ally her with Philip of Spain; who thus already exercised that unhappy influence on her fortune which was destined to overshadow her later years.

The ambitious views which Francis cherished, now induced him to propose an alliance between Jeanne and the Duke of Cleves, utterly regardless either of her inclinations or her parents' wishes. The Duke was a Lutheran, and such an alliance would cement the friendly relations subsisting between France and the German Protestants, while it would prove a constant thorn in the side of the Emperor Charles, the father of Philip of Spain. The Duke was no uncomely bridegroom; he was tall and handsome, skilful in all martial and chivalrous exercises, magnificent in his attire, liberal in his habits, and a lover of art and letters. But Jeanne, when brought acquainted with the projected match, displayed the warmest resentment. The Duke's accomplishments and personal gifts availed him nothing. She made her way into the presence of her uncle, and with tears implored him that she might not be constrained to marry the Prince. But to all her solicitations Francis replied with a stern expression of his will.

When introduced to the Duke, Jeanne exhibited the coldest indifference; and though but a child, conducted herself with so much haughtiness of demeanour, as to excite her uncle's displeasure. Madame de Silly remonstrated with her on her want of graciousness, and her apparent insensibility to the advantages of the projected match. 'I deem it no advantage,' she replied, 'to leave France, and my own inheritance of Béarn, to wed a Duke of Cleves.' She protested with vehemence that she should die if the alliance were carried out: and as she had been brought up in the Roman Catholic faith, she manifested great repugnance to the Duke's heretical opinions. The resolution with which this child of twelve years old opposed the royal mandate was indeed extraordinary ; and when she found herself finally compelled to submit, she resorted to the strange expedient of drawing up a secret protest against the unwelcome nuptials —a document which she caused three of the officers of her household to witness :—

'I, Jeanne de Navarre, persisting in the protestations I have already made, do hereby again affirm and protest, by these presents, that the marriage which it is desired to contract between the Duke of Cleves and myself, is against my will ; that I have never consented to it, nor will consent ; and that all I may say and do hereafter, by which it may be attempted to prove that I have given my consent, will be forcibly extorted against my wish and desire, from my dread of the King, of the King my father, and of the Queen my mother, *who had threatened to have me whipped* by the Baillive of Caen (Madame de Silly), my governess.*

'By command of the Queen my mother, my said governess has also several times declared that if I do not all in regard to this marriage which the King wishes, and if I do not give my consent, I shall be punished so severely as to occasion my death ; and that by refusing I may be the cause of the ruin and destruction of my father, my mother, and of their house ; the which threat has inspired me with such fear and dread, even to be the cause of the ruin of my said father and mother, that I know not to whom to have recourse, excepting to God, seeing that my father and my mother abandon me, who both well know what I have said to them —that never can I love the Duke of Cleves, and that I will not have him.

'Therefore, I protest beforehand, if it happens that I am affianced, or married, to the said Duke of Cleves in any way or manner, it

* What a curious glimpse of life and manners ! Here is the betrothed bride of a duke threatened with ignominious whipping.

will be against my heart, and in defiance of my will; and that he shall never become my husband, nor will I ever hold and regard him as such, and that my marriage shall be reputed null and void; in testimony of which I appeal to God and yourselves as witnesses of this my declaration, that you are about to sign with me; admonishing each of you to remember the compulsion, violence, and restraint employed against me, upon the matter of this said marriage.

(*Signed*) 'JEANNE DE NAVARRE.
'J. D' ARROS.
'FRANCES NAVARRO.
'ARNAULD DUQUESSE.'

Who will not pity this poor child of twelve forced into a marriage against which her soul revolts? Who will not sympathize with the evident sincerity and earnestness of grief that reveals itself in every line of her childlike protest? Alas, human happiness or sorrow is never an obstacle to the cruel ambition of kings; and the ceremony of betrothment between the Princess Jeanne and the Duke of Cleves took place in the great hall (*regia aula*) of the Castle of Alençon, the Bishop of Séez officiating. Immediately it was concluded, and before she was conveyed to Châtelherault, where the public nuptials were to be solemnized, the unhappy Jeanne placed on record a second protest as emphatic as the first, but with which it is unnecessary to fatigue our readers.

The marriage-ceremony between the unwilling Princess and the eager Duke was performed on the 15th of July 1540, when Jeanne was about twelve and a half years old. In those days such sacrificial rites were always invested with luxurious pomp and splendour, as if a wealth of leaf and blossom could conceal the depths of the chasm into which the victim fell! The bride was dressed in a robe of cloth of gold, sparkling with precious stones. A ducal coronet pressed her fair white brow; the train of her mantle was edged with ermine. All the great officers of state attended; and so bright and gorgeous was the show, that it cost a far greater sum than even the coronation-pageant of the Emperor Charles V. When King Francis stood forward to lead the bride to the altar, she rose from her chair reluctantly, and suddenly declared herself unable to walk under the burthen of gold and jewels with which her robes were loaded. Then, at the King's command, though not a little to his discomfort, the Constable de Montmorency took her up in his arms, and carried her to the chapel, where the rites were duly solemnized.

At the splendid banquet and ball which terminated these strange proceedings, Jeanne was constrained to appear. She was then allowed to retire, with aching heart and heavy head, to her mother's apartments, where the Duke of Cleves formally entrusted her to the guardianship of Queen Marguerite and Madame de Silly, until she should have arrived at a suitable age to fulfil the conjugal engagements she had solemnly contracted.

Eight days of rejoicing now ensued—rejoicings in which, you may be sure, the Princess took no part, nor would she ever see her husband. 'In the meadow of Châtelherault,' says the chronicler,[*] 'jousts and tourneys were holden; for which halls, galleries, triumphal arches, and palaces were constructed of verdant boughs, and in these armed knights were placed to defend them in honour of the ladies of their hearts, whose devices were blended

---

[*] Paradin, 'Histoire de Notre Temps.'

in the foliage with the arms of the cavaliers, and with
such trophies as they captured from their assailants.
Close to these said structures stood verdant bowers,
occupied by hermits, clad in green or gray velvet, and
other colours, whose duty it was to serve as guides to
any stranger-knights who might present themselves.
In other parts of the meadow ladies were placed, who
personated nymphs and dryads, attended by their dwarfs;
all ordered according to the mode and fashion of bygone
days. This joust, for novelty and splendour, was the
most memorable thing of the kind that had been done
or heard of in our days. These knightly encounters
were celebrated in the day-time; but, that pastime
might not be lacking for the nights, lists were erected,
and the joustings continued by torchlight—a thing never
before heard of in France.'

At the close of these festivities the Duchess of Cleves
joyfully took leave of her uncle, who loaded her with
costly gifts, and proceeded with her parents to their
castle of Nérac, from whence they retired to pass the
winter at Pau.

Here she remained for two years in the happy society
of her excellent mother—two years which gave a beneficial direction to her tastes, and exercised a subduing
and softening influence on her character. Under the
wise and anxious superintendence of her mother she
learned to control the impetuosity of her temper, to
restrain her passions, to distinguish between obstinacy
and firmness, and to practise the great lesson of endurance —

"To suffer, and be strong."

Thrown, moreover, into constant association with the

divines of the Reformed Church who had sought an asylum in Béarn, she acquired a knowledge of their doctrines and was powerfully impressed by the moral of their lives—that principle must never be repudiated or compromised for the sake of expediency.

She studied theology daily under the guidance of her mother and the excellent Gérard Roussel, Bishop of Orleans—'a prelate of singular piety, and who asserted under the Roman purple a liberality of sentiment, and a boldness in discussing theological tenets, worthy of Calvin himself.' The doctrines which she now imbibed were as bread cast upon the waters, and in later years wrought a happy result.

Meanwhile, a great change took place in the Princess's fortunes. The Duke of Cleves had made peace with the Emperor Charles, and Francis, indignant at his defection to his great rival, determined to annul the marriage he had contracted with the Princess Jeanne. He therefore desired his niece to return to France, and take up her residence at Fontainebleau, while the necessary measures were in progress.

With unspeakable joy Jeanne received this unexpected intelligence, and signified her ardent desire for the dissolution of her marriage-bond. The Duke himself was by no means unwilling to be freed from a wife who had treated him with the most marked contumely, and eagerly seconded the applications for a divorce which now poured in upon the Roman pontiff. Some delay was interposed by the Papal court, and it was not until the spring of 1545 that Jeanne found herself released from the alliance that had proved so distasteful to her.

'And now,' says the old Béarnese historian, 'the countenance of our Princess once more grew serene, her deportment became cheerful, and she readily consoled herself for the loss of her husband. For it had seemed to her very grievous to quit France as the spouse of a simple duke, when she might choose among the greatest princes of the blood-royal.'

On the 31st of March 1547, died Francis I., an event which caused a complete change in the political views of the French court, and greatly affected the present position and future destinies of the Princess Jeanne. The Queen, her mother, now lost all her political influence, and a new star rose on the horizon—the beautiful Diana of Poitiers, Duchesse de Valentinois, who ruled Henry the Second as with a spell of magical power.

But we here open up a second stage in the Princess's career, and, accordingly, pass on to a new section of our brief biographical summary.

II.

Two of the most brilliant nobles of the French court —Antoine, Duke de Vendôme, and François, Duke de Guise—now presented themselves as suitors for the hand of the Princess, who had ripened into a beautiful and accomplished woman. As the former was eventually successful in his suit, the reader will probably be glad to learn what manner of man he was.

Antoine de Bourbon was the eldest son of Charles, Duke de Vendôme, who died at Amiens in 1536, and of Françoise, sister of the Duke d'Alençon—the first husband of the mother of the Princess Jeanne. The most intimate friendship existed between the Queen of Navarre and her sister-in-law, the Duchess de Vendôme; a fact which, doubtless, encouraged Antoine to press his suit with the Princess. He was born in the castle of La Fère, on the 18th of April 1518; and had therefore entered his twentieth year when he sought the hand of Jeanne D'Albret.

But as boy and man he presented that not infrequent combination, a defective moral sense and 'a goodly outside:' but the utmost fascination of address combined with grave moral deficiency. Superficial and frivolous, he yet disarmed censure by his frank admission of ignorance, and his good-natured condescension. 'His disposition was vacillating and uncertain; perpetually wavering, and devoid of principle, he invariably became the victim of those who last possessed his ear—being himself totally regardless of antecedent engagements. His temper was excitable; in the first heat of passion his resentments appeared unbridled, and his energy irresistible. His anger pacified, all sense of wrong to himself, and of justice to others, passed away, and Antoine again became the luxurious, effeminate prince.'[*]

As a soldier, however, he had shown himself able and intrepid; while he possessed all those graces of manner which spell-bind a woman's fancy, however clear may be her judgment, and however vivid her perception of character.

Contrast would seem to give the keenest zest to love, and that poetry of sentiment which dwells upon the delight of congenial minds and sympathizing hearts we may dismiss as mere exaggeration. One could hardly

* M. W. Freer, 'Life of Jeanne D'Albret,' p. 40.

imagine a greater discrepancy than existed between Jeanne D'Albret and Antoine de Bourbon. He, capricious and vacillating; she, decided and unbending. He, devoted to pleasure; she, controlled by a strong sense of duty. He, irascible and impetuous; she, energetic but composed. If it is difficult to understand the attraction which Antoine de Bourbon exercised over the clear intellect of Jeanne D'Albret, it is not, however, impossible to explain the secret of the influence which Jeanne soon acquired over the volatile duke. When Marie de Concini was accused of sorcery, from the powerful command she had enjoyed over the French queen, she replied that the only magic she had used was 'the influence of a strong mind over a weak one.' This was Jeanne D'Albret's talisman—added to which she was beautiful, vivacious, and witty.

The course of true love does not always run smooth, and Jeanne found the match discountenanced by the King and Queen, who encouraged the suit of the Duke de Guise; and by her father, who disapproved of Duke Antoine's frivolity, extravagance, and love of pleasure. But this opposition was finally removed, and the marriage-contract signed at Moulins, on the 20th of October 1548, in the presence of Henry II. and his Queen—the famous, shall we not say the *in*famous, Catherine de Medicis—the King and Queen of Navarre, the Duchess de Vendôme, the Cardinal de Bourbon, and other illustrious personages. The King and Queen of Navarre bestowed upon their daughter a dowry of one hundred thousand gold crowns, and the Duke settled lands on his future bride to the annual value of twelve thousand livres, besides presenting her with costly jewels.

The bridal ceremony was performed on the following day, in the chapel of the castle of Moulins. The King gave away the bride. Apprehensions had arisen whether even, at the last moment, the marriage would have taken place, for the Duke had conceived some sudden doubts as to the validity of Jeanne's alliance with the Duke of Cleves. He burst into a frenzy of jealous rage, which was only soothed by the solemn and reiterated protestations of Queen Marguerite and Madame de Silly that the Princess had never seen or conversed with the Duke of Cleves after the termination of the marriage-ceremony at Châtelherault.

When the bridal pageantry was concluded, the Duke and Duchess retired from court to his castle of La Fère, in the province of Picardy. There they made a brief and pleasant sojourn during *la lune des noces*—the honeymoon—and afterwards proceeded to Pau to receive the homage of the states of Béarn, and public recognition of her rights as heiress to the crown of Navarre. The reception of the young wedded pair was enthusiastic, and the Duke won golden opinions by his deference towards Queen Marguerite, and the predilection he professed for the doctrines of the Reformed Church. His name was, therefore, associated with that of Jeanne in the public edict by which the States acknowledged the successor of Henry and Marguerite.

But while all went merry as a marriage-bell, and the blossoms of Love and Hope sprang up about the young couple's path, a great affliction was preparing for the Princess. After a brief and sudden illness Queen Marguerite died at the castle of Odos, in Bigorre, on the 21st of December 1548. It was Jeanne's first heavy sorrow, and it fell upon her like a crushing blow. On the mind of the bereaved King its effect was still more terrible, and thenceforward he utterly neglected the interests of his kingdom.

Consolation came to the Princess, on the 21st of September 1550, in the birth of a son—an event eagerly desired by her aged father, no less than by her sumptuous husband. The child was named Henry, and bore the title of Duke de Beaumont.

In those days the art of rearing children was not very well understood, and many a poor infant was put to death by the injudicious attentions of its nurse. The young prince was consigned to the care of Madame de Silly, now old and infirm, but whose loyal attachment seemed to merit such a proof of confidence and regard. Madame de Silly looked upon the infant as a gardener might upon an exotic transplanted from some tropical clime, as a precious thing to be shielded from the air, and to be kept in a hot-house. The poor child was never allowed, even in the finest weather, to bask in the open sunshine; and when the gouvernante was remonstrated with for so injudicious a course of treatment, she contented herself with replying, 'Laissez l'enfant! il vaut mieux suer que trembler!'—Let the child alone, it is better for it to sweat than to shiver. The reader will not be astonished to learn that under such a regimen the young duke wasted away. Apprised of his dangerous condition, the Duchess hastened to Orleans to see him, and bitterly reproached Madame de Silly for her cruel thoughtlessness. She carried the prince to the castle of Gaillon, in Normandy, where she was sojourning in expectation of her second *accouchement.* But it was too late: his constitution had been completely ruined, and he died when little more than a year and a half old.

Jeanne gave birth to a second son in August 1552, who received the title of Count de Marle. Brought up under her own eye, he proved a robust and healthy child; and his mother was able to promise the old king of Navarre that she would present him to the Béarnois at the ensuing Christmas festival.

Accordingly, the Duke and his consort, with the young heir of Navarre, set out for Pau. The gray-haired King hastened to meet his daughter—*sa bonne fille,* as he called her—at Mont de Maison, and contemplated his vigorous little grandson with proud satisfaction. He never wearied of exhibiting him to the good Béarnois, who fully sympathized with his affectionate pride.

But all these proud hopes were doomed to be shattered. While the Duke and Duchess, and the King, were out one day on a hunting expedition, the young prince was left in charge of the nurse and chamberlain. During the afternoon, the nurse carried him to an open window, where she was recognized by one of King Henry's gentlemen of the chamber, who approached and conversed from without. Observing the sleeping prince, he requested permission to hold him. The lady complied, and the babe was several times tossed, in sport, from her arms to those of the cavalier. This pastime was continued for a while, when the nurse, thinking that her companion held the child, suddenly relinquished her grasp, and the babe, falling on a flight of marble steps beneath, fractured a rib. In alarm at the result, they agreed to conceal the accident: but the poor child sickened, and, after suffering extreme agony, died. It was not until four days after his death that its cause was discovered, and the guilty parties visited with the punishment their criminal folly had deserved.

The mortification and grief of the old King were excessive, and he vented his rage on his daughter, reproaching her with neglect, and stigmatizing her as *marâtre* and inhuman—epithets which certainly her conduct never justified. He declared he would marry a second time, and that Jeanne should never inherit his kingdom. Nor was he pacified until his daughter promised that if Heaven again blessed her with offspring, she would repair to Pau, and place her child entirely under his charge.

The Duchess's prayers were many and earnest, and Providence in its wisdom deigned to answer them. On the 13th of December 1553, was born the famous Henry of Navarre —the future hero of many a well-fought field— whose life seems rather the romance of some chivalrous poet than a matter-of-fact portion of European history; and whose memory is still dear to the heart of every true child of France. Exultant and joyous, the old King conveyed the babe to his own apartments, and before consigning him to the nurse's care, performed an ancient ceremony generally in use among the Béarnnois. First, he took a clove of garlic, with which he just touched the infant's lips; then he presented him with wine in a cup of gold. On smelling the wine, the young prince, it is said, lifted his head, and otherwise displayed his gratification. The King then put a few drops of wine on his tongue, and he immediately swallowed them. "*Va*," exclaimed the old King, in a rapture of delight, "*tu seras un vrai Béarnois.*" Go, thou wilt be a true son of Béarn!

The young prince flourished mightily and throve apace, giving promise of an energetic disposition and a stalwart frame. The old King was proud of his grandson—the Béarnois of their future sovereign—and in joy and sunshine opened a career which was destined to resound with the incessant clang and clash of battle

When he was about a year and a half old, his grandfather died (May 25, 1555), bequeathing to Queen Jeanne the inheritance of a kingdom assailed by many enemies. When she had somewhat recovered from the deep grief she experienced in the loss of her father, she despatched a courier to her husband, who was with the camp at Estrée-le-Pont, requesting his presence at Baran, that she might salute him as King of Navarre.[*]

III.

Our limits will not permit us to write the history of Jeanne D'Albret's reign, which, through the jealousies of the French court, and the intrigues of the Spanish government, was clouded with trouble, anxiety, and danger. Both powers menaced the independence of the crown of Navarre, and it required all the Queen's firmness, and all her indomitable courage to transmit it safely to her son. We must confine ourselves, however, to a narration of those events which most vividly illustrate the high qualities of her character, and justify us in speaking of her career as a heroic life.

Such an event was her profession of the Lutheran religion, a step which was the result of matured thought and sincere conviction, and assuredly militated against her worldly prospects. It was in 1560 that she publicly avowed her renunciation of the Catholic faith, and received the holy communion, according to the Reformed ritual, in the cathedral at Pau. At that time her husband professed a warm attachment to Protestant principles; but Catherine de Medicis and the Papal legate succeeded in warping his easy and impressionable mind by alternate menaces and bribes. They promised him a divorce from the Queen on the ground of her pre-contract with the Duke of Cleves, and to negotiate his marriage with Mary Stuart. Thus the triple crowns of England, Scotland, and Navarre would eventually devolve upon his brow, a royalty certainly not unworthy the acceptance of a French prince of the blood.

At this period, says Miss Freer, the Queen had only completed her thirty-third year. But sorrow was her heritage; and it had long ago subdued the buoyant spirit of her youth. Her nature had never been softened by basking in the sunshine of love and sympathy. Endowed with the faculty of command, her mind had been divested of many of its feminine attributes by the philosophical bias of her education, while the solitary state in which she had passed several years at Plessis-les-Tours, and the objects and associations which had surrounded her, had developed the intellect while hardening the heart. Torn with anxiety, and circled round with dangers, she nevertheless preserved a serene composure, and no outward sign betrayed the working of the proud spirit within.

Antoine now insisted that the Queen should attend mass, and when she refused, even ventured to try compulsion. On one occasion, when she was about to step into her litter to attend the prelections of one of her Lutheran ministers, the King presented himself, and,

taking her by the hand, commanded the litter to be dismissed, and led her back to her apartments. He then
required that she should outwardly conform to the rites
and services of the Roman Catholic Church. Jeanne
undauntedly replied that she would not barter her immortal soul for territorial aggrandizement, and that she
would not be present at mass, nor at any other ceremony
of the Romish creed.

Antoine now, in his wrath, avowed all the details of
the intrigue designed to crush her both as a Queen and a
woman, and threatened, if she still opposed his commands, to sue for a divorce. Tears of scorn fell from
her eyes, tears proceeding from the bitterness of a proud
spirit that felt at last the unworthiness of the object on
which its early affection had been lavished. But regain-
ing her composure, she eloquently exposed the insidious
designs of Antoine's councillors, and warned him that
their real object was to accomplish his degradation, and
elevate his hereditary enemies, the princes of the house
of Guise. She appealed to his better feelings. 'Sir,' she
said, ' if you have no pity for me, your wife, at least have
mercy upon your two children. Know you not that in
repudiating me you disgrace *them !* That the blow
aimed at *my* fame, must also fall upon *their* honour!'

To such appeals, as well as to political arguments,
Antoine, dazzled by the will-o'-the-wisp dream of ambition which hovered before him, turned a deaf ear; and
thenceforward, Jeanne, as she herself said, closed her
heart for ever against the affection which she still
cherished for her husband, and devoted its every impulse
to perform her duty. She would not forsake the faith
which she believed to be the truth, and dedicated herself

to the high and holy mission which Providence seemed to have devolved upon her. 'To obtain for all men liberty of conscience,' she wrote to one of her advisers, 'I am minded to do good battle, and not to relax my efforts. The cause is so holy and sacred, that I believe God will strengthen me by his mighty power; and although I may not at once avow my full and entire sentiments, I will conduct myself with such dexterous energy, as greatly to aid by my endeavours the common cause, to the glory of the Eternal, and the public weal; for it is high time to quit the land of Egypt, to traverse the Red Sea, and to rescue the Church of Christ from amid the ruins of that throne of all pride, unclean Babylon!'

Under her auspices the principles of the Reformation made great progress in Béarn, and thither flocked the persecuted Huguenots from every province of France. Jeanne received them with a kindly welcome, provided them with food and necessaries at her own expense, and, though at the peril of her crown, assured them of her protection.

On the 14th of November 1562, Jeanne lost her husband. He died of fever, and the inflammation of a gunshot wound received at the siege of Rouen. On his death-bed he professed himself a Lutheran. But, a faithless husband and a fickle friend, neither wife, child, nor ally, shed a tear over his untimely grave.

'Queen Jeanne,' says Miss Freer, 'was thirty-four years old when she became a widow. From the time that she bade farewell to the King of Navarre in Paris—after her open declaration of the Lutheran faith—she seems to have had a presentiment that she should never more behold her husband. She too well knew the un-

scrupulous daring of the dominant parties at court, to
doubt that the life of the nominal chief of the trium-
virate would be sacrificed upon the first symptoms of his
vacillation in the cause which he had been prevailed
upon to support; "for," says Le Grain, "this Princess
was a woman of great discernment." It was always
doubted by Queen Jeanne whether the bullet, fatal to
her husband's life, was fired from the ramparts of Rouen,
or whether it proceeded from a hand which Antoine had
recently grasped in friendship. From the very earliest
days of her widowhood, the Queen protested that she
would never more enter into the bonds of matrimony.
Her life had been embittered by Antoine's neglect, her
power as a sovereign princess curtailed, and her fine and
noble spirit, so susceptible of good in its aspirations, had
been wounded. Outraged and disappointed in her hopes
of domestic happiness, Jeanne, concentrating those admirable talents with which Nature had endowed her,
became the dauntless and politic princess, against whose
genius such a character as that of Antoine de Bourbon
was helpless as a straw tossed on the waves of the
ocean.'

IV.

The Huguenots sustained a terrible defeat at Jarnac
(in January 1569), which threatened to overwhelm their
cause in irretrievable ruin. But a yet greater blow was
the death of Condé, foully murdered after the battle—
Condé, their ablest soldier, and one of the most illustrious military commanders of the age. Great generals are
not sown broadcast over the world; they are the rare
but happy accidents of nature; and to supply the place of

a leader so eminent and so beloved might well be deemed impossible. Coligny, who succeeded to the command of the Huguenot army, viewed with alarm the depression which had seized upon his soldiers. He perceived that they needed some fresh stimulus to rouse them to exertion, and therefore despatched a messenger to the Queen entreating her presence in the camp. But she was already on her way thither, filled with grief for the loss she and her kingdom had sustained.

By Coligny's orders, the whole army was drawn up in battle-array to receive their sovereign. With sad eyes she gazed on the gloom that clouded every brow, the drooping banners, the mourning veil which everywhere concealed the escutcheon of the fleur-de-lis; but she suffered no feeling of sorrow to interfere with the discharge of an imperative duty, and did not allow the woman to prevail over the queen. She was somewhat cheered, moreover, by the welcome shouts which hailed her as she rode along the front ranks of the army, and the joyous cries which saluted the gallant presence of her son, the Prince of Béarn. In the train of the sovereign rode many a gallant Lutheran: Coligny, D'Andelot, La Rochefoucauld, Fontrailles, De Piles, Rohan, Pontivy, and Genlis. Jeanne advanced, with Condé's son on her left and the young Henri of Navarre on her right, and, sustained by her high heart and lofty resolute spirit, she addressed her soldiers in language of stirring eloquence:—

'Children of God, and of France, Condé is no more. That prince who has oft-times set you the example of courage and of stainless honour; who was ever ready to combat for his king, his country, and his faith; who never

took up arms except to defend himself against implacable foes; that heroic prince, whom even his enemies
were constrained to reverence, has sacrificed his life for
the noblest of causes! Instead of receiving from our
hands the laurel wreath which would justly have rewarded
his valour, a crown of immortal glory now shines upon
his brow. Condé has given up his breath on the battle-
field, cut short in his career of fame. He is dead! A
murderous hand has severed the thread of life. His
enemies have perfidiously assassinated him. What do I
say? Have they not heaped their insults upon his cold
corpse? Oh, how, by this shameful outrage, have they
increased his glory, and eternally sullied the laurels they
sought to gather on the field of Jarnac!

'Soldiers, you weep!

'But does the memory of Condé demand nothing
more than tears? Will you be satisfied with vain regrets?
No; let us unite, let us recall our courage, to defend a
cause which can never die, and to avenge him who was
its most illustrious supporter! Does despair unnerve
your arms? Despair! that shameful vice of weak natures
—can it be known to you, noble soldiers and Christian
heroes? When I, your Queen, have not abandoned hope,
do you still fear? Because Condé is dead is all lost?
Does our cause lose its justice and its sanctity? No;
God who placed arms in his hand for our defence, and
who has already rescued you from innumerable dangers,
he has provided us with brothers-in-arms worthy to suc-
ceed him, and to fight for the cause of religion, of truth,
and of our fatherland! Not only princes of royal blood
are enrolled amongst our leaders, but Coligny, La Rochefoucauld, La Noue, Nohan, De Piles, D'Andelot, Mont-

gomery! To these brave soldiers I add my son. Prove ye his courage! The blood of Bourbon and of Valois flows in his veins. He burns with holy ardour to avenge the death of Condé. Behold, also, Condé's son, whom henceforth I adopt among my own children. He is the worthy heir of his father's virtues. He inherits his name and his renown. Soldiers! I offer ye everything which it is in my power to bestow—my dominions, my treasures, my life, and that which is dearer to me than all—my children! Here do I solemnly vow before ye all—and ye know me too well to doubt my word—here do I solemnly swear to defend to my last sigh the holy cause which now unites us—the cause of honour and of truth!'

For a moment after the Queen ceased speaking a solemn silence prevailed, then a burst of enthusiastic cheering rose from every part of the 'tented plain.' Breaking from their ranks, the soldiers pressed eagerly round the Queen, and demanded to be led at once against their enemies. The young prince of Navarre rode into their midst, his brow flushed with the light of coming triumph. By an unanimous impulse the army hailed him as their chief and leader in the place of Condé, and Jeanne signifying her assent, he was saluted on the spot as generalissimo of the confederated forces.

'Soldiers!' he exclaimed, 'your cause is mine—our interests are the same. I swear to you on the salvation of my soul—by my honour and by my life—never to abandon you!'

Proclamation was then formally made that the command of the army would thenceforth be vested in the Prince of Navarre, assisted by the veteran Coligny. By the Queen's directions the young Prince de Condé took the same oath as Henry had done, of life long fidelity to the cause.

Thus, says the historian, Queen Jeanne, by her cour-age and intrepidity, dissipated the dejection and appre-hensions of our soldiers, so that the army, after hearty cheering, and a great salvo of artillery, dispersed, every man retiring in 'measureless content' to his allotted quarters.[*]

V.

Yet another incident we may quote in illustration of Jeanne's nobility of character. It will throw a light on its more womanly qualities.

During the succeeding campaigns the Huguenots were generally successful in every engagement with their ene-mies. On the 12th of June 1570, under the command of the gallant La Noue, they completely defeated Puy-Gailliard and his Catholics at Ste. Gemme, a village close to the town of Luçon. The slaughter was considerable —five hundred killed were counted on the field of battle. It was a misfortune for the Huguenots, however, that La Noue's right arm was fractured by a musket-ball, and he compelled to retire to La Rochelle. Jeanne and the Rochellois welcomed him as his fame and services merited, and his sufferings were lamented as a public calamity. The royal physicians exercised their craft in vain; the wound mortified; and La Noue was informed that, to save his life, he must submit to the amputation of his arm. No tidings could be more sorrowful to so brave and impetuous a soldier. He refused to submit to the operation—'Better death,' he exclaimed, 'than a maimed and mutilated existence which could be of little benefit to his Queen or country.'

Finding all their remonstrances and entreaties power-less to shake his determination, his friends besought the interference of the Queen. Jeanne immediately repaired to her wounded general's bedside, soothed his grief, chided his impatience, encouraged his hopes. 'Brave La Noue,' she exclaimed, 'ought you to hesitate in this matter? If you reject all the solicitations of your friends your death is inevitable, and you are lost for ever to our cause, to your brothers-in-arms, and to the faith which your virtue has adorned and your heroism supported. But, on the other hand, if you follow the advice of men skilled in their art, if you listen to the voice of duty and the pleadings of friendship, that precious life, which is at once an inspiration to my soldiers and a support to our holy cause, will probably be saved. Beloved La Noue, a hero so dear to his country and his friends, ought, when in danger, to welcome every gleam of hope. Then, if he succumbs after all, he bears with him to his grave the consciousness of having done his duty to the last.'

This appeal, and the emotions which his sovereign manifested, overcame the warrior's resistance, and he con-sented to submit himself to the surgeon's knife. At a sign from the Queen the leeches made their appearance. With her own hands Jeanne then removed the bandages, and with noble fortitude supported the sufferer's arm, and encouraged him with consoling words while the ope-ration was performed. In later life, when La Noue told the tale of this heroic act of sympathy, tears would roll down his bronzed and battle-scarred cheeks; and he proved his gratitude by the most brilliant devotedness.

During his convalescence Jeanne continued her gentle care, and by her directions an ingenious mechanician fabricated an iron arm of such cunning workmanship that La Noue was enabled to guide his horse with it. Thenceforth the warrior was known as La Noue Bras de Fer— La Noue of the Iron Arm.

Among the noble deeds of noble women surely this act of generous sympathy and chivalrous fortitude deserves to be enrolled. It is one of the brightest gems in the regal crown of fame that circles the brow of Jeanne D'Albret.

VI.

Jeanne inherited from her accomplished mother a passionate love of letters, and, according to the standard of the age, was a woman of extensive erudition. Once, when on a visit to Paris, she found an opportunity of visiting the printing establishment of Henri Etienne (Stephen), son of the famous printer, Robert Etienne, who died at Geneva in 1559. In the annals of typography the Stephens are honourably distinguished for the excellence of their workmanship, and for their careful and excellent editions of many of the Greek and Roman classics.

Jeanne examined every part of the establishment with the greatest interest. Her powerful mind could fully appreciate the vast and important influence which the discovery of the new art was destined to exercise on the minds of men and the affairs of nations, and could acknowledge the growth of a new power in Europe—as yet but dimly seen and seldom heard—the power of Public Opinion.

She spoke Latin with freedom and classic elegance, and had also attained an extensive acquaintance with the language of ancient Greece. A life of storm and contention left her but little leisure to cultivate her poetic talents; yet that she was a worshipper of the muse may be inferred from the pleasant Impromptu, in praise of printing, which she composed on the occasion of her visit to the Etiennes. It is the only specimen extant of her skill in versification :—

IMPROMPTU: BY THE QUEEN OF NAVARRE.

' Art singulier, d'ici aux derniers ans
Representez aux enfans de ma race,
Que j'ai suivi des Craignans-dieu la trace,
Afin qu'ils soient des mêmes pas suivants.'

Translation:

Wonderful art, from now to later years make known to the children of my race that I have followed in the footsteps of God-fearing men, so that they may pursue the same path.

In acknowledgment of this royal quatrain, Etienne presented the Queen with the following sonnet :—

REPONSE EN FORME DE SONNET AU NOM DE L'IMPRIMERIE
A LA DITE DAME ROYNE.

' Princess, que le ciel de graces favorise,
A qui les Craignans-dieu * souhaitent tout bonheur,
A qui les grands esprits ont donné tout honneur,
Pour avoir doctement la science conquise.

' S'il est vrai qui au temps la plus brave entreprise,
Au devant des vertus abbaise sa grandeur,
S'il est vrai que les ans n'offusquent la splendeur
Qui fait luire partout les enfans de l'Eglise.

* A nickname given to the Lutherans by their opponents.

'Le ciel, les Craignans-dieu et les hommes savants
Me feront raconter aux peuples survivans,
Vos graces, et votre heur et louange notorie.
Et puisque vos vertus ne peuvent prendre fin,
Par vous je demeurerai vivante, à cette fin
Qu'aux peuples à venir j'en porte la mémoire.'

Translated:

ANSWER IN THE FORM OF A SONNET, AND IN THE NAME OF
THE PRINTING ESTABLISHMENT, TO THE SAID QUEEN.

Princess, whom heaven has graciously favoured, to whom all
Lutherans wish happiness, on whom the greatest minds have bestowed every honour for having mastered the secrets of knowledge ;

If it be true that in time the boldest enterprise becomes as nothing
in the presence of virtue ; if it be true that years cannot dim the
splendour which surrounds and glorifies the children of the Church ;

Heaven, the God-fearing and the wise, will bid me recount to
posterity your eminent praises and your brilliant qualities. And
since your virtues will never die, I through you shall live for ever,
to the end that I may transmit their memory to future ages.

VII.

We now come to the last scene of Jeanne D'Albret's
eventful career. She had been summoned to Paris by
Charles IX., to be present at the nuptials of her son
Henry with the King's sister, the fair but frail Marguerite.
On arriving in the capital, she took up her abode at the
Hôtel de Condé, Rue de Grenelle Saint Honoré. Her
health, which for several years had been failing, now
seemed completely broken, and a melancholy which she
could not overcome took possession of her mind.

The magnificence of the pomp which was preparing
for the reception of the young prince of Navarre, seemed
for awhile to recall some flashes of the old spirit. Her
gracious address conciliated the citizens of Paris. Her

eloquent words won the hearts of those to whom they were addressed. Attended by the Marshal de Montmorency, the governor of Paris, she visited the *ateliers* of the artists, and the warehouses of the most celebrated *marchands* of the capital. She gave lavish orders for gold, and gems, and sumptuous habiliments, and under her immediate superintendence everything was selected that could enhance the splendour of the approaching festival. Amongst other shops visited by the Queen, was that of Maître Réné, the perfumer—and let us add the poisoner —to Queen Catherine de Medici; of whose darkest secrets he was the repository, and of her foulest intrigues the instrument. Here, it is said, Jeanne purchased a quantity of drugs, perfumes, embroidered ruffs, and gloves. It was an unfortunate visit, for Catherine's hatred of the Queen of Navarre was intense; she was capable of conceiving the most criminal designs, and Réné was equally capable of carrying them into execution.

On Wednesday evening, the 4th of June 1572, the Queen of Navarre, on her return from one of her laborious progresses, complained of pain in her limbs, and of excessive lassitude. She passed the ensuing night in feverish restlessness, disturbed by an excruciating agony in the chest, which no applications seemed able to relieve. On the second day her breathing became impaired, and such alarming symptoms presented themselves that her medical attendants summoned the King's physicians, but their united skill availed nothing. The Queen at once declared herself convinced that her illness was mortal, and when all around her were convulsed with grief, preserved the serenest composure. Not all her sufferings could extort from her lips a complaint, **and her** tranquillity in these solemn hours attested her **consciousness** of a well spent life.

'I know,' she exclaimed, 'that the prayers of **the** righteous avail much. I resign myself to God's **holy** will, taking all evils from him as chastisements **from the** hands of a living Father. I have never feared **Death;** still less dare I murmur at the dispensations of **Provi-** dence, though he afflicts me with these most **grievous** pains. Nevertheless, I mourn deeply to leave the **chil-** dren whom God has given me, in their tender **age,** exposed to so many perils and such adversity; **but in** God's providence I trust!'

Addressing her weeping attendants: 'Ought **you to** mourn for me?' she cried. 'Have you not all **witnessed** the extreme wretchedness of my past life? **Should you** weep when, at length, God takes pity upon me, **and** summons me to the enjoyment of a blessed **existence,** for the which I have unceasingly prayed?' With **such** sublime contentment she calmly awaited the **supreme** moment, and never ceased to testify to the 'faith **that** was in her'—the faith, that star-like lighted her **soul** through the Valley of the Shadow of Death!

On Sunday, the 8th, the violent sufferings of the **Queen** were sensibly mitigated, but it was evident that **she was** rapidly losing her strength. Towards evening she **made** her will, appointing the Cardinal de Bourbon and **the** Admiral de Coligny her executors. The **ministers,** Merlin and Espina, then prayed by her bedside, **and** read, at her request, the 14th, 15th, and 16th **chapters** of St. John's Gospel—a portion of the Scriptures which **to** Jeanne, as to all other troubled and weary spirits, **has** always breathed the balm of consolation. 'O my Saviour!' she cried, at intervals, 'hasten to release my spirit from the thraldom of life, and from its prison in this suffering body, so that I may offend thee no more, but enter joyfully into the glorious rest which thou hast promised, and my soul longs for!'

Throughout the early hours of the 9th of June, the Queen spoke little; but lay exhausted, fatigued, apparently not in pain, and with her eyes closed. This brief pause of repose was followed by a severe paroxysm; her attendants raised her in their arms; her difficulty of breathing increased, and her hands and feet became cold and pulseless. After awhile her sufferings decreased, but her dissolution was evidently near at hand. Her mind, however, remained unclouded to the last; and presently she made a gesture to her chaplains to continue their intercessions on her behalf to God. A ray of light seemed to flit across her countenance, when one of them commenced the psalm: 'In te, Domine, speravi'—In thee, O Lord, have I put my trust. Throughout the remaining period of her existence she gradually continued to sink; and between the hours of eight and nine, on the morning of Monday, June 9th, 1572, the pure and heroic spirit of the Queen of Navarre passed into its rest.

The suddenness of the Queen's decease, and its occurring so quickly after her visit to the notorious Réné, not unnaturally suggested to the excited imaginations of the Huguenots— who grieved over her death as children over the death of a beloved mother—that she had fallen a victim to the hatred of Catherine de Medicis. It was

said that she had been poisoned by a subtle scent communicated to a pair of gloves. By Charles the Ninth's
directions her body was subjected to a post-mortem
examination, in the presence of several Huguenot officers
of the deceased Queen's household; but, it is said, no
traces of poison were discovered. Medical science, however, in those days, was frequently baffled by the poisoner,
and despite the declarations of the surgeons, the Huguenots still affirmed, and Henry of Navarre himself believed,
that the great Queen had been foully and treacherously
slain.

Jeanne D'Albret was forty-four years old at the time
of her decease. Her obsequies were performed with
splendid pomp, the body being carried to Vendôme,
where it was interred in the Cathedral, in the mausoleum
of the Bourbons, and by the side of her husband, Antoine,
King of Navarre. We subjoin in a note the inscriptions
carved upon their tomb.*

The Huguenot poets celebrated the memory of their
lamented Queen in divers odes and epitaphs, of which
two of the more notable have been preserved by Miss
Freer in her interesting pages.

* *Inscriptions on the tomb of Antoine de Bourbon and Jeanne D'Albret,
King and Queen of Navarre:—*

' Icy dessus gist ensepulturé Antoine de Bourbon, Roy de Navarre, Souverain
de Béarn, Duc de Vendômois, Lieutenant pour le Roy Charles IXème de ce nom.
Lequel Saigneur fut fils du très haut, très puissant, et tres magnanime prince,
Monseigneur Charles de Bourbon Ier. Duc de Vendôme, et de Madame Françoise
d'Alençon, son épouse, et deceda à Andely le VIIème jour d'Octobre 1562.

' En ce même sepulchre gist très haute, très sage, et très vertueuse Dame
Madame Johanne D'Albret, Royne de Navarre, Souveraine de Béarn, et Duchesse de Vendômois, fille unique et seule heritière de Henry D'Albret, Roy de
Navarre, et de Madame Marguerite de France, laquelle deceda à Paris la IXème
jour de Juin 1572 '

EPITAPH ON JEANNE D'ALBRET.

' S'ébahit-on pourquoy la Royne de Navarre,
En sagesse, en bonté, en pieté, si rare,
N'a languy que cinq jours à s'envoller au ciel?
C'est le peu qu'elle avoit en elle de mortel.'

Translated:

Dost thou wonder why the Queen of Navarre, so gifted in wisdom, goodness, and piety, lingered but five days before she flew to heaven? It was because so little of her was mortal.

LATIN EPITAPH.—DE EADEM.

' Dum mens continuò cœlestia spirat, anhelum
Deficiens corpus, cessit, humique jacet.'

While the mind continually breathes celestial things, the body, lacking breath, gives way, and lies i' the earth.

Here endeth the story of the life of Jeanne D'Albret—where all stories end—in the grave, and under the melancholy legend, HIC JACET; pomp, and power, and virtue, and heroism, and ambition; sorrow and mirth, suffering and pleasure, all terminating in 'cold obstruction:' a fact which is obvious to every one of us, and yet by too many is constantly forgotten, though life, for you as for me, dear reader, should be but a preparation for that great change which clothes mortality with immortality, and the human with the Divine!

X

Enthusiasm in Woman.

THE STORY OF MADAME ROLAND.

'Enthusiasm is the fundamental quality of strong souls; the true nobility of blood, in which all greatness of thought or action has its rise. *Quicquid vult valde vult*, is ever the first and surest test of mental capability.'

CARLYLE, *Life of Schiller*.

i.

ADAME ROLAND was one of the most remarkable women of the French Revolution— an era which was rich in remarkable women— remarkable for the purity of her character, the elevation of her motives, the loftiness of her aim, and the intensity of her genius. She may be said to have symbolized all that was best and brightest in republicanism, as Marie Antoinette was, to a certain extent, the representative of all that was best and brightest in aristocracy. Her influence was extensive; and around her gathered the boldest intellects, the most ardent spirits of France, intent on her eloquence, spell-bound by her beauty, animated by the same glorious but delusive dreams of a Golden Age. Yet it was not so much her eloquence, though her language throbbed with poetry, and was uttered by a voice of the richest and sweetest music; nor her beauty, though her personal charms were of rare excellence—a graceful person, a broad open brow, eyes thoughtful and tender, and richly curling tresses of a dark brown hue, combining, with extraordinary grace of manner, to fascinate the beholder; it was not so much her eloquence or her beauty that secured her social power and her influence over her contemporaries, as the magic force of her earnestness, and the spotlessness of her womanly character. It is difficult to resist the contagion of enthusiasm. Believe what you preach, and your hearers will be infected by your own faith. Madame Roland had consecrated her soul to liberty; and she was so evidently sincere in her devotion, that those who listened to her, and saw her daily life—who had opportunities of observing her truthfulness—fell insensibly under the spell of an enthusiasm so generous and so absorbing. When a woman was prepared to do all, to dare all, for the sake of national freedom,—even to the last sublime act of self-sacrifice,—what man could refuse to follow in her steps? Like Joan D'Arc, she was ever in the van; and craven, indeed, must have been the knight who would not couch his lance in behalf of a cause exalted by such a heroine! Her career is a note-worthy illustration of the influence, in times of doubt and confusion and shattered faith, exerted by the individual whose heart is resolute, whose character is unblemished, and whose enthusiasm is above suspicion.

Manon Phlipon was born at Paris in 1754. She was the second child of Gratien Phlipon and Marguerite

Philipon, and the only survivor of a family of five children. Her father was an engraver of some talent, who also dealt in jewels and objects of *vertu*. His circumstances were those of an opulent tradesman, and Manon's childhood passed in considerable comfort. Nursed by a strong peasant woman near Arpajon, she returned to her parents a healthy and robust child, and early gave proof of the firmness of her will when opposed by force, as of the gentleness of her disposition when guided by affection. She was grave, reserved, meditative; she was also of an inflexible temper. When about six years old she had refused, during an illness, to take a nauseous dose of medicine. Her father, a man of rigid sternness, immediately corrected her, and bade her obey; again she refused, and the chastisement was repeated; a third time she was ordered to drink the medicine; silent but determined, she offered herself for the expected punishment. Her mother then interfered, with a few mild words of reproof and prayer. The child immediately drank off the potion, and hazarded no further objection. Struck by the peculiar obstinacy of his daughter's temper, M. Phlipon henceforth abandoned her management to his wife, and forbore to practise a system of tyranny which would only be fruitful in ill results.*

Madame Phlipon was a woman of sincere piety, and Manon's childhood was consequently subjected to the most beneficial influences. Every Sunday she attended the Catechism class, whose members the curé of the parish duly prepared for confirmation. The quaint old French version of the Bible became her daily study; and the marvellous stories which enrich the pages of the

* Miss Kavanagh, 'Woman in France,' p. 345.

'Lives of the Saints' she perused with as much eagerness as an English child her 'Tales of the Genii' or
'Arabian Nights' Entertainments.' She read incessantly,
history, geography, fact, fiction—when all else failed her,
she dipped into the abstruse mysteries of heraldry, and
began, but could not thoroughly understand, a treatise
on contracts! The Abbé Bimont, her maternal uncle,
promised to teach her Latin; but he was a gay, rubicund,
indolent priest, and Manon made little progress under
his instructions. Her favourite companion was an old
volume of Plutarch's Lives; those famous biographies
which have inspired so many noble minds to noble deeds.
Seated in a quiet corner of her father's workshop, she
would pore for hours over the magic page, and, with a
spirit in advance of her years, would often let the book
drop from her hands, while the tears streamed down her
cheeks, and she fell into rapt musings over the glories of
Athens, Thebes, Sparta, Rome. Why was I not a Greek,
she would exclaim, born in the free bright land of Hellas?
Or a countrywoman of the godlike Cincinnatus and the
virtuous Scipio? Of the future which awaited her—the
scaffold and the martyr's crown—she was all unconscious;
yet was her youthful soul fired with a burning ardour to
emulate the example of the 'brave men of old,' and she
felt that all sacrifices would be as nothing which were
made in the cause of liberty. A strange childhood was
this of Manon's! It passed away among books and flowers,
the twin objects of her passionate devotion; it passed
away, like a dream of enthusiasm, fervour, romance, and
mystery. As there seemed no prospect of her rivalling
the heroes of Rome and Sparta, she fell back, in her
intense absorption, on a life of religious martyrdom. She

would imitate Xavier and Loyola, St. Elizabeth or St. Theresa. From the pages of Plutarch she turned to those of the *Aurea Legenda.* She read of devout men and women who had borne all things for the love of God; obloquy and poverty, hunger, thirst, and wretchedness; consummating their lives of suffering and endurance by a painful death. She longed to follow in their footsteps, even if they led to the stake! It is evident that the great feature of her character was a capacity of self-sacrifice; and the most careless observer would scarcely have predicted for this dreamy and enthusiastic child a happy life or a peaceful end. She was always aspiring after some radiant ideal, and at length she fancied she saw it within her reach. She resolved to devote herself to the service of the Church.

At her earnest request, her parents allowed her to enter a convent for a twelvemonth, preparatory to her receiving the first communion. They selected the establishment of La Congregation, in the Rue Neuve St. Etienne, in the Faubourg St. Marcel. She entered it as a pupil in May 1765.* She found herself one of four and thirty young ladies, varying in age from seven to eighteen; and though nearly the youngest, soon outstripped them all in the acquisition of knowledge and the strict performance of religious duties. Her poetical intellect—for though it never found expression in rhyme and rhythm, her mind was eminently poetical—took an intense pleasure in the visionary world of quiet and meditation that now surrounded her. She loved the

* 'Mémoires de Madame Roland,' by Herself (Discours Préliminaire). See also 'An Appeal to Impartial Posterity,' translated from the French original, London, 1796.

dimly-lighted chapel, the roll of the glorious organ, the melody of matin and vesper, the silent prayer, the subdued air of celestial calm that was present ever and everywhere. She shunned the society of her companions, and sat apart under the trees to read and meditate, or paced the silent cloisters, musing over the grave of some fair young nun who had early passed away from the solitude of the convent. All this was not true religion; not the religion of faith and knowledge; but the mysticism of an excited imagination. Manon, however, knew not how widely she erred from the true path; and it must be owned that the influence of this religious *sentimentality* tended to purify and refine her character throughout her later life, and probably imparted that tenderness of feeling and nobility of motive which raised her so far above the other heroines of the French Revolution.

These sacred dreams and this happy solitude she left with regret. On her return home she found her father immersed in political cares, and her mother compelled to devote herself to the management of her father's business. She was therefore placed in the charge of her grandmother, a woman of moderate means, who lived a retired but comfortable life in the Ile St. Louis, then a quiet cluster of old and mossy streets in the bosom of the Seine. For several years Manon lived in herself, and 'made no sign.' She studied assiduously, meditated constantly, and occupied herself at other times with household duties. Her chief pleasure was in an active correspondence which she maintained with two of her former convent-companions, Henriette and Sophie Cannet, and which vividly illustrates the peculiar bias of her exalted and imaginative genius. She now began to experience that transformation which at some time or other all thoughtful minds are conscious of. At first we believe everything, for such is the credulity of ignorance; then we doubt everything, for such is the arrogance of imperfect knowledge. Happy he who has finally passed through Doubt into Faith—the faith of reason and conviction—has faced the spectres of the mind, and laid them. Thus he comes at length

> ' To find a stronger faith his own.

Thus does he learn—

> ' That life is not as idle ore,
>
> ' But iron dug from central gloom,
>   And heated hot with burning fears,
>   And dipt in baths of hissing tears,
>   And battered with the shocks of doom,
>
> ' To shape and use ' *

Manon Phlipon had now to undergo this great trial and torment of the soul. Her religion, as we have hinted, had been a thing of the heart and imagination; a dream, pure and bright enough, it is true, but lacking that substance which faith alone can give. Conscious of how much she wanted, she commenced a course of studious inquiry. In France, and in those days of gathering infidelity and unreason, there was no safe guide for her anxious spirit. She devoured the works of the so-called philosophers, — Descartes, Diderot, Voltaire ; and in abandoning the credulity of childhood plunged into a miserable scepticism. She flung aside a creed which did not seem capable to her of logical proof, but embraced no other. For a while she doubted the immortality of

---

* Tennyson, ' In Memoriam,' cxvii.

the soul; for a while she even disbelieved the existence of a God; yet is it characteristic of her natural purity and loftiness of soul, that in this dreary unbelief she still clung to as severe a standard of duty as the most conscientious Christian could adopt. She declared that the Gospel was the best code of morals she knew, and that her whole conduct should be regulated by it. In fact, it was her understanding that went astray; her heart remained steadfast to the truth; and when she listened to its impulses, she rejected the cold and cheerless doctrines of the atheist. 'In the contemplation of nature,' she wrote, 'my heart, moved by it, rises towards that vivifying Principle which animates it; that high Intelligence which governs it; that Goodness which, through its means, provides me with so many pleasures. And when,' she added, writing in her gloomy prison, 'impenetrable walls separate me from all I love, and the crimes and vices of society seem to unite in punishing me for having desired its highest good, I look beyond the limits of this life to the reward of our sacrifices hereafter, and the intense joy of a future re-union!'* This pure and noble woman erred with her age and her country; but when true to herself, she rose above both, and acknowledged the ideal excellence of the Christian's creed.

Her lot, indeed, was cast in a stormy time. France, worn and spent with the sufferings of generations, was on the brink of a terrible convulsion. Sick of vice in high places, of the masquerade of religion, of sham glory, of a degraded aristocracy, of the worship of wealth, of pageantry and imbecility, the great nation was preparing to throw off the incubus that had so long oppressed it.

* Madame Roland, 'Mémoires,' i. (Discours Préliminaire).

In its disgust at the crimes of priestcraft, it had learned
to loathe religion; in its hatred of the tyranny of the
throne, it had begun to dream of the glories of the
ancient democracy.   Extremes meet.   Shocked and
indignant at what it saw and suffered, France longed for
some grand, some superb ideal—it knew not what—it
cared not what—so long as it was ridded of kings, and
nobles, and priests; of corruption, and hypocrisy, and
shame.   Philosophers preached the virtues of Grecian
stoicism; politicians descanted on the natural equality of
man—on universal brotherhood—on social regeneration
—and professed to see at hand

> 'The dawn of mind, which, upwards on a pinion
> Borne, swift as sunrise, far illumines space,
> And clasps this barren world in its own bright embrace!' *

Alas! the dawn which coloured the distant skies, and
misled their vision, was but the reddening of a terrible
conflagration, wherein all that was good and beautiful
and true perished in common with the base, false, and
mean!

Manon Phlipon saw with the delight of an enthusiastic
nature the old order changing and the coming of the
new.   Her austere and pure soul revolted at the vice
which surrounded her; her warm imagination was kindled
by the remembrance of Greek and Roman glories; she
longed for her country to throw off the chains that fettered its native manliness.   When her parents took her
to Versailles, she was disgusted with the ridiculous pagean-
tries and adulation of the court; she thought of Athens,
and the simplicity of the happier times of that great
republic.   Like many other dreamers, she forgot the

* Shelley, 'The Revolt of Islam.'

dark passages of Athenian history, and remembered only those which an heroic spirit animates. She thought of Aristides, to forget that his countrymen ostracized him; of Socrates, to forget the day of trial and the cup of poison. Burning with a love of duty and of truth, keenly feeling the nobleness of life, she rebelled against the social conventionalities that fettered her. 'O Liberty!' she cried; 'idol of earnest souls, thou art but a name for me!'

She was now seventeen, and she was beautiful. Her personal appearance has been sketched in few but graphic words by a great master. 'Reader,' he says, 'mark that queenlike burgher-woman: beautiful, Amazonian-graceful to the eye—more so to the mind. Unconscious of her worth (as all worth is), of her greatness, of her crystal clearness; genuine, the creature of sincerity and nature, in an age of artificiality, pollution, and cant; there, in her still completeness, in her still invincibility, *she*, if thou knew it, is the noblest of all living Frenchwomen!'* Her face was rather round, the nostril thick, the mouth large; but the brow was broad, high, and open; the hair parted over it in dark-brown glossy tresses; the eye-brows, full and dark, were arched over deep-blue eyes, of that peculiar hue which, in some lights, changes to brown; the smile was radiant with sweetness, the glance lofty and commanding, the whole expression that of an exalted and serene intellect. In stature she was above the ordinary standard; her figure was slight but dignified; she looked, she moved—a queen; queen by virtue of her genius, her enthusiasm, and her elevation of thought. Such a woman could not but have suitors; they made,

---

* Carlyle, 'The French Revolution,' i 261.

however, little progress in their suits. The idea of uniting herself, says Miss Kavanagh,* to a man with tastes and feelings inferior to her own revolted her; to remain single was, in her opinion, a far more preferable fate. She watched with jealous care over every feeling of her heart, and, as though actuated by a foreknowledge of her high destiny, proudly avoided indulging in aught resembling an unworthy affection. She owns that a young man named De Blancherie produced some impression upon her, but circumstances revealing his real character, she cast aside the illusion. Other lovers came—some inspired by her beauty, some by her supposed fortune—but she calmly dismissed them all.

The death of her mother, in the spring of 1775, was a great blow. Soon afterwards her father fell into a career of dissipation and extravagance, which wasted not only his own means but his daughter's. Manon turned for consolation to the writings of the great French divines, Massillon, Bourdaloue, Bossuet; but it was with great regret she found them devoted to the mysticisms of their creed rather than to lessons of practical Christianity. The want she felt she endeavoured to supply by a sermon, of her own composition, on loving one's neighbour, which, unfortunately, has not descended to posterity.

It was at this time that she made the acquaintance, through Sophie Cannet, of M. Roland de la Platière. Her beauty, capacity, and generous warmth of feeling, at once made a powerful impression upon him; and she in her turn could not but respect his integrity and admire the force of his character. He was hardly one of Plutarch's heroes; for he was elderly, tall and thin in person.

* Miss Kavanagh, 'Woman in France.' p. 351.

of reserved manners, and with a grave harsh countenance and yet he had so much of the heroic in him that he could love truth and worship liberty. No fair young girl could identify him with the ideal of her dreams, and yet no sensible woman would hesitate to accept him as her life companion.

For some unexplained reason, M. Phlipon refused his consent to his daughter's marriage. Manon had long felt it desirable she should quit the paternal roof, and she seized the opportunity afforded by this interference with her happiness to retire to the Ursuline convent, where she had formerly spent so blest a twelvemonth. The narrow income (about £20 per annum) bequeathed by her mother did not permit her to enter La Congregation as a boarder; she only rented a small garret, where she cooked her own food, consisting of the cheapest vegetables. Even in this period of privation, however, she enjoyed many luxuries which the wealthy do not always possess, and found a constant source of unalloyed enjoyment in her books, her music, and her drawing.

After an interval of prudent reflection, M. Roland once more offered her his hand. She accepted it, without being under any delusion as to the nature of their mutual feelings, and in 1781 they were married. Her high sense of duty made her married life a not unhappy one; yet was it such a life as few women would envy. The love of Roland, says Miss Kavanagh,* was a love selfish and domineering, to which he expected every feeling of his wife to yield. Such was his jealousy of her exclusive affection, that he required her to put aside all the friendships of her youth. A severity so injudicious

---

* Miss Kavanagh, ‘Woman in France,’ p. 354.

and so selfish would have alienated the hearts of most
women; but Madame Roland was sensible of his many
virtues, of the implicit confidence he reposed in her, of
what was due to her own honour.   A year after her
marriage she accompanied him to Amiens, where he was
appointed inspector of several important manufactories.
It was there she gave birth to her daughter and only
child—the Eudora on whom she lavished all the love of
her passionate nature.   Her leisure she devoted to her
husband's assistance; transcribing his literary labours,
correcting the proofs, and occasionally vivifying the dry
mass with a spark of her own enthusiastic imagination.

From Amiens, after a four years' residence, they removed to the Clos la Platière, near Lyons, the home of
the Roland family. She pursued here the same calm life of
self-control, notwithstanding the annoying interference of
her husband's relatives, a younger brother, and an aged
mother-in-law; gaining the golden opinions of the poor
by her charity, her medical skill, her patience, and un-
selfish devotion.   She would go three or four leagues,
whenever needed, to relieve the wants of a sick peasant.
Nor was she one of those women who spend all their
charity abroad. When, in 1789, her husband was stricken
with a dangerous illness, she watched by his side for
twelve dreary days and nights, with a gentle patience
which completed her conquest over him.*   Who will·
laugh at enthusiasm when it inspires such noble deeds as
these?

But domestic peace and lettered ease were now to
give way to public duties.   France in 1789 was all
a-flame.   'Equality,' 'Fraternity,' 'Liberty,' were the

---

* Madame Roland, 'Mémoires' (Discours Préliminaire).

watchwords on every tongue. Madame Roland and her husband believed that at length the golden age of freedom had dawned on man. She was not insensible to the perils which inaugurate every great popular movement. ' Blood may be shed,' she wrote to a friend, ' but tyranny will not be re-established: her iron throne is tottering throughout Europe. The efforts of the despots can only hasten its fall. Let it fall! even though we should perish beneath its ruins. A new generation will arise to enjoy the freedom we shall have bequeathed, and to bless our endeavours in their behalf.' Heart and soul she devoted herself to a cause which she felt to be sublime--yet to which she had a dim foreboding she should fall a martyr.

The advanced political opinions of M. Roland secured his election as deputy for the city of Lyons to the Constituent Assembly, and early in 1791 the husband and wife repaired to Paris. Henceforth Madame Roland's life belongs to history, and history shows how high and glorious a life it was.

Her clear intellect soon arrived at a correct estimate of the state of parties and the condition of public affairs. She saw that the diseases of the commonwealth could only be cured by a violent remedy, and though willing to assist in the establishment of a constitutional monarchy, her prescience told her that the seas were too stormy for the safe voyage of so trim a barque. When, however, the unfortunate Louis XVI. determined on the experiment of a purely Patriot Ministry, under the leadership of the gallant, able, but surely unprincipled Dumouriez—afterwards the hero of Valmy—she did not dissuade her husband from joining it as Minister of the

Interior (March 1792).   For Roland was a man of influence, and the friend of Brissot, Barbaroux, Vergniaud, and others, the acknowledged chiefs of the famous party of the Girondins.*

On accepting office, Roland, as austere in his dress as in his principles, and therefore nicknamed the *Quaker endimanché*, or 'Sunday Quaker,' repaired to the Tuileries to kiss the royal hand, in a round hat, a black coat, and dusty shoes without buckles.   The chamberlain gazed on the unaccustomed apparition with horror, and made complaint of it to General Dumouriez.—'He wears no buckles to his shoes!' The soldier laughed blithely. 'All is lost, then!' cried he ; 'no more etiquette, no more monarchy !' +

Carlyle has painted, with characteristic force, this period in Madame Roland's life: 'She now removes,' he says,‡ 'from her upper floor in the Rue Saint Jacques, to the sumptuous saloons once occupied by Madame Necker.   Nay, still earlier, it was Calonne that did all this gilding; it was he who ground these lustres, Venetian mirrors ; who polished this inlaying, this veneering and *or-moulu*.   The fair Roland, equal to either fortune, has her public dinner on Fridays, the Ministers all there in a body : she withdraws to her desk (the cloth once removed), and seems busy writing ; nevertheless loses no word ; if, for example, Deputy Brissot and Minister Clavière get too hot in argument, she, not without timidity, yet with a cunning gracefulness, will interpose.

* So named because Vergniaud, their leader, was from that part of France known as the Gironde.   He and his associates were moderate in their opinions, and hence opposed to the extreme Jacobins.

† Madame Roland, 'Mémoires,' ii. 80-115.

‡ Carlyle, 'The French Revolution,' ii. 77, 78.

Envious men insinuate that the wife Roland is Minister, and not the husband : it is happily the worst they have to charge her with. Serene and queenly is she here, as of old in her own hired garret of the Ursulines' convent! She who has quietly shelled French beans for her dinner; being led to that, as a young maiden, by quiet insight and computation ; and knowing what that was, and what she was : such a one will also look quietly on *or-moulu* and veneering, not ignorant of these either.'

It soon became evident that the Patriot Ministry could not long work in harmony with the vacillating Louis. Madame Roland from the first mistrusted the king, and still more the despotic tendencies of Marie Antoinette, while she perceived that Dumouriez was playing a double game for his own personal aggrandizement. Her suspicions to some extent made her unjust ; but it is easier for posterity to be cool and calm in its judgments than for those who live in the throes of national convulsion. The ministers demanded of Louis that he should sign certain decrees of the Assembly for the exile of malignant priests, and the establishment of a civic force ; but the king refused. Madame Roland thereupon advised her husband to address the sovereign in a letter of remonstrance, which, if ineffectual, would be a guarantee to the nation of their representative's sincerity. The letter was written, and by herself. Its language was bold, vigorous, vehement ; its representations were unanswerable ; yet had the tone been milder and more generous, it would have better become a minister remonstrating with his king on public affairs.

Louis listened to the reprimand in silence : the next day he dismissed his ministers. Roland, who, says

Thiers,[*] possessed all the nerve necessary for executing what the bold spirit of his wife conceived, repaired immediately to the Assembly, and read to it the letter which had caused his dismissal. It was a sign of open hostility between the Girondists and the king. The Assembly bestowed the warmest plaudits on the eloquent remonstrance; ordered it to be printed, and circulated throughout France; and declared that the displaced ministers possessed the confidence of the nation (June 13, 1792)—a declaration which that nation ratified with the loudest applause.

Madame Roland now retired to humbler apartments in the Faubourg Saint Jacques, whither her power and social influence went with her. She became the acknowledged centre of the Girondists, whom her enthusiasm inspired with visions, beautiful but baseless, of the approaching regeneration of mankind. Brissot and Vergniaud, Buzot and Clavière, listened with admiration to her lofty utterances. And among those who visited her most frequently was the handsome and impetuous Barbaroux, who seemed to Madame Roland a realization of her earlier fancies of Greek heroism, and who, in his turn, saw in the lovely and generous-souled woman a goddess of liberty, at whose feet the haughtiest soul might bow. Each appreciated the other's greatness, but no breath of calumny ever sullied the pure fame of Manon Roland.

We are not writing the history of France, and we must pass very briefly over the astonishing incidents of the Reign of Terror. Enraged at what they conceived to be the perfidy of Louis, and convinced that their country

[*] M. A. Thiers, 'History of the French Revolution.' i. 284.

could only be saved by a republic, the Girondists united with the Mountain, as the extreme party was named,* to effect the overthrow of the throne. They succeeded. On the 20th of June the populace of Paris paraded before the Tuileries, rejoicing in the humiliation of their sovereign. On the 20th of July Barbaroux brought up his chosen band of six hundred from Marseilles, and on the 10th of August the Tuileries were assaulted and stormed. In vain the Swiss Guards stood firm in the defence of the throne; · how could they resist the strength of an infuriate people? They were massacred to the last man, and the French monarchy, on that day of carnage, ceased to exist.

And now that the Girondists had won the victory, did it bring the universal happiness which they had so ardently desired? Alas, they found that their efforts had but inaugurated an era of anarchy and bloodshed, and instead of peace, of regeneration, of ennobling patriotism, there prevailed the unscrupulous ambition of bad men, and the insatiable greed of mean souls. The Golden Age had not yet returned, but an age of cruelty dawned on unhappy France, whose annals were written in blood, to the horror and execration of the latest time. In vain the Girondists sought to check the Mountain in their sanguinary projects. They might as well have attempted to stay the avalanche in its course. The passions of the mob were aroused, and the leaders of the extreme faction, undeterred by any scruples, and hungering after supreme power, did not hesitate to make them subserve their own purposes. Those who refused to tread with

* Carlyle, 'The French Revolution,' ii. 115-121; Thiers, 'History of the French Revolution,' i. 370, *et seq.*

them their path of blood and crime, they denounced as enemies of their country, and ruthlessly swept away. In that prolonged massacre—which men still call the Reign of Terror—virtue and valour, the purest patriotism, the most stainless innocence, youth, sex, age, honour, availed you nothing. The whirlwind was let loose, and the frail blossom as well as the stalwart tree fell before its fury. Blood—more blood! Such was the cry, until such time as the people themselves sickened of the cruel work.

Madame Roland looked on aghast at this rude awakening from her enthusiastic dreams. She had hoped to revive the palmy times of free and liberal Hellas; she found France wallowing in the worst of all tyrannies— the tyranny of the mob. Her husband, though re-appointed to the Ministry of the Interior, was powerless to check this Saturnalia of murder and rapine. The Girondists wept with shame at the fatal error they had committed. The supreme authority was now virtually placed in the hands of the unscrupulous Danton. Under his auspices took place the frightful massacre of the 2nd of September—that black Sabbath-day which, in the annals of man, is reckoned with the hours of the Bartholomew Butchery, of the Armagnac Massacres, and of the Sicilian Vespers—hours of woe and frenzy, which show how much of the demon lurks beneath the polish of humanity! An attempt was made, after this hideous slaughter, to effect a reconciliation between the Mountain and the Girondists; but Barbaroux loftily said: No alliance was possible between crime and virtue.* Roland, in the National Convention, did not hesitate to

---

* Thiers, ' History of the French Revolution.'

denounce, with a noble eloquence which his wife inspired, the barbarous outrages. that had disgraced France and dishonoured the Revolution. But it must be owned that these men were unequal to deal with the crisis. They kept their hands too clean. They could not guide a revolution, when they had only meditated a reform. 'The men of action on their side,' says Alison,* 'strove in vain to rouse them to the necessity of vigorous measures. Their constant reply was, that they would not be the first to commence the shedding of blood. Their whole vigour consisted in declamation, their whole wisdom in abstract discussion. They were too honourable to believe in the wickedness of their opponents; too scrupulous to adopt the means requisite to crush them.'

'We are under the knife of Robespierre and Marat,' wrote Madame Roland; 'you know my enthusiasm for the Revolution; alas, I am ashamed of it now; it has been profaned by monsters; it has grown hideous.'

The French Republic was proclaimed on the 22nd of September. In the evening, the Girondists met to celebrate an event from which so much had been anticipated at the house of Madame Roland. When the supper was ended, the hostess, in imitation of a custom of antiquity, and with a touch of poetical feeling, scattered rose leaves over the wine. Vergniaud rose, and drank to the eternity of the Republic. All honoured the toast; but the orator, as he sat down, remarked to Barbaroux, with a sorrowful smile: 'It is not rose leaves, but cypress leaves, we should drink in our wine to-night. Who knows, but that in pledging a republic whose birth is stained with the blood of

* Sir A. Alison, ' History of Europe during the French Revolution.'

September, we are drinking to our own deaths? Not the less, were this wine my life-blood, I would drain it to liberty and equality.' *

This word soon came true. Danton, Marat, Couthon, Robespierre—differing widely in their aims and views—were united in hatred of the Girondists and the Rolands. The enthusiast, still cherishing her fond fancies of human regeneration, regarded Danton with especial horror, and would suffer no alliance with him. She employed her passionate eloquence and fervid thought in the noble enterprise of purifying the Revolution from the stains of blood and crime which profaned it. Alas, in such an enterprise she could not but fail, and failing, suffer! She became, however, the heart, if not the brain, of the Girondists, and the Jacobins lavished upon her their bitterest virulence. Her life and her husband's life were in danger. She slept constantly with a pistol under her pillow. Her friends urged her to fly, but the brave woman refused. She was prepared to sacrifice herself, if the necessity arose, on the altar of liberty, in the vain hope that such an act might rouse her country to a sense of its degradation.

Urged by Madame Roland, the Girondists ventured to attack Robespierre; and Louvet, in an oration of remarkable eloquence, exposed his secret ambition. The attack failed, and recoiled on those who made it. They attempted to save Louis XVI. from the scaffold, but the Convention by a large majority determined on the trial of the unfortunate monarch. ' Alas!' exclaimed Roland, 'the Convention is both accuser and judge; it is dishonoured!' In their eager desire to ruin a woman whose

---

* Madame Roland, 'Mémoires,' *ut ante*

genius they feared, and whose lofty patriotism was a constant reproach, the Jacobins next endeavoured, through
the agency of a worthless spy, named Viard, to involve
her in a pretended Royalist conspiracy. She was summoned before the Convention. She came, in 'her high
clearness,' and with few clear words 'dissipated this
Viard into despicability and air.' The members ap-
plauded her vindication of herself, and the President
decreed that the honours of the sitting belonged to her.
The Jacobins in the galleries, however, maintained a
gloomy silence. Marat rose, and pointing to them, exclaimed, 'Look at the people; they are wiser than you
are.' *

On the 23d of January 1793, two days after the King's
execution, Roland resigned his post as Minister of the
Interior, unwilling to appear even nominally implicated
in deeds which he condemned and shuddered at. His
wife lived in mournful seclusion, while the Jacobin press
assailed her with incessant calumnies, and Danton stigmatized her as the Circe of the Republic. The Mountain
determined on one final effort to crush her and her
associates. Excited by atrocious libels, the Parisian
mob furnished the pretext that was required. They
gathered with arms in their hands around the Hall of the
Convention, and demanded the arrest of the Gironde
leaders—twenty-two in number. On the 31st of May all
was over; the Jacobins triumphed. The Girondists,
except Roland, who had succeeded in making his escape,
were placed under arrest in their own houses, whence

* For the general history of this period, the reader should consult Lacretelle,
Mignet, and Thiers, among French authors; or Lamartine's eloquent 'History
of the Girondists;' and in English, the great work of Carlyle.

they were soon afterwards removed to the Conciergerie,
and, on the 31st of October, to the scaffold. There
they sang in unfaltering chorus, as their death-hymn, the
martial strains of the Marseillaise ; and, one by one, fell
beneath the sickle of the guillotine.

Madame Roland was arrested on the 31st of May.
In the pride of her innocence and the fulness of her
enthusiasm, she had disdained to fly. Worn with fatigue,
on this particular evening she had retired early to her
room, in the hope of enjoying a little repose. Her
servant entered, and informed her that her attendance
was required by some armed men. Knowing how
intensely her enemies hated her, she listened to the
summons without surprise. She rose, dressed herself
with more than her usual care, and appeared before the
gendarmes. They showed her a warrant for her arrest.
It was illegal, but she knew that resistance was useless.
She made her preparations with perfect composure, bade
her daughter and her servants farewell, and passed out
into the darkness and the night.

A tumultuous crowd had meanwhile forced their way
into her chambers, and now gathered round the fiacre in
which she was placed, with boisterous cries of ' A la
guillotine ! ' One of the guards, touched by her tranquil
meekness, inquired, ' Shall we draw down the blinds ? '
' No,' she replied ; ' oppressed innocence must not put
on the aspect of crime. I fear the looks of none.' 'You
have more strength than most men,' said the gendarme
admiringly. ' Yet I groan for my country,' she answered ;
' I regret the error which made me think it worthy of
happiness and freedom.' ' Wait patiently, and justice
will be done you.' ' Justice ! ' she exclaimed, with lofty

scorn; 'were justice done to me, I should not be here to-day; but I shall walk as calmly to the scaffold as I now proceed to the prison.' *

A few minutes more, and the doors of the Abbaye closed upon the unfortunate enthusiast, whose high hopes and radiant visions had been so rudely swept away.

II.

Madame Roland was fortunate in a humane gaoler, who did all he dared to make her confinement endurable. She herself displayed the serenity of a brave spirit, conscious of its innocence, and too proud to indulge in useless complaints. She made, however, every necessary exertion to procure her release. She wrote to the Convention, denouncing the illegality of her arrest, and sent remonstrances to the municipal authorities. When these proved unavailing, she submitted to her fate with composure. She had obtained a few books: Thomson's 'Seasons,' whose fresh descriptions of Nature lit up her prison-cell with living landscapes; Tacitus, in whose eloquent pages she studied the meditations of a profound and subtle intellect; and Plutarch, whose noble biographies renewed her enthusiasm and her belief in liberty. With characteristic energy, she began a perusal of Hume's ' History of England,' and endeavoured, by the aid of Sheridan's ' Dictionary,' to improve her knowledge of English. Her gaoler daily decked her cell with flowers, and she was occasionally visited by a few particular friends, with whom she arranged for the removal of her daughter to the care of a Madame Creuze la Fouche, and through whom she obtained some tidings

* Madame Roland, 'Mémoires;' Thiers, ' History of the French Revolution, &c.

of the outer world. Alas, they were ill-calculated to cheer or console a heart like hers, which was always dreaming dreams of a regenerated earth! France was rushing headlong into the whirlpool of social and political anarchy, and its noblest men were perishing on the fatal Place de la Revolution. She found, too, that her own name was inscribed upon Robespierre's death-list. She knew that her enemies were powerful, and she felt they would not spare her.

Suddenly, after a captivity of four and twenty days, she was released. She left her cell—afterwards tenanted by Charlotte Corday—with eager delight, and hastened to her home. She had scarcely entered it before she was again apprehended. Her first arrest having been too shamelessly illegal, her persecutors adopted this method of fastening their hold upon her. The son of her landlady bravely protested against the foul deed. He expiated his crime on the guillotine. Madame Roland was removed to Sainte Pelagie, the prison generally reserved for dissolute and abandoned women. At first her courage gave way under the shock; but she soon recovered her usual tranquillity, and that power over her thoughts and feelings which, to use her own words, 'a strong soul preserves even in chains, and which, above all things, disappoints the malice of its enemies.'

The heart of Madame Bonchaud, her gaoler's wife, was affected by the serenity with which this noble woman endured her fate, and by the heroism with which she prepared to sacrifice herself on the shrine of liberty. She caused her to be placed in a more comfortable chamber, where the window-bars were hidden by the starry blossoms of the jessamine; provided her with flowers; and obtained the loan of a piano. Her captivity thus brightened and alleviated, Madame Roland set herself down to make good use of the little time that remained to her, and began those 'Memoirs'—'which all the world still reads'*—on the 9th of August 1793. It was her object in this to clear her fame from the calumnies cast upon it by the malignity of unscrupulous tongues, and to reveal the whole course of her life from childhood to its last sad days. Of all autobiographies, it is at once the most eloquent, the most touching, and the most truthful. Written in a fervid and picturesque style, which insensibly charms the reader like a strain of wayward music, its great merits arise from the fidelity with which, as in a photograph, it reproduces every feature of the writer's character—her scorn of tyranny; her love of freedom; her sympathy with all that was bright and beautiful; the clearness of her intellect, and the force of her imagination. It is a wonderful picture of a human soul, drawn in the very shadow of death, on the very threshold of a premature grave.† Hurriedly written, for the writer never knew how soon her task might be arrested by the guillotine, it nevertheless remains a noble memorial to her literary ability as well as to her heroic genius.

Helen Maria Williams, a celebrity of whom these later ages have been persistently forgetful, has left on record some interesting details of a visit which she paid to Madame Roland at Sainte Pelagie: 'She conversed with

* Carlyle, 'The French Revolution,' ii. 289.

† Madame Roland, 'Mémoires,' with Introduction, &c., translated into English with the title which she originally chose, 'An Appeal to an Impartial Posterity."

me,' writes the poetess, 'with as great a cheerfulness in
her little cell as ever she preserved in the saloons of her
husband's hotel. She had supplied herself with a few
books, and I found her reading Plutarch. She told me
that she well knew she should die; and the smile of
placid resignation with which she said it, convinced me
that she was prepared to meet death with a firmness
worthy of her exalted character. When I inquired after
her daughter, she burst into tears; and at the over-
whelming recollection of her husband and child, the
courage of the martyr of liberty was lost in the feelings
of the wife and the mother.' *

Madame Roland might have escaped from the prison,
but every offer of assistance she steadily refused. She
feared to bring disgrace on the good cause for which she
had lived, and for which, if need were, she was ready to
die. Henriette Cannet, her old convent friend, would
fain have taken her place, and exchanged attire with her;
but neither her prayers nor her tears could shake the
enthusiast's resolution. 'They would kill thee, my good
Henriette,' she exclaimed; 'thy blood would ever rest
upon my soul. Sooner would I suffer death a thousand
times, than have to reproach myself as the author of
thine!' †

On the same day that her friends and fellow-labourers,
the leaders of the Gironde, were hurried to the scaffold,
Madame Roland was removed to the Conciergerie, the
prison they had just left. She was treated there with
unrelenting cruelty. Her dungeon was damp and dark;
she had no bed, until a prisoner gave her up his own;

* Helen Maria Williams, 'Letters from France, &c.' (London, 1792-96.)
† Miss Kavanagh, 'Woman in France,' p. 419.

and, though the weather was cold, no coverings were
provided for her. The adjoining cell was that which
Marje Antoinette had occupied previous to her execution.
'There was a strange link,' observes a recent writer,
'between the destinies of those two women. Born
within a few months of each other—one in the sheltering
obscurity of the French bourgeoisie, the other on the
steps of an imperial throne—they met in antagonism on
the stormy path of the French Revolution. Both were
beautiful, ardent, and heroic, and helped to ruin, by their
imprudence, the opposite causes to which they clung.
In her republican ardour, Madame Roland hastened the
fall of Marie Antoinette; but it was, after enjoying a brief
triumph, to end by following the fallen queen to her
dungeon, and to perish on the same scaffold. Opposed
in life, the two rivals met in death : the revolutionary
axe knew no distinction of victims.'

Even while standing on the threshold of a terrible
death, Madame Roland's courageous spirit did not quail.
She read; she meditated; she continued the composition of her ' Mémoires ;' and her heart returned to that
holy gospel of Christianity which had been the light of
her early womanhood. She possessed an extraordinary
faculty of self-absorption, and the storm which raged
around could not withdraw her from her solitary studies.
She was frequently seen in her prison by the philosopher
Riouffe; and to his eyes, not easily dazzled or blinded
by mere show, she appeared veritably heroic. 'Something more,' he says,[*] 'than is usually found in the looks
of women shone in those large black eyes of hers, full of
expression and sweetness. She spoke to me often at the

---

[*] Riouffe. ' Mémoires sur les Prisons,' i. 55, *et seq.*

grating (which divided the women's portion of the prison
from that allotted to the men), and we listened attentively,
in a sort of admiration and astonishment. Her discourse
was dignified, but animated; frank and courageous as
that of a great man. She expressed herself with a purity,
with a harmony and prosody that made her language like
music, of which the ear could never have enough. She
never spoke of the Girondists who had perished but with
respect; yet, at the same time, without any effeminate
pity. She even deplored that they had not adopted
sufficiently vigorous measures. She generally designated
them as "our friends." She frequently sent for Clavière,
and conversed with him. Sometimes she gave way to
the natural feelings of her sex, and traces of tears showed
that she had been weeping at the memory of her child
and her husband. The woman who attended her said
to me one day, "Before you she summons up all her
strength; but in her own room she will, now and then,
sit for three hours, leaning on her window, and shedding
tears."'

For my own part, I reverence those tears; they were
of the woman, womanly. In the true hero, gentleness,
and the wealth of household feelings, and the capacity
of divine sorrow, will always be combined with courage,
intrepidity, the most resolute will. Madame Roland was
no splendid virago, no imperial Semiramis—hard, cold,
unimpressionable, dead to the tenderer emotions, heroic
only in her ambition—but

> 'A dearer being, all dipt
> In angel instincts, breathing Paradise.'

As such, she claims our sympathies no less than our
admiration.

She prepared for her trial by taking notes, collecting evidence, and drawing up a defence. She knew her care would avail her nothing; but she believed it to be her duty. To her most intimate friends, and to her well-beloved daughter, she addressed farewell letters of the most touching eloquence. The day before her trial she received her counsel, Chauveau de la Garde, the defender of Marie Antoinette and Charlotte Corday. At the close of the interview, she pressed upon him a ring, and said, ' To-morrow I shall be no more. I know the fate which awaits me. Your kind assistance can do nothing for me, and would but imperil you. I pray you, therefore, not to appear before the tribunal, but to accept of this last token of my regard.'

Early on the following morning she was summoned before the judges. She was dressed in simple white, her long rich tresses of raven blackness falling about her neck and shoulders, and down to her very waist. Never had she looked more beautiful or more radiant. She seemed like a queen going forth to her marriage-pomp, rather than a persecuted woman treading the thorny path of death. Her very beauty was felt as a reproach by her enemies, and they loaded her with the foulest abuse. She endured their invectives with equanimity, until they ventured to asperse her moral character. Then the woman's nature was touched, and she gave way to tears. But, recovering herself, she answered with such contemptuous eloquence, that the judges silenced her, fearful of the effect it might produce upon the crowd. She boasted that she was the wife of Roland, and the friend of the martyred Girondists. She gloried in all she had done for the liberty, happiness, and regeneration

of France. She accused her persecutors of having betrayed the good cause to serve the purposes of their own
mean ambition and vulgar selfishness.

Two days later she was again called before the Revolutionary Tribunal. Her enemies, unable to prove
against her any crime which even their own cruel edicts
could recognize, now called upon her to reveal her husband's place of concealment. 'There is no law,' she
exclaimed, ' which can compel a betrayal of the holiest
feelings of nature.'

'With such a babbler,' interrupted Fouquier Tin-
ville, the public prosecutor, ' we shall never have done.
Close the interrogatory.'

She turned upon him a glance of scorn.

' How I pity you!' she cried; ' you can send me to the
scaffold, but cannot deprive me of the blessing of a good
conscience, and the assurance that posterity will acquit
Roland and myself, while it devotes our foes to everlasting infamy!'

She was condemned; her crime, concealing the hiding-
place of an enemy of the republic. Immediate execution was ordered.*

Her friends stood without, waiting to receive her.
She drew her finger across her neck, to intimate that her
sentence was death, and then re-entered her cell for a
few hours of meditation and prayer.

On that fatal day, the 8th of November 1793, the
tumbrel had incessantly traversed the road between the
prison and the scaffold. It was on its last journey when
it received Madame Roland, and a weak, infirm, old

---

* Thiers, 'History of the French Revolution;' Madame Roland, 'Mémoires,
Introduction, i. 67, 68, 69, et seq.

man, named Lamarche, 'Director of Assignat Printing.'
As they approached the scaffold, which was erected in
the Place de la Revolution, now known as the Place de
la Concorde, he wept and moaned bitterly. She sought
to cheer him with words of noble consolation. At the
foot of the guillotine she sprang lightly from the cart,
close beneath a huge clay statue of Liberty—Liberty!
Shall we not rather call it a Moloch, which was never
weary of demanding victims? She asked for pen and
paper, ' to write the strange thoughts that were rising in
her;' strange thoughts of the past and future, of the life
so nearly ended, and that *other* life which was so soon
to begin. Her request was refused, and the executioner
pulled her by the arm towards the scaffold. 'Stay,' said
she—that noble self-sacrifice which had been the motive.
principle of her whole career still powerful in the last
supreme moment—' I would ask a favour, but not for myself. Spare yonder poor old man the pain of seeing me
die.' 'It is contrary to my orders,' answered Samson.
'You cannot,' she said, with a radiant smile, ' refuse the
last request of a lady;' and the executioner complied.

But it soon became her turn to ascend the scaffold.
For a moment she gazed on the great clay image of
Freedom, and, bowing gravely before it, pronounced the
well-known words, ' O Liberty, Liberty! what crimes
are committed in thy name!' Then she submitted herself to the executioner, and in a few seconds her head
rolled into the fatal basket.

' Noble white vision,' exclaims Carlyle,* ' with its high
queenly face, its soft proud eyes, long black hair flowing
down to the girdle; and as brave a heart as ever beat in

Carlyle, 'The French Revolution: a History,' ii. 289, 290

woman's bosom! Like a white Grecian statue, serenely
complete, she shines in that black wreck of things—long
memorable. Honour to great Nature who, in Paris city,
can make a Jeanne Philipon, and nourish her to clear
perennial womanhood. Biography will long remember
that trait of asking for a pen "to write the strange
thoughts that were rising in her." It is as a little light-
beam, shedding softness and a kind of sacredness over
all that preceded: so in her, too, there was an Unname-
able; she, too, was a daughter of the Infinite; there
were mysteries which philosophism had not dreamt of!'

So perished, in her thirty-ninth year, Jeanne Marie
(better known as Manon) Roland, her death not unworthy of her life, as her life had been a fitting prelude to
such a death. The glorious enthusiasm of her soul shone
out in all she said and did, exalted every thought, purified
every feeling. She was incapable of mean motives or
selfish aims; her whole career was one of self-devotion to
the happiness of others. The virtues she at first exhibited
and practised in a narrow circle and on a confined stage,
circumstances eventually afforded her an opportunity of
cultivating in the eyes of the world, and never spot nor
stain was found by the most envious scrutiny upon her
bright renown. Some critics have pronounced her heroism unwomanly; but we have seen that she was capable
of the gentlest emotions, that she was no stranger to
'sacred tears.' She met death, it is true, with almost
stoical composure, because she felt herself supported by
an ardent faith in the future, and a grand belief that she
fell a martyr to one of the noblest causes ever consecrated by the blood of the innocent. The love of truth
was her over-mastering passion. To be faithful to the

truth was her conception of a woman's noblest duty. Speak the truth she must, even if death were to be the issue. A generous, trustful woman, a sublime enthusiast, a tender mother, a loyal and devoted wife, surely the annals of heroic womanhood can produce few names as glorious as that of Manon Roland!

She had predicted that her husband would not long survive her. The news of her death soon reached him at Rouen, where he was lying concealed. In his first frenzy he would have gone straight to Paris, and in the Convention itself have denounced the murderers of his wife, to perish, like her, upon the scaffold. But he remembered that if he were tried and judicially condemned, all his property would be forfeited to the State, and his child left penniless.

Still, he felt that he could not survive the extinction of all his hopes of happiness.

On the 16th of the month, a week or so after his wife's death, some four leagues from Rouen, and near Bourg Baudoin, on the road to Paris, there was seen sitting at the foot of a tree, and leaning against its trunk, the figure of an aged and wrinkled man. The wayfarers, approaching, found it stiff and cold in death, with a cane-sword run through the heart; the whole attitude and expression of the pale face tranquil and composed—the tranquillity and composure of sleep. A paper pinned on his breast explained who he was, and had been:—

'Whoever thou art that findest me lying here, respect my remains; respect them as those of a virtuous man, who consecrated all his life to being useful, and who died, as he had lived, virtuous and honest. Not fear, but indignation, made me quit my retreat, on learning

that my wife had been murdered. I wished not to re
main longer on an earth polluted with crimes.' *

Had this worthy but mistaken patriot been inspired by
the spirit of a true religion, he would have known that
life was not a plaything to be flung away at will; he
would have felt that he had duties to perform which only
cowardice could evade; duties towards a daughter left
motherless, in a time of unreason, restlessness, and social
confusion. To have fallen by the guillotine, as his wife
had done, would have been far nobler, and more useful;
for every unjust death is a sacrifice in the cause of
humanity. But peace to his ashes! Recalling the sins
and follies of the age in which he lived, and the ignorance which everywhere prevailed of the sublime truths
of Christ's gospel, we may judge him leniently, we may
deal with his memory tenderly, and own that he did his
duty with calm courage and singular honesty, so far as
he understood it. May as much be said of *us*, O reader,
when *our* careers are spent, and our life-work done!

Let us, then, thank God devoutly for the example
and teaching of such lofty souls as Manon Roland.
Let us be grateful that mankind is ever and anon made
happy by the inspiration of so exalted an enthusiasm.
The Heavens, says Carlyle, cease not their bounty; they
send us generous hearts into every generation.—The
torch passes on from hand to hand, and its light is never
wholly wanting even in the darkest night.

---

* Madame Roland, 'Mémoires,' Introduction, i. 88.

XI

The Patience of Genius.

THE STORY OF CHARLOTTE BRONTË.

> ' A soul tempered with fire,
> Fervent, heroic, and good,
> Helper and friend of mankind.'
>
> MATTHEW ARNOLD.

AMONG the women of letters who lend so much lustre to the records of English literature, a foremost place will always be allotted to Charlotte Brontë, the author of ' Jane Eyre.'

She resided at Haworth, near Keighley, in Yorkshire. Of her birthplace it is necessary to give a brief description, because her genius, and indeed her life, were strongly influenced by its character and surroundings. It is a small village, with houses mostly built of a dull gray stone, which stretch irregularly along the main road. A ' beck ' or stream washes the base of the hill, which forms a steep ascent, crowned by the steeple of the little and venerable church. Access to the church is obtained by a small lane that diverges from the main road, and passes one side of an oblong area, where stand the church, the parsonage, and the belfried schoolhouse. The parsonage

is a two-storied house of gray stone, with a small garden in front, which a stone wall separates from the
churchyard. This churchyard has a dull, forbidding aspect, and is unrelieved, as churchyards are in the south,
by flowers, or flowering shrubs, or fine old trees. The
church itself is of great antiquity, but has been modern-
ized into a plain, uninteresting building. In the interior
the pews are of black oak, with high divisions. Brasses,
altar-tombs, and monuments are wholly wanting; and
the visitor's attention is necessarily concentrated on a
plain mural tablet on the right-hand side of the com-
munion-table. It bears an inscription, as he discovers,
to Maria Brontë, wife of the Rev. P. Brontë, who died in
the thirty-ninth year of her age, on the 15th of September
1821. Also to her two daughters;—Maria, who died in
the twelfth year of her age; and Elizabeth, who died in
the eleventh year of her age. Lower down, the same
tablet is inscribed with the names of Patrick Branwell Brontë, died in 1848, aged thirty; Emily Jane
Brontë, died in the same year, aged twenty-nine; Anne
Brontë, died in 1849, aged twenty-nine. Another
tablet, below the first, bears an inscription to Charlotte Brontë, who died in 1855, in the thirty-ninth year
of her age.

The scenery in the immediate neighbourhood of Haworth is as little prepossessing as is the village. The
air is dim with the smoke of factories; the vegetation is
meagre—'it does not flourish, it merely exists;' and
bushes and shrubs take the place of trees. Instead of
fresh green hedges, bright with woodbine or honey-
suckle, the fields are divided by stone dykes; and what
crops there are consist of pale, hungry-looking, stunted,

gray-green oats. But if the traveller fare a little further, he comes upon an expanse of dun and purple moors, bounded by a line of wave-like hills ; the 'scoops' into which they fall revealing other hills beyond, all alike in shape and colour, and all suggesting, with their wild, bleak look, a strange feeling of solitude and desolation. A little further, and he finds the breezy moorland furrowed by glens or ravines, each watered by a brawling stream, and each so rich in leafiness as to seem an Eden in the 'boundless waste.' The slopes are thickly clothed with brushwood and dwarf oaks, which, near the top, are replaced by tall green firs. In the shady depth the noisy brook takes a restless and erratic course : now breaking in foam against tiny promontories, now eddying round some gnarled and twisted tree-root, now splashing and dashing over a rocky ledge. The turf is everywhere besprinkled with sweet wild-flowers, — with blue-bells, bright as the arch of heaven, or pearl-white blossoms that spangle the grass like humble emblems of 'some starlit spot in space.'

The reader familiar with the writings of Charlotte Brontë knows how deep an impression such scenes as these made upon her mind, and with what freshness and accuracy she has reproduced them on her vivid pages.

The father of Charlotte Brontë, the Rev. Patrick Brontë, was a native of the county of Down in Ireland. Having been educated at St. John's College, Cambridge, he took orders in the Church of England, and obtained a curacy in Essex, whence he removed to Hartshead, in Yorkshire. Here he married Maria Branwell, a woman

of considerable mental power and much gentleness of
disposition; and here were born to him two daughters,
Maria and Elizabeth, both of whom died in childhood.
From Hartshead Mr. Brontë was preferred to Thornton,
the birthplace of Charlotte, her brother Patrick, and her
sisters Emily and Anne. After the birth of their last
daughter, Mrs. Brontë's health began to decline; and it
may be supposed that it was not improved by the translation of the family to Haworth, which took place in
February 1820. She died in September 1821, when
Charlotte was scarcely five years old.

Mr. Brontë, a man of strong and peculiar character,
and reserved habits, was thus left alone with a family of
five daughters and one son. The childhood of motherless children is always wanting in sunshine; and certainly it is impossible to conceive of a more singular
training than that to which the Brontës were subjected.
They were all of them endowed with more than average
ability, and they were bound together by the bonds of a
more than average affection. They lived within themselves, and for one another. Maria, the eldest, read the
newspapers, and reported to the others such intelligence
as they contained; so that at an age when most children
are playing with dolls and thinking upon trifles, this extraordinary family discoursed 'high politics,' and gravely
conversed upon affairs of State. Almost as soon as they
could read and write, they were accustomed to invent
and act little plays of their own composition, in which
the Duke of Wellington, who was Charlotte's hero—probably on account of his sublime sense of duty—invariably
appeared as conqueror; and long debates were held upon
the comparative merits of the Duke, Napoleon, Hanni-

bal, and Cæsar.   Mr. Brontë has put on record a striking illustration of their intellectual precocity :—On one
occasion, gathering them around him, he asked Anne,
the youngest, what a child like her most wanted ; she
answered, 'Age and experience.'   Then he inquired of
Emily what he had best do with her brother Branwell,
who was sometimes ill behaved ; she replied. 'Reason
with him ; and when he won't listen to reason, whip
him.'   Of Branwell he asked what was the best way of
knowing the difference between the intellects of man and
woman ; he answered, 'By considering the difference
between them as to their bodies.'   Then he desired
Charlotte to inform him what was the best book in the
world ; she replied, 'The Bible.'   And the next best ?
'The Book of Nature.'   What was the best mode of
education for a woman ?   'That which would make her
rule her house well.'   Lastly, of Maria he asked what
was the best mode of spending time ; she answered,
'By laying it out in preparation for a happy eternity.'
If these were singular questions to address to children,
the eldest of whom was not eleven years old, the answers
were still more singular, and throw a vivid light on the
reflective habits and thoughtful moods of the young
members of the Brontë family.

The superintendence of this strange household was
practically vested in the hands of Miss Branwell, an
elder sister of the deceased mother ; but she seems not
to have been a person adapted to win the loving confidence of the children.   Their education was at first
undertaken by their father, but they gathered a vast
amount of information for themselves from miscel-
laneous and assiduous reading   But in 1824 Maria also

Elizabeth Brontë were placed at a school which, a year
or two before, had been opened at Cowan Bridge for the
daughters of clergymen. It was avowedly conducted on
economical principles, but the economy was of a kind
which approximated towards starvation. We do not
think it necessary to dwell on its mistakes of management; for in the pages of 'Jane Eyre' such a picture is
presented of its internal details as could be presented
only by one who had suffered keenly and observed
closely. But it may be conceded that the Brontës were
delicate children, and therefore more susceptible than
others to the unfavourable influences of the place. It
is enough to say that Maria and Elizabeth grew daily
weaker, though they were cheered during the latter portion of their stay at Cowan Bridge by the company of
their sisters, Charlotte and Emily. In the spring of 1825
Maria grew so ill that her removal became imperative:
she died a few days after her return home. Five or six
weeks afterwards she was followed by Elizabeth. As it
was evident that the damp situation of the house at
Cowan Bridge did not suit the health of the Brontës,
Charlotte and Emily were brought back to Haworth in
the autumn of this fatal year.

The amusements of the four children thus once more
compelled to be all in all to each other, and utterly
deprived of the companionship of children of their own
age, continued to be of an intellectual and sedentary
character. They wrote plays, poems, dramas, romances,
they read all the books they could anywhere procure;
they conducted impassioned debates on great men and
historical events. Charlotte was the guide, philosopher

and friend in these curious avocations; and we cannot
do better than put before the reader her 'History of the
Year 1829' in illustration of the nature of her pursuits
and of the conditions under which her character and
genius were developed :—

'Once papa lent my sister Maria a book. It was an
old geography book: she wrote on its blank leaf, "Papa
lent me this book." This book is a hundred and twenty
years old: it is at this moment lying before me. While
I write this I am in the kitchen of the parsonage,
Haworth; Tabby, the servant, is washing up the break-
fast-things ; and Anne, my youngest sister (Maria was
my eldest), is kneeling on a chair, looking at some cakes
which Tabby has been baking for us. Emily is in the
parlour brushing the carpet. Papa and Branwell are
gone to Keighley. Aunt is upstairs in her room, and I
am sitting by the table writing this in the kitchen.
Keighley is a small town four miles from here. Papa
and Branwell are gone for the newspaper, the *Leeds Intelligencer*, a most excellent Tory newspaper, edited by Mr.
Wood, and the proprietor, Mr. Henneman. We take
two and see three newspapers a week. We take the
Leeds Intelligencer (Tory), and the *Leeds Mercury* (Whig),
edited by Mr. Baines, and his brother, son-in-law, and
his two sons Edward and Talbot. We see the *John
Bull:* it is a high Tory, very violent. Mr. Driver lends
us it, as likewise *Blackwood's Magazine*, the most able
periodical there is. The editor is Mr. Christopher
North, an old man seventy-four years of age ; the 1st of
April is his birthday: his company are Timothy Tickler,
Morgan O'Doherty, Macrabin Mordecai, Mullion, War-
nell, and James Hogg, a man of most extraordinary

genius, a Scottish shepherd.* Our plays were established: "Young Men," June 1826; "Our Fellows," July
1827; "Islanders," December 1827. These are our
three great plays that are not kept secret. Emily's and
my best plays were established the 1st of December 1827;
the others, March 1828. Best plays mean secret plays;
they are very nice ones. All our plays are very strange
ones. Their nature I need not write on paper, for I
think I shall always remember them. The "Young
Men" play took its rise from some wooden soldiers Branwell had; "Our Fellows" from "Æsop's Fables;" and
the "Islanders" from several events which happened.
I will sketch out the origin of our plays more explicitly
if I can. First: "Young Men." Papa bought Branwell
some wooden soldiers at Leeds. When papa came home
it was night, and we were in bed; so next morning Branwell came to our door with a box of soldiers. Emily
and I jumped out of bed, and I snatched up one and
exclaimed, "This is the Duke of Wellington! This shall
be the duke!" When I had said this, Emily likewise
took up one, and said it should be hers; when Anne
came down, she said one should be hers. Mine was the
prettiest of the whole, and the tallest, and the most perfect in every part. Emily's was a grave-looking fellow,
and we called him "Gravey." Anne's was a queer little
thing, much like herself, and we called him "Waiting-
Boy." Branwell chose his, and called him "Buona-
parte."'

Was there ever such a quaint and elf-like little com-

---

* This sentence is amusing as shewing the entire good faith with which Charlotte Brontë accepted the brilliant mystifications of Professor Wilson, whose
papers, 'Noctes Ambrosianæ,' were then the life and soul of *Blackwood.*

pany as the four children of whom Charlotte was evidently the guiding and directing spirit ?

And now we must attempt a description of this extraordinary girl. She was very small in figure, but not at all dwarf-like or stunted ; for her limbs and head were in exact proportion to her slight and fragile body. Her hair was soft, thick, and brown ; her eyes large, well-shaped, and of a reddish brown, though, when closely examined, the iris seemed to be composed of a great variety of tints. Usually their expression was intelligent, but tranquil ; on occasion, however, they shone out with a sudden light like that of a lamp new kindled. 'I never saw the like,' says Mrs. Gaskell, 'in any other human creature.' The rest of her features were irregular and plain ; but it was impossible to dwell on the large nose and crooked mouth while you were under the spell of those wonderful eyes and of the power that pervaded every lineament of her countenance. Her hands and feet were marvellously small. 'When one of the former was placed in mine,' says Mrs. Gaskell, 'it was like the soft touch of a bird in the middle of my palm.' In her personal attire Charlotte Brontë was remarkably neat; and though free from the slightest touch of personal vanity, she had a lady's liking for well-fitting shoes and gloves.

In January 1831 she went to school again. Her teacher was a Miss W——, residing at Roe Head, on the Leeds and Huddersfield road ; a woman of ability and tact, by whose lessons Miss Brontë largely profited, and who took a keen interest in her thoughtful and industrious pupil. She remained under her charge for about a twelvemonth, and then returned again to the monotony of

Haworth parsonage. Her course of life is sketched by
herself. In the morning, from nine till half-past twelve,
she taught her sisters, and practised drawing. A long
walk occupied the time until dinner. Between dinner
and tea the needle was industriously and skilfully plied;
after tea she either wrote, read, drew, or did a little fancy-
work. The usual social dissipations were unknown in
this quiet household; but occasionally a neighbour
'dropped in' to take tea, or one or other of Mr.
Brontë's brother clergymen. It is not to be wondered
at that a mind like Charlotte Brontë's was driven, by a
life like this, to feed upon itself, and indulge in its own
creations. But she read continually, and she read
miscellaneously,—an excellent plan when the intellectual
digestion is strong and healthy; and she not only read,
but analyzed what she read, forming her own indepen-
dent judgments, and cultivating that faculty of close,
keen observation and criticism, to which her novels owe
so much of their power.

We gain a good idea of her course of reading, as well
as of the soundness and clearness of her judgment, from
the advice which, when she was still a reserved and bash-
ful maiden of eighteen, she gave to a dear friend, who
had been her schoolfellow at Roe Head. The counsel
is so excellent that our readers will do well to profit by it.

'You ask me,' she says, 'to recommend you some
books for your perusal. I will do so in as few words as
I can. If you like poetry, let it be first-rate; Milton,
Shakspeare, Thomson, Goldsmith, Pope (if you will,
though I don't admire him), Scott, Byron, Campbell,
Wordsworth, and Southey. Now don't be startled at
the names of Shakspeare and Byron. Both these were

great men, and their works are like themselves. You will know how to choose the good and to avoid the evil : the finest passages are always the purest, the bad are invariably revolting ; you will never wish to read them over twice. Omit the comedies of Shakspeare, and the *Don Juan,* perhaps the *Cain,* of Byron, though the latter is a magnificent poem, and read the rest fearlessly ; that must indeed be a depraved mind which can gather evil from *Henry VIII.,* from *Richard III.,* from *Macbeth,* and *Hamlet,* and *Julius Cæsar.* Scott's sweet, wild, romantic poetry can do you no harm. Nor can Wordsworth's, nor Campbell's, nor Southey's—the greatest part at least of his ; some is certainly objectionable. For history, read Hume, Rollin, and the 'Universal History,' if you *can;* I never did.* For fiction, read Scott alone ; all novels after his are worthless. For biography, read Johnson's "Lives of the Poets," Boswell's "Life of Johnson," Southey's "Life of Nelson," Lockhart's "Life of Burns," Moore's "Life of Sheridan," Moore's "Life of Byron," Wolfe's "Remains." † For natural history, read Bewick and Audubon, and Goldsmith, and White's "History of Selborne." ‡ For divinity, your brother will advise you there. I can only say, adhere to standard authors, and avoid novelty.'

It was about this time, or perhaps a little earlier, that Miss Brontë wrote the following poem, which seems to

---

* This, of course, was written before the days of Macaulay, Froude, Gardiner, Forster, Carlyle, Professor Green, Dr. E. A. Freeman, and other eminent historical writers.

† Miss Brontë refers to the 'Remains' of the Rev. Charles Wolfe, author of the beautiful lyric on 'The Burial of Sir John Moore.'

‡ The reader will learn little from Goldsmith, but a good deal from White and Audubon.

us instinct with true poetic feeling, and coloured by the
light of a vivid though sad imagination :—

THE WOUNDED STAG.

' Passing amid the deepest shade
   Of the wood's sombre heart,
Last night I saw a wounded deer
   Laid lonely and apart.

' Such light as pierced the crowded boughs
   (Light scattered, scant, and dim,)
Passed through the fern that formed his couch,
   And centred full on him

Pain trembled in his weary limbs,
   Pain filled his patient eye,
Pain-crushed amid the shadowy fern
   His branchy crown did lie.

' Where were his comrades? where his mate
   All from his death-bed gone !
And he, thus struck and desolate,
   Suffered and bled alone.

' Did he feel what a man might feel,
   Friend-left and sore distrest ?
Did Pain's keen dart and Grief's sharp sting
   Strive in his mangled breast ?

' Did longing for affection lost
   Barb every deadly dart ;
Love unrepaid, and Faith betrayed,
   Did these torment his heart ?

' No ! leave to man his proper doom !
   These are the pangs that rise
Around the bed of state and gloom
   When Adam's offspring dies !'

Mrs. Gaskell is of opinion that these lines were written
before 1833.   If so, the force and clearness of the scene
they embody are all the more remarkable.

In July 1835 Charlotte, then in her twentieth year, went as a teacher to Miss W——'s at Roe Head, accompanied by Emily as pupil. The latter, however, so yearned after her beloved moors that she fell ill, and had to return home. During her brief sad life she left the quiet parsonage but twice after this pathetic incident; once, for six months, when she served as teacher in a school at Halifax, and once when she accompanied her sister Charlotte to Brussels for ten. She was endowed with a most subtly sensitive organization; one apparently unfitted to bear the slightest contact with the outside world. Yet her strength of will was supreme: she could endure without a murmur; she could labour without hope; she yielded neither to weakness of body nor sorrow of heart; and, intellectually, she was in some respects the most gifted member of a gifted family.

Miss Brontë was quite happy at Miss W——'s, until over-study and a too unremitting attention to her duties brought on an attack of ill health. As her physical strength failed, she became subject to religious depression and a general despondency, which acted unfortunately on her strong and quick imagination. The Christmas holidays, however, which brought to her the solace of the companionship of her beloved sisters, restored her considerably; and she once more joined with them in literary efforts. Having written much poetry, of which they desired to obtain a candid estimate, they consulted Southey, and received from the veteran man of letters a kind and thoughtful reply, in which he expressed his sense of the abilities of his correspondents, while dissuading them from making 'literature the business of a woman's life.'

In 1853, the state of her health compelled her to resign her engagement at Miss W——'s, and take up her abode once more at Haworth. Here she renewed the old routine of the quiet daily life; but there was much to darken it, and render it less happy than of yore. Her mother Branwell had turned out ill, and her sister Anne was ailing, with a slight cough, a pain in her side, and a difficulty of breathing,—the signs, alas, of insipient consumption. No mother could have watched over a child more tenderly or vigilantly than Charlotte watched over her dearly beloved sister. She knew how Maria and Elizabeth had been taken away, and when she looked at Anne a cold fear struck to her loving heart. It was probably her profound reverence for the law of duty which influenced her rejection of an advantageous offer of marriage made to her at this period. She knew she was the light and life of her little family circle. Her services were necessary to her father, whose eccentricity was yearly growing more pronounced; and to her sisters, who deferred in all things to her sound judgment and practical intellect. But the means of the Brontë household were very straitened, and they could not all live at home. So, in 1839, both Anne and Charlotte obtained situations as governesses. Their lines did not fall into pleasant places. They had to learn that sometimes the bread earned by the sweat of the brow is very bitter. 'I have striven hard,' writes Charlotte, 'to be pleased with my new situation. The country, the house, and the grounds are, as I have said, divine; but, alack-a-day! there is such a thing as seeing all beautiful around you—pleasant woods, shady paths, green lawns, and blue sunshiny sky —and not having a free moment or a free thought left to enjoy them. The children are constantly with me. As for correcting them, I quickly found that was out of the question;—they are to do as they like! A complaint to the mother only brings black looks on myself, and unjust, partial excuses, to screen the children. I have tried that plan once, and succeeded so notably, I shall try no more........I now begin to find Mrs. —— does not intend to know me,—that she cares nothing about me, except to contrive how the greatest possible quantity of labour may be got òut of me; and to that end she overwhelms me with oceans of needle-work—yards of cambric to hem, muslin night-caps to make, and, above all things, dolls to dress.' It is to be feared that the position of governesses has not very greatly improved since the time of Charlotte Brontë ; and that parents are still forgetful of the respect and regard which are due to those engaged in the arduous and responsible work of tuition.

Miss Brontë soon wearied of this uncongenial employment, and returned to Haworth. Here she found that her father, through an increase of duty, rendered more difficult of discharge by failure of health, had secured the assistance of a curate ; the first of a long series of clerical subordinates, who thenceforth added somewhat to the life and activity of the parsonage, and furnished Charlotte with fresh materials for the study of character. Her experiences in the matter of curates were mostly amusing. One of these she relates in a letter to a friend, with her usual graphic freedom of style :—

'The other day, Mr. ——, a vicar, came to spend the day with us, bringing with him his own curate. The latter gentleman, by name Mr. B——, is a young Irish clergyman, fresh from Dublin University. It was the first time we had any of us seen him; but, however, after the manner of his countrymen, he soon made himself at home. His character appeared quickly in his conversation; witty, lively, ardent, clever too, but deficient in the dignity and discretion of an Englishman. At home, you know, I talk with ease, and am never shy—never weighed down and oppressed by that miserable *mauvaise honte* which torments and constrains me elsewhere. So I conversed with this Irishman, and laughed at his jests; and, though I saw faults in his character, excused them because of the amusement his originality afforded. I cooled a little, indeed, and drew in towards the latter part of the evening, because he began to season his conversation with something of Hibernian flattery, which I did not quite relish. However, they went away, and no more was thought about them. A few days after, I got a letter, the direction of which puzzled me, it being in a hand I was not accustomed to see. Evidently, it was neither from you nor Mary, my only correspondents. Having opened and read it, it proved to be a declaration of attachment and proposal of matrimony, expressed in the ardent language of the sapient young Irishman!'

Such an adventure seems to prove that, in spite of Miss Brontë's lack of what are generally known as personal charms, she possessed a great power of attractiveness. This was due to the varied expression of her countenance, its unmistakable evidence of a high, pure intellect, and the vivacity of her conversation.

Mrs. Gaskell's memoir of Miss Brontë leaves upon the mind of the reader an impression of gloom and melancholy which, we are persuaded, is not a little exaggerated. That she suffered bitterly from the sorrows which fell upon her family, from the havoc which death made in the home-circle, cannot be doubted; but her genius was too strong and healthy, and her faith too living and sincere, to be wholly clouded by any misfortunes, however heavy. The mind which has resources in itself is never overcome by external conditions; it bends, but it does not break. It was impossible for Charlotte Brontë, with her quick imagination, her strenuous intellect, her self-mastery, her vivid perception of nature, to yield to the pressure of any worldly burden. That she had a rich fund of natural humour is as clearly shown in her letters as in her published works. Here is a specimen; interesting not only because of its liveliness, but because of the glimpse it gives us of her surroundings. It was written in August 1840 to one of her dearest friends :—

'"The wind bloweth where it listeth. Thou hearest the sound thereof, but canst not tell whence it cometh, nor whither it goeth." That, I believe, is Scripture; though in what chapter or book, or whether it be correctly quoted, I can't possibly say. However, it behoves me to write a letter to a young woman of the name of E——, with whom I was once acquainted, "in life's morning march, when my spirit was young." This young woman wished me to write to her some time since, though I have nothing to say—I e'en put it off, day by day, till at last, fearing that she will "curse me by her gods," I feel constrained to sit down and tack a few lines together, which she may call a letter or not, as she pleases. Now if the young woman expects sense in this production, she will find herself miserably disappointed. I shall dress her a dish of salmagundi—I shall cook a hash—compound a stew—toss up an *omelette soufflée à la Française*, and send it her with my respects. The wind, which is very high up on our hills of Judæa, though, I suppose, down in the Philistine flats of B—— parish it is nothing to speak of, has produced the same effect on the contents of my knowledge-box that a quaigh of usquebaugh does upon those of most other bipeds. I see everything *couleur de rose*, and am strongly inclined to dance a jig, if I knew how. I think I must partake of the nature of a pig or an ass—both which animals are strongly affected by a high wind. From what quarter the wind blows I cannot tell, for I never could in my life; but I should very much like to know how the great brewing-tub of Bridlington Bay works, and what sort of yeasty froth rises just now on the waves.

'A woman of the name of Mrs. B——, it seems, wants a teacher. I wish she would have me; and I have written to Miss W—— to tell her so. Verily it is a delightful thing to live here at home, at full liberty to do just what one pleases. But I recollect some scrubby old fable about grasshoppers and ants, by a scrubby old knave yclept Æsop : the grasshoppers sang all the summer, and starved all the winter.

'A distant relation of mine, one Patrick Branwell, has set off to seek his fortune in the wild, wandering, adventurous, romantic, knight-errant-like capacity of clerk on the Leeds and Manchester Railroad. Leeds and Manchester—where are they? Cities in the wilderness, like Tadmor, *alias* Palmyra—are they not?

'There is one little trait respecting Mr. W—— ' [a

brother clergyman of Mr. Brontë's] 'which lately came
to my knowledge, which gives a glimpse of the better
side of his character. Last Saturday night he had been
sitting an hour in the parlour with papa; and, as he
went away, I heard papa say to him, "What is the matter
with you? You seem in very low spirits to-night."—
"Oh, I don't know. I've been to see a poor young girl,
who, I'm afraid, is dying."—"Indeed; what is her name?"
—"Susan Bland, the daughter of John Bland, the super-
intendent." Now Susan Bland is my oldest and best
scholar in the Sunday school; and when I heard that,
I thought I would go as soon as I could to see her. I
did go on Monday afternoon, and found her on her way
to that 'bourn whence no traveller returns.' After sitting with her some time, I happened to ask her mother
if she thought a little port wine would do her good. She
replied that the doctor had recommended it, and that
when Mr. W—— was last there, he had brought them a
bottle of wine and jar of preserves. She added, that he
was always good-natured to poor folks, and seemed to
have a deal of feeling and kind-heartedness about him.
No doubt, there are defects in his character, but there
are also good qualities....God bless him! I wonder
who, with his advantages, would be without his faults?
I know many of his faulty actions, many of his weak
points; yet, where I am, he shall always find rather a
defender than an accuser. To be sure, my opinion will
go but a very little way to decide his character. What
of that? People should do right as far as their ability
extends. You are not to suppose from all this, that Mr.
W—— and I are on very amiable terms; we are not at
all. We are distant, cold, reserved. We seldom speak;

and when we do it is only to exchange the most trivial
and commonplace remarks.'

In March 1841 Miss Brontë obtained her second and
last engagement as a governess; an engagement fully as
felicitous as her former one had been the reverse.   Her
employers treated her with the utmost consideration,
which she repaid by giving them of her best and most
willing service.   But the delicate health of her sister
Anne began again to trouble her.   It was evident that she
needed the constant, watchful, and tender attention of
her eldest sister.   Yet how was that to be given?   Mr.
Brontë's income, after he had paid a curate, was insuffi-
cient to meet the wants of even that small family.   His
daughters must help themselves.   The thought occurred
to Charlotte that she and her sisters might successfully
conduct a school, and with characteristic energy she set
to work to realize it as far as her means allowed.   It
happened that at this time Miss W—— was desirous of
relinquishing her school at Dewsbury Moor, and she
offered it to the Brontës on very advantageous terms.
But then reflection showed them that with all their knowledge and intellectual wealth they lacked that precise and
definite information in certain branches which was almost
indispensable in the successful conduct of a school.
They therefore altered their plans; and, obtaining some
pecuniary assistance from their aunt, resolved that Charlotte and Emily should go to Brussels in order to
'improve' themselves in the study of French and music.
They were fortunate enough to obtain an introduction to
M. Héger, a man of rare ability, who agreed to receive
them into his *pensionnat* at a very moderate charge, and

to whose skilful method of tuition both were greatly indebted for the development of their mental resources.

Their life at Brussels has been portrayed with extraordinary vividness by Charlotte Brontë in her novel of 'The Professor.' It was, on the whole, a happy period, during which the genius of the future novelist ripened rapidly, and she accumulated vast stores of observation and reflection for after use. All that she saw was photographed distinctly on her memory; she studied closely every aspect of character which presented itself to her scrutinizing eye. The novelty of the scenes that passed before her gaze in the medieval city, the gay crowds in varying costumes, the religious processions, the national festivals, these refreshed her greatly. She had the true artist's love of art, and the ancient churches and picturesque mansions, with their fine carvings and rich architectural details, were a source of constant delight.

M. Héger was greatly interested in his pupils. He quickly discerned that they possessed no ordinary powers, and he appreciated, moreover, their force of character. Of Emily's genius he formed the higher estimate, and, we think, correctly. He was struck by her tenacity of will, and not the less by her capacity for the abstrusest reasoning. He spoke of her afterwards as one who ought to have been a man, a great navigator. Her powerful reason, he said, would have deduced new spheres of discovery from its knowledge of the old; and no opposition or difficulty would have daunted her strong, imperious resolve. His mode of instruction he adapted to their unusual capabilities. Dispensing with grammar and vocabulary, he read to them and carefully analyzed the masterpieces of the most famous French authors; after-

wards requiring from them, in French, a statement of
their impressions, or a criticism on the characteristics of
the writer they had been engaged in studying.

The school-hours at M. Héger's were from nine to
twelve. Then the boarders and half-boarders, generally
about thirty-two in number, repaired to the refectoire to
partake of bread and fruit, the *externes* or morning-pupils
enjoying such refreshment as they had brought with
them, in the garden. From one to two fancy-work was
the order of the day, a pupil reading aloud some entertaining book ; from two to four, lessons again. At four
the *externes* retired ; and the boarders dined in the refectoire, along with M. and Madame Héger. An hour was
allotted to recreation ; then, from six to seven, preparation for lessons ; and after that, the *lecture picuse*, or
devotional reading. At times M. Héger himself would
be present, when he invariably substituted a book of a
more interesting kind. At eight a slight meal of water
and *pistolets* (or light rolls) was served up. Prayers
followed ; and then to bed.

Towards the end of the year the two sisters were recalled to England by the death of their aunt. The little
family at Haworth was afterwards united at Christmas,
and enjoyed a few happy days together. ' Branwell was
with them,' says Mrs. Gaskell : ' that was always a pleasure at this time : whatever might be his faults, or even
his vices, his sisters yet held him up as their family hope,
as they trusted that he would some day be their family
pride. They blinded themselves to the magnitude of the
failings of which they were now and then told, by per-
suading themselves that such failings were common to
all men of any strength of character ; for, till sad experi-

ence taught them better, they fell into the common error of confounding strong passions with strong character.'

In the following year Charlotte Brontë returned to Brussels; this time not as a pupil, but as a teacher. Her remuneration was scanty enough; board, lodging, and £16 a year, out of which she had to pay for her German lessons. She had but little leisure for self-improvement, and altogether the change she had made was not one for the better, but she accepted its disagreeable vicissitudes with her usual fortitude and patience. Her chief source of unhappiness, however, was her separation from her family; for she knew how sadly her sisters missed her sympathy and guidance. Here again we shall leave her to speak for herself, and to describe in her own graphic language the peculiarities of her position. Reserved as she was, Charlotte was eminently truthful, and her letters afford a clear insight into both the strength and the weakness of her character. She was incapable of disguise, and as she felt she wrote, though she did not write all she felt:—

'Mary —— urges me very much to leave Brussels and go to her; but, at present, however tempted to take such a step, I should not feel justified in doing so. To leave a certainty for a complete uncertainty, would be to the last degree imprudent. Notwithstanding that, Brussels is indeed desolate to me now. Since the D——s left, I have had no friend......I am completely alone. I cannot count the Belgians anything. It is a curious position, to be so utterly solitary in the midst of numbers. Sometimes the solitude oppresses me to an excess. One day lately I felt as if I could bear it no longer, and I went to Madame Héger and gave her notice. If it had depended on her, I should certainly have soon been at liberty; but

M. Héger, having heard of what was in agitation, sent for me the day after, and pronounced with vehemence his decision, that I should not leave. I could not, at that time, have persevered in my intention without exciting him to anger: so I promised to stay a little while longer......Sometimes I ask myself how long I shall stay here; but as yet I have only asked the question, I have not answered it. However, when I have acquired as much German as I think fit, I think I shall pack up bag and baggage and depart. Twinges of home-sickness cut me to the heart every now and then. To-day the weather is glaring, and I am stupified with a bad cold and head-ache. I have nothing to tell you. One day is like another in this place. I know you, living in the country, can hardly believe it is possible life can be monotonous in the centre of a brilliant capital like Brussels; but so it is. I feel it most on holidays, when all the girls and teachers go out to visit, and it sometimes happens that I am left during several hours quite alone, with four great desolate school-rooms at my disposition. I try to read, I try to write; but in vain. I then wander about from room to room, but the silence and loneliness of all the house weigh down one's spirits like lead.'

To her sister Emily she writes with an infinite home-longing:—

'This is Sunday morning. They are at their idolatrous *messe,* and I am here—that is, in the refectoire. I should like uncommonly to be in the dining-room at home, or in the kitchen, or in the back kitchen. I should like even to be cutting up the hash, with the clerk and some register people at the other table, and you standing by, watching that I put enough flour, not too much pepper, and, above

all, that I save the best pieces of the leg of mutton for
Tiger and Keeper, the first of which personages would be
jumping about the dish and carving-knife, and the latter
standing like a devouring flame on the kitchen-floor. To
complete the picture, Tabby blowing the fire, in order to
boil the potatoes to a sort of vegetable glue! How
divine are these recollections to me at this moment!
Yet I have no thought of coming home just now. I lack
a real pretext for doing so. It is true this place is dismal
to me, but I cannot go home without a fixed prospect
when I get there ; and this prospect must not be a situation—that would be jumping out of the frying-pan into
the fire. *You* call yourself idle! Absurd! absurd! Is
papa well? Are you well? and Tabby? You ask about
Queen Victoria's visit to Brussels. I saw her for an
instant flashing through the Rue Royale in a carriage and
six, surrounded by soldiers. She was laughing and talking very gaily. She looked a little stout, vivacious lady,
very plainly dressed, not much dignity or pretension
about her. The Belgians liked her very well on the
whole. They said she enlivened the sombre court of
King Leopold, which is usually as gloomy as a conven-
ticle. Write to me again soon. Tell me whether papa
really wants me very much to come home, and whether
you do likewise. I have an idea that I should be of no
use there—a sort of aged person upon the parish. I pray
with heart and soul, that all may continue well at Haworth ;
above all, in our gray, half-inhabited house. God bless
the walls thereof! Safety, health, happiness, and prosperity to you, papa, and Tabby. Amen.'

Her return home took place much sooner than she had
expected, being rendered necessary by domestic reasons,

of which not the least was the increasing blindness of her
father. She arrived at Haworth on the 2nd of January
1844. After a brief rest, her active mind was busy with
schemes for adding to the limited income of the family.
The most hopeful seemed that of taking a limited number
of pupils as boarders; and for this purpose she printed
and circulated cards of terms, and addressed herself to
all the friends and acquaintances whom she thought likely
to be interested in her venture. Unfortunately, nothing
came of it. The Brontès had no influential connections;
they could not afford to spend much money in advertising,
and Haworth was a place remote, melancholy, and little
known. The brave little woman persevered, however,
and refused to be mortified by defeat. Yet she had cause
enough for depression, if it were only from the anxiety
induced by her brother's wretched conduct, and the pressure entailed upon her by her father's helpless condition.
Wonderful it is that her energy yielded so little; that her
intellect maintained all its force and brilliancy; and this
too in spite of her own ill-health. At times, indeed, the
cross seemed almost too heavy to bear, but from an
occasional fit of depression she was quickly recalled by
her loving trust in God, and by the marvellous patience
and self-control which she had assiduously cultivated.
We can never think without admiration of the noble life
of Charlotte Brontë; of its unostentatious heroism and
generous self-devotion. Its study has much the same
effect as that of a good book; one is all the better for it;
one learns the beauty of the virtues which it so vividly
sets forth; one feels how much there is of truth and
rectitude in human nature, when that nature finds its
inspiration in the religion of the Christ.

In the autumn of 1845, melancholy as many circumstances rendered it, a novel and cheerful interest entered
into the life of the three sisters. It happened that Charlotte came upon a manuscript volume of verse written
by her sister Emily. On perusing it, she was impressed
with a deep conviction that the verse was no common
verse ; that it was not such as ordinary rhymsters write,
but that it breathed a spirit of genuine poetry. She
thought it condensed and terse and vigorous. To her
ear it had also a peculiar music, wild, melancholy, and
elevating. Emily, like all the Brontës, was not of a
demonstrative disposition, nor one into the recesses of
whose mind and feelings even those nearest and dearest
to her could with impunity intrude. It was with no
slight difficulty her sister reconciled her to the discovery
she had made ; and it was with much greater difficulty
she persuaded her that poems of so conspicuous a merit
deserved publication.

Meantime, the gentle Anne quietly produced some of
her own compositions ; and these, too, on examination,
seemed to the critical eldest sister to have no small
sweetness and sincerity of pathos. So that, after much
discussion, it was resolved to arrange a small selection
of the poems of all three aspirants, who also agreed
to hide their identity under the names of Currer, Ellis,
and Acton Bell ; the ambiguous choice, says Charlotte,
being dictated by a sort of conscientious scruple at
assuming Christian names positively masculine, while
they did not like to declare themselves women. For
though they did not then suspect that their mode of writing and thinking could possibly be stigmatized as un-
feminine, they had a vague impression that authoresses

are liable to be looked on with prejudice; they noticed
how critics sometimes used for their chastisement the
weapon of personality, and for their reward a flattery
which was not true praise.

At the outset of their literary career they met with the
obstacles which have so often baffled the endeavours of
true genius; but after some seeking and not a little dis-
appointment, they found publishers for their small volume
in Messrs. Ayton and Jones, of Paternoster Row, London. It made its appearance about the end of May
1846, but attracted scarcely any attention. Yet there
was much in it that rose far above the standard of verse
which has secured the ear of the public.

A month or two later Charlotte was in Manchester,
zealously attending on her father, who underwent an
operation for cataract, and required the tenderest and
most watchful care. On her return, she busied herself
with further literary labours, conscious that she had
something to say worth listening to, if she could get the
opportunity of saying it. Each sister had written a prose
tale,—'Wuthering Heights' was Emily's, 'Agnes Grey'
was Anne's, and 'The Professor' was Charlotte's, and
they now conceived the idea of issuing the three in one
volume. Accordingly they were despatched to publisher
after publisher, only to come back again to their authors
with a more or less civil letter of declinature. Undis-
couraged by these failures, Charlotte Brontë began
'Jane Eyre,' as if resolved to compel a hearing from the
public. There was true courage in the attempt; nay,
there was something heroic in this absolute defiance of
the most discouraging circumstances. 'Think,' says her
biographer, 'think of her home, and the black shadow

of remorse lying over her brother, till his very brain was mazed, and his gifts and his life were lost;—think of her father's sight hanging on a thread ; of her sister's delicate health, and dependence on her care ; and then admire, as it deserves to be admired, the steady courage which could work away at "Jane Eyre," all the time that the one-volume tale was plodding its weary round in London.'

Yet her happiest hours, and the happiest hours of her two sisters, were undoubtedly those which they occupied in discussing each other's plots, and the characters to be introduced, and in exchanging criticisms upon their different works as they progressed towards conclusion. In thus creating a world within a world,—an ideal world free from cares and anxieties and sorrows,—they took the best means of gaining strength to endure the trials of the real work-a-day life around them. They could forget the pressure of poverty, and the shame and agony entailed upon them by their brother's dissoluteness, while they traced the imaginary fortunes of the heroes and heroines evolved from their vivid imaginations. This is one of the rarest gifts of Genius, this power of self-absorption, this faculty of escaping from the clouds and shadows of the world into a bright and beautiful fairy-land, peopled by airy shapes and visionary creatures.

In the course of these home-debates. Miss Brontë decided on making her heroine, 'Jane Eyre,' plain and unattractive, in opposition to the time honoured practice of novelists, who have always lavished on their Clarissas and Amelias all the personal graces of Venus and all the intellectual gifts of Minerva. She told her sisters that they were wrong, even morally wrong, in endowing their heroines with beauty as if it were a necessity. And when they argued that in no other way could they be made interesting, she answered, 'I will prove to you that you are wrong; I will show you a heroine as plain and as small as myself, who shall be as interesting as any of yours.' Hence 'Jane Eyre,' who, however, was not identical with her creator in any other respect. As the work went on, it engaged more and more of the writer's enthusiasm, so that when she came to 'Thornfield,' she was utterly unable to pause. The fervour of her genius hurried her on. Being excessively short-sighted, she wrote in little square paper books, held close to her eyes, and in a truly microscopic handwriting. On she went, plying her pen incessantly for three weeks; by which time, it is said, she had carried her plain little heroine away from Thornfield, and worked herself into a fever which compelled her to take some rest.

Meantime, 'The Professor,' in its weary round of the London publishers, had fallen into the hands of Messrs. Smith and Elder, who were struck by its merits, and though they declined for various reasons to undertake its publication, they held out hopes that any work from its author's pen in the then indispensable 'three volumes,' would meet with their immediate attention. This courteous encouragement induced her, in August 1847, to forward the manuscript of 'Jane Eyre.' It was examined without delay by a gentleman connected with the firm, upon whom it produced so strong an impression, that he recommended it in terms of unusual warmth. Mr. Smith was thus induced to read it himself, with the result that it was instantly accepted. In the course of the autumn it was published. At first it was not very eagerly welcomed

by the literary organs, but little by little it rose in popularity, and by Christmas the writer's fame was insured.
'Jane Eyre' was recognized as one of the most powerful works of fiction which for years had been given to the
world. There was a freshness, an originality about it
which commended it to the most cultured judges; while
the striking evolutions of its plot, and its deep interest,
inthralled the ordinary reader. The heroine, 'Jane
Eyre,' was an entirely new conception in the region of
fiction: here was a woman represented as plain, unattractive, small of figure, without those adventitious attractions so freely bestowed on their heroines by preceding
novelists, and yet the reader's sympathies were enlisted on
her behalf, and he followed her fortunes from first to last
with the most intense and even painful curiosity. Then
'Rochester' was as unconventional a hero as 'Jane
Eyre' was abnormal as a heroine. Moreover, the scenes
through which the plot of the tale was carried bore the
same stamp of absolute novelty, and were depicted with
a pencil of extraordinary firmness and precision. It was
noted, too, that the new writer had at his (or her) command a style of much strength, variety, and eloquence,
and that the incidental descriptions of nature were as brilliant as they were true in their colouring. The present
writer well remembers the eagerness with which he devoured page after page of this fascinating fiction, and the
consciousness that broke upon him of being face to face
with an extraordinary genius, from which in the course of
time much admirable work might reasonably be expected.
He remembers, too, that conjecture as to the authorship
was very busy, though, of course, it never hit the mark.
'People in London, smooth and polished as the Athenians

of old, and like them "spending their time in nothing
else, but either to tell or to hear some new thing," were
astonished and delighted to find that a fresh sensation, a
new pleasure, was in reserve for them, in the uprising of
an author capable of depicting with accurate and Titanic
power the strong, self-reliant, racy, and individual characters which were not, after all, extinct species, but lingered still in existence in the North.'

Charlotte's literary work had been carried on without
her father's direct knowledge; for she was unwilling to
add to his anxieties by acquainting him with her ambition
to obtain the suffrages of the public.   As soon, however,
as her success was insured, she desired that he should
participate in it; and accordingly, one day after dinner,
she entered his study with a copy of the novel, and some
of the critiques passed upon it in the public journals.

'Papa, I've been writing a book.'

'Have you, my dear?'

'Yes; and I want you to read it.'

'I am afraid it will try my eyes too much.'

'But it is not in manuscript; it is printed.'

'My dear! you've never thought of the expense it will
be!   It will be almost sure to be a loss, for how can you
get a book sold?   No one knows you or your name.'

'But, papa, I don't think it will be a loss; no more
will you, if you will just let me read you a review or two,
and tell you more about it.'

And then her father became aware of the astonishing
fact that his daughter had leaped at one bound into a
reputation which will endure as long as English literature
itself endures.

In December 1847 appeared the novels of 'Wuther-

ing Heights,' by Ellis Bell, and of 'Agnes Grey,' by
Acton Bell. Neither attracted the attention it deserved;
partly owing, perhaps, to the confusion caused by the
pseudonyms, for the critics seemed unable to agree
whether the three Bells were three brothers, or three
appearances of a single writer. As to 'Wuthering
Heights,' it was generally said that it was an earlier and
ruder attempt from the same pen which had produced
'Jane Eyre.' And, perhaps, in the rugged power per-
vading it one may trace a certain resemblance to the
strength and masterfulness of Currer Bell's work. In
most respects, however, it is entirely *sui generis*. It is
not a pleasant book, but, with all its faults, it is a great
one ; and it is difficult to conceive to what elevation the
genius might not have attained, had its career been prolonged, that gave to English fiction such creations as
Heathcliff, as Earnshaw, as Catherine. Had she but
lived, says her sister Charlotte, with a judgment un-
warped by affection, her mind would of itself have grown
like a strong tree,—loftier, straighter, wider-spreading,—
and its matured fruits would have attained a mellower
ripeness and sunnier bloom ; but on that mind time and
experience alone could work,—to the influence of other
intellects it was not amenable. It must always remain
a psychological problem how a woman who mixed so
little with the outer world, knew so little of the darker
aspects and more complex relations of social life, could
imagine such a character as Heathcliff, and present it
with so startling a distinctness. He is no shadowy
villain, such as flits, for instance, across the picturesque
pages of Mrs. Radcliffe, but as real almost, and is true
in every detail, as Shakspeare's Iago.

Our rapid survey of Charlotte Brontë's career brings us now to the year 1848, perhaps the saddest and darkest in a life in which so many years were sad and dark. Not that it opened unfavourably; for their literary ventures enforced upon Charlotte and her sister Agnes— whose second and last novel, 'The Tenant of Wildfell Hall,' was in the press—a first journey to London. They were most cordially received by Messrs. Smith and Elder, who hitherto had been unaware whether Currer Bell was man or woman, a real name or a fictitious one, and enjoyed their brief visit greatly. But as the year wore on, a heavy cloud hung over the little household. Branwell, who had shattered his constitution and dimmed a brilliant intellect by shameful excess, grew rapidly worse. Subject to frequent delirious attacks, and terrible fits of depression, he required assiduous watching; and the trial was equally hard for his aged father and delicate sisters,—it wrung their very hearts. At last, on the 9th of October, Charlotte had to write to her friend:— 'Branwell died, after twenty minutes' struggle, on Sunday morning, September 24th. He was perfectly conscious till the last agony came on. His mind had undergone the peculiar change which frequently precedes death, two days previously; the calm of better feelings filled it; a return of natural affection marked his last moments.' She adds: 'He is in God's hands now; and the All-Powerful is likewise the All-Merciful. A deep conviction that he rests at last—rests well after his brief, erring, suffering, feverish life—fills and quiets my mind now. The final separation, the spectacle of his pale corpse, gave me more acute, bitter pain, than I could have imagined. Till the last hour comes, we never know how much we can forgive, pity, regret a near relative. All his vices were and are nothing now. We remember only his woes.'

A greater pang awaited her loving heart. Emily and Anne, always delicate, showed signs of daily increasing feebleness. Emily was the first to pass away. Her illness, so to speak, was characteristic of her. Always accustomed to practise a stern self-control, she would not yield one jot or tittle even in her latest hours. She was without pity for her failing strength, her fading energies. The spirit struggled hard against the flesh. From hands that trembled, and eyes that were dim, and limbs that were unnerved, she exacted the same service that they had rendered in health. She would accept of assistance from no one. The stern, masterful nature, spurned every sign of weakness. On Tuesday morning, the 19th of December, the last morning she was to see on earth, she rose as usual. As usual she dressed herself, though with many a pause imposed upon her by her physical weakness. She even took up her needle, and attempted to perform her daily task; while her sisters and servants looked on with dread and wonder at this frail creature's defiance of death, and scorn of its rapid advance. But about noon she grew so ill that the strong will was forced to surrender. In a broken whisper she said to Charlotte, ' *Now*, if you will send for a doctor, I will see him.' But medical science could do nothing. Her feet already trembled on the verge of the dark river, and at two o'clock she was no more.

There is a touching passage in Mrs. Gaskell's admirable biography of Charlotte, referring to the last scene of Emily

Brontë's strange, restless, and, in the higher sense of the word, romantic career : —

'As the old, bereaved father and his two surviving children followed the coffin to the grave, they were joined by Keeper, Emily's fierce, faithful bulldog. He walked alongside of the mourners, and into the church, and stayed quietly there all the time that the burial service was being read. When he came home, he lay down at Emily's chamber-door, and howled pitifully for many days.

'Keeper figures in Charlotte Brontë's novel of "Shirley," and the incident recorded, in illustration of the heroine's firmness and self-reliance, really occurred between Keeper and his mistress.'

Even yet the cup of bitterness which Providence held to the lip of Charlotte Brontë was not full. She had still one sister left; but now she came to see that there was little chance of retaining her long. Anne's delicacy from her very childhood seems to have blinded the eyes of her family to the really dangerous symptoms that year after year presented themselves; and it was quite a surprise, a dreadful surprise, when in March 1849 the doctor, after examining her, pronounced that her lungs were affected, and that she was suffering from tubercular consumption. For a while some hopes were entertained of her recovery; but the patient and gentle invalid, bearing her cross with Christian meekness, slowly faded away. She was removed to Scarborough, in the expectation that she might derive benefit from the sea-air. This was on the 24th of May; on the 28th she died. We are unable to refrain from borrowing the

following description of her last hours; for it cannot but
convey a precious suggestion of peace and comfort to
our readers:—

'Nothing occurred to excite alarm until about 11 A.M.
She then spoke of feeling a change. "She believed she
had not long to live. Could she reach home alive, if we
prepared immediately for departure?" A physician was
sent for. Her address to him was made with perfect
composure. She begged him to say, "How long he
thought she might live; not to fear speaking the truth,
for she was not afraid to die." The doctor reluctantly
admitted that the angel of death had already arrived, and
that life was ebbing fast. She thanked him for his
truthfulness, and he departed to come again very soon.
She still occupied her easy-chair, looking so serene, so
reliant: there was no opening for grief as yet, though
all knew the separation was at hand. She clasped her
hands, and reverently invoked a blessing from on high;
first upon her sister, then upon her friend, to whom she
said, "Be a sister in my stead. Give Charlotte as much
of your company as you can." She then thanked each
for her kindness and attention.

'Ere long the restlessness of approaching death appeared, and she was borne to the sofa. On being asked
if she were easier, she looked gratefully at her questioner,
and said, "It is not *you* who can give me ease, but soon
all will be well, through the merits of our Redeemer."
Shortly after this, seeing that her sister could hardly
restrain her grief, she said, "Take courage, Charlotte;
take courage." Her faith never failed, and her eye
never dimmed till about two o'clock, when she calmly,
and without a sigh, passed from the temporal to the

eternal. So still and so hallowed were her last hours
and moments. There was no thought of assistance or
of dread. The doctor came and went two or three
times. The hostess knew that death was near, yet so
little was the house disturbed by the presence of the
dying, and the sorrow of those so nearly bereaved, that
dinner was announced as ready, through the half-opened
door, as the living sister was closing the eyes of the dead
one. She could now no more stay the welled-up grief of
her sister with her emphatic and dying "Take courage,"
and it burst forth in brief but agonizing strength. Charlotte's affection, however, had another channel, and there
it turned in thought, in care, and in tenderness. There
was bereavement, but there was not solitude; sympathy
was at hand, and it was accepted. With calmness came
the consideration of the removal of the dear remains to
their home resting-place. This melancholy task, however, was never performed; for the afflicted sister decided
to lay the flower in the place where it had fallen. She
believed that to do so would accord with the wishes of
the departed. She had no preference for place. She
thought not of the grave, for that is but the body's garb,
but of all that is beyond it.

‘ Her remains rest—

" Where the south sun warms the now dear sod,
  Where the ocean-billows lave and strike the steep and turf-covered rock."

Miss Brontë's next work was the daring and richly
coloured ‘Shirley.’ She bestowed upon it no ordinary
labour, determined to hold by the reputation her first
work had won for her. And, probably, she pursued her
task with the more loving interest, because in Shirley

Keeldar she had attempted to present her beloved sister Emily with those modifications of character which a happier fortune might have been expected to bring about. The second volume was taken up early in 1848, and was just finished when Branwell died. During the dark months that followed, the pen was idle; and when, after the death of Anne, it resumed its task,—a task which had lost so much of its pleasure when it could be no longer shared with loving sisters!—she who wielded it might well entitle the first chapter, 'The Valley of the Shadow of Death.'

Those who saw Miss Brontë, after she had passed through the furnace of affliction, could not but admire her self-restraint and her sublime patience;—so frail, so feeble, and yet enduring her weight of sorrow with an eye that had lost none of its brightness, a countenance that bore no mark of nervousness or irritability. In her neat dress of the deepest mourning, with her beautiful smooth brown hair, her eloquent eyes, and her calm, intelligent face indicating the control and firmness of a lofty nature, she seemed a perfect household image. To look at her was instantly to recall Wordsworth's fine description of

> ' A being breathing thoughtful breath,
> A traveller betwixt life and death :
> The reason firm, the temperate will,
> Endurance, foresight, strength, and skill
> A perfect woman, nobly planned,
> To warn, to comfort, and command :
> And yet a spirit still, and bright,
> With something of an angel-light.'

It is to be noted with respect to Charlotte Brontë as an author, that she was in no haste to produce. So

great was the attraction of her name that she might
easily have enriched herself had she chosen to publish
two or three novels a year, regardless of the finish and
excellence of her work. But, as Miss Martineau has
remarked, she held fast to the conviction that the publication of a book is a solemn act of conscience, and she
had a high sense of the dignity and usefulness of her
art. She was not a demonstrative woman, not given to
self-confession or to talking of her conscience; but at
times she disclosed some of her inmost feelings to a
few cherished friends, and among these rare utterances
was one that explains the long interval between her
works. She said that she thought every serious delinea-
tion of life ought to be the product of personal experience and observation,—experience naturally occurring,
and observation of a normal, and not of a forced or
special kind. She had a conscientiousness, remarks
Miss Martineau, which could not be relaxed by praise,
or even sympathy—dear as sympathy was to her keen
affections. She had no vanity that praise could ex-
aggerate or censure wound. She read every adverse
review of her works with the desire to profit by them;
and if at times she disputed the justice of the criticism,
she was not so much wounded or angry as she was perplexed. The flatteries which wait upon literary success
she satirized with easy grace; while such occasional
severity as literary women suffer under in the outset of
their career, she accepted with a truly dignified humility.
'From her feeble constitution of body,' adds Miss Martineau, ' her sufferings by the death of her whole family,
and the secluded and monotonous life she led, she became morbidly sensitive in some respects; but in her

high vocation she had, in addition to the deep intuitions of a gifted woman, the strength of a man, the
patience of a hero, and the conscientiousness of a
saint.'

'Shirley' was published on the 26th of October, and
took the public by storm. Everybody read it, and
most people praised it. By many it was pronounced, as
we hold it to be, superior in force of characterization,
delicacy of touch, glow of description, and variety of
interest, to 'Jane Eyre.' The secret of the identity of
the author was now revealed ; and when she paid a visit
to London towards the end of the year, she was recognized
by society as 'a lion,' and but for her natural modesty
would have been overwhelmed with adulation. To all
such display, however, she was unaffectedly averse ; but
in converse with such men as Thackeray, who had always
been one of her heroes, Lewes, Sydney Dobell, and other
litterateurs and critics, she took an intense delight. It
was at this time that she made the acquaintance of Miss
Martineau, with whom she thenceforth maintained a very
cordial and sympathetic friendship.

Returning to Haworth, she soon had experience of
what it is to be famous. Even that remote and quiet
Yorkshire village was wild with excitement. Here is her
own description of the turmoil of local celebrity :—

'Mr. ——, having finished "Jane Eyre," is now crying
out for the "other book ;" he is to have it next week......
Mr. —— has finished "Shirley:" he is delighted with it.
John ——'s wife seriously thought him gone wrong in
the head, as she heard him giving vent to roars of
laughter as he sat alone, clapping and stamping on the

floor. He would read all the scenes about the curates aloud to papa.......Martha came in yesterday, puffing and blowing, and much excited. "I've heard sich news!" she began. "What about?" "Please ma'am, you've been and written two books—the grandest books that ever was seen. My father has heard it at Halifax, and Mr. G—— T—— and Mr. G—— and Mr. M—— at Bradford; and they are going to have a meeting at the Mechanics' Institute, and to settle about ordering them!" "Hold your tongue, Martha, and be off!" I fell into a cold sweat. "Jane Eyre" will be read by J—— B——, by Mr. T——, and B——. Heaven help, keep, and deliver me!......The Haworth people have been making great fools of themselves about "Shirley;" they have taken it in an enthusiastic light. When they got the volumes at the Mechanics' Institute, all the members wanted them. They cast lots for the whole three, and whoever got a volume was only allowed to keep it two days, and was to be fined a shilling *per diem* for longer detention. It would be mere nonsense and vanity to tell you what they say.'

Yet with all her great and well-deserved renown, and with her genial correspondence with such friends as Lewes, Thackeray, Mrs. Gaskell, Miss Martineau, the career of Charlotte Brontë was scarcely, from the world's point of view, a happy one. It was overshadowed by sad memories of the past, and by the weariness arising from feeble health. Then, too, she was virtually alone. Her father, owing to his age and retired habits, confined himself almost all day to his own chamber, and Charlotte Brontë's solitude was seldom shared except by the phantoms of those who had gone before. After dinner she read to her father for an hour or so; at eight o'clock family prayers were said; Mr. Brontë then retired, and was soon followed by the two servants. Charlotte, less eager for sleep and less able to enjoy it, stopped up to a late hour; reading or sewing until her weak eyes failed her, and afterwards recalling the beloved faces of the dead, or seeking a charm for her melancholy in the exercise of her inventive faculty.

'No one on earth,' says her biographer, 'can ever imagine what these hours were to her. All the grim superstitions of the North had been implanted in her during her childhood by the servants who believed in them. They recurred to her now—with no shrinking from the spirits of the dead, but with such an intense longing once more to stand face to face with the souls of her sisters, as no one but she could have felt. It seemed as if the very strength of her yearning should have compelled them to appear. On windy nights, cries, and sobs, and wailings seemed to go round the house, as of the dearly-beloved striving to force their way to her. Some one conversing with her once objected, in my presence, to that part of "Jane Eyre" in which she hears Rochester's voice crying out to her in a great crisis of her life, he being many, many miles distant at the time. I do not know what incident was in Miss Brontë's recollection when she replied, in a low voice, drawing in her breath, "But it is a true thing; it really happened."'

We imagine, however, that this depressed and sensitive condition did not endure for many months after the publication of 'Shirley.' The letters recently published in Mr. Wemyss Reid's monograph on Charlotte Brontë show her in a somewhat less melancholy light than that which Mrs. Gaskell has thrown about her. And, indeed, we do not think that there was much of the melodramatic in our heroine's life or character. Her intellect was so strong, her judgment so sound, her habits were so practical, that we cannot conceive of her as yielding, except in hours of physical suffering, to unavailing regrets. Through endurance she conquered. Her love of nature, her enjoyment of books, the cultivation of her prompt and fertile genius, would all help to raise her above the attacks of a sickly despondency. Hers was an eminently noble life, a healthy and a generous life, which spent itself freely for others, and, though darkened by many sorrows, was not without a brightness and a beauty of its own.

In 1851 she paid another visit to London, and met again with her friends Thackeray and Lewes. Afterwards she travelled north to Edinburgh, making excursions to Abbotsford, the home of Scott, and the glorious ruin of Melrose. Of her pilgrimage she retained a very pleasant recollection, and wrote to one of her friends in the following terms:—

'The six weeks of change and enjoyment are past, but they are not lost; memory took a sketch of each as it went by, and, especially, a distinct daguerreotype of the two days I spent in Scotland. These were two very pleasant days. I always liked Scotland as an idea, but now, as a reality, I like it far better; it furnished me with some hours as happy almost as any I ever spent. Do not fear, however, that I am going to bore you with description; you will, before now, have received a pithy and pleasant report of all things, to which any addition of mine would be superfluous. My present endeavours are directed towards recalling my thoughts, cropping their wings, drilling them into correct discipline, and forcing them to settle to some useful work : they are idle, and keep taking the train down to London, or making a foray over the Border. Especially are they prone to perpetrate that last excursion ; and who, indeed, that has once seen Edinburgh, with its couchant crag-lion, but must see it again in dreams, waking or sleeping? My dear sir, do not think that I blaspheme when I tell you that your great London, as compared to Dun-Edin, "mine own romantic town," is as prose compared to poetry, or as a great rumbling, rambling, heavy epic, com-pared to a lyric, brief, bright, clear, and vital as a flash of lightning. You have nothing like Scott's Monument ; or, if you had that, and all the glories of architecture assembled together, you have nothing like Arthur's Seat; and, above all, you have not the Scotch national char-acter,—and it is that grand character, after all, which gives the land its true charm, its true greatness.'

The extracts with which we have enriched our pages will give the reader an idea of the delightful letters, full of happy bits of description and suggestion, of thought and criticism, which Charlotte Brontë wrote. And if he turns to those which Mrs. Gaskell, and, more recently, Mr. Wemyss Reid, have collected, he will come to the conclusion, we think, that among English letter-writers Charlotte Brontë is entitled to hold almost as high a place as she occupies amongst English novelists.

Here is one more extract ; a felicitous combination of the conversational and the critical. It is dated August

the 27th, and was addressed to Mrs. Gaskell, herself a
novelist of no inconsiderable power :—

'Papa and I have just had tea : he is sitting quietly in
his room, and I in mine : "storms of rain" are sweeping
over the garden and churchyard : as to the moors, they
are hidden in thick fog. Though alone, I am not unhappy : I have a thousand things to be thankful for, and,
amongst the rest, that this morning I received a letter
from you, and that this evening I have the privilege of
answering it.

'I do not know the "Life of Sydney Taylor;" whenever I have the opportunity I will get it. The little
French book you mention shall also take its place on the
list of books to be procured as soon as possible. It
treats a subject interesting to all women—perhaps more
especially to single women ; though, indeed, mothers,
like you, study it for the sake of their daughters. The
Westminster Review is not a periodical I see regularly,
but some time since I got hold of a number—for last
January, I think—in which there was an article entitled
"Woman's Mission" (the phrase is hackneyed), containing a great deal that seemed to me just and sensible.
Men begin to regard the position of woman in another
light than they used to do ; and a few men, whose sympathies are fine and whose sense of justice is strong,
think and speak of it with a candour that commands
my admiration. They say, however—and, to an extent,
truly—that the amelioration of our condition depends on
ourselves. Certainly there are evils which our own efforts
will best reach ; but as certainly there are other evils—
deep-rooted in the foundations of the social system—
which no efforts of ours can touch ; of which we cannot

complain; of which it is advisable not too often to think.

'I have read Tennyson's "In Memoriam," or rather part of it; I closed the book when I had got about half-way. It is beautiful; it is mournful; it is monotonous. Many of the feelings expressed bear, in their utterance, the stamp of truth; yet, if Arthur Hallam had been somewhat nearer Alfred Tennyson—his brother instead of his friend—I should have distrusted this rhymed, and measured, and printed monument of grief. What change the lapse of years may work I do not know; but it seems to me that bitter sorrow, while recent, does not flow out in verse.'

Here we think the writer unjust to our great nineteenth-century poet. She herself was not accustomed to express her feelings in verse. It does not appear that she continued her poetical efforts after the publication of the little volume by 'Currer, Ellis, and Acton Bell.' Prose was to her the natural vehicle for the conveyance of her thought; and her novels are full of the records of her own personal experience. Tennyson's 'In Memoriam' is as genuine in its commemoration of Arthur Hallam as Charlotte Brontë's 'Shirley' in its commemoration of her sister Emily. The poet made use of the forms with which he was most familiar; so did the novelist. Poets learn in suffering what they teach in song; novelists, like Miss Brontë, embody the results of their bitter apprenticeship in prose.

A visitor to Haworth, in October 1850, describes Miss Brontë as putting her in mind of the novelist's own 'Jane Eyre.' She looked smaller than ever, and moved about so quietly and noiselessly, just like a little bird, as 'Rochester' calls her, except that birds are joyous, while it seemed to the visitor as if joy could never have entered the small, dull, gray stone parsonage since it was first built. About the same time, Mrs. Gaskell describes her as 'undeveloped,' thin, and more than half a head shorter than herself; soft brown hair, not very dark; eyes, very good and expressive, with an open straightforward look, and of the same colour as her hair; a large mouth; the forehead square, broad, and rather overhanging. Her voice was very sweet: she hesitated a little in choosing her expressions, but when chosen they seemed without an effort admirable, and just befitting the occasion; never exaggerated, but always perfectly simple. And Miss Martineau depicts her as youthful-looking, almost a child in stature,—dressed in a deep mourning robe,—the very model of neatness,—with, as already stated, fine eyes and beautiful brown hair.

Towards the end of 1852, this child-like woman put into the hands of her publishers the third, and not the least extraordinary, of her novels, 'Villette.' Its heroine, Lucy Snowe, is identified with herself by Mr. Wemyss Reid; and probably certain features of her own character are woven into it, just as many of her Brussels adventures are woven into the plot. And if Mr. Wemyss Reid be correct in his conjecture, that the work describes Miss Brontë's sufferings from a profound attachment for some one whom she met at Brussels, we shall then be better able to understand, what has always perplexed her critics, the power and energy with which she depicts the passion of love. But who was M. Paul Emmanuel? If such a man had really crossed her path in life, we think some record of him would have been found in her correspond-

ence. For our own part, Miss Brontë seems to us something more as well as something less than 'Lucy Snowe.'
No doubt she put a portion of herself, so to speak, into
the heroine of 'Villette,' just as she did into the heroine
of 'Jane Eyre;' but she herself was better and nobler
than both or either. In 'Lucy Snowe,' for instance,
there is, as her creator points out, much that is morbid
and weak,—her character sets up no pretensions to un-
mixed strength; but who can say, with any degree of
truth or justice, that Charlotte Brontë, throughout her
life of trial and shadow, showed weakness or morbidity?

In December 1852, she received a proposal of marriage
from Mr. Nicholls, her father's curate, who had known her
for years, and whose affection had deepened and strengthened with his knowledge. 'In silence he had watched her,
and loved her long;' and the love of a man so honourable, so conscientious, and so cultured, was not to be
despised even by a woman like 'Currer Bell.' She did
not despise it; but before she would allow herself to
accept it, she went to her father, and he, always sternly
protesting against marriages, and unwilling, perhaps, in
his old age to lose his only daughter, the stay and solace
of his life, induced her to give a distinct refusal. This
was in accordance with her prevailing sense of duty and
readiness to self sacrifice; but there can be no doubt that
she felt it deeply. Mr. Nicholls resigned his curacy; and
to gain some respite from sad thoughts, Charlotte Brontë
paid a visit to her friends in London, and afterwards to
Mrs. Gaskell, at Manchester. Happily, by degrees Mr.
Brontë grew reconciled to the idea of his daughter's
marriage. Friends on both sides interfered; and the
result was, that in the spring of 1853 Mr. Nicholls

resumed his curacy at Haworth, on the understanding
that his proposals were accepted.

The marriage took place on the 29th of June; and
after the ceremony, Mr. Nicholls and his bride went to
visit his friends and relatives in Ireland. They also
made a tour from Killarney to Cork, through scenery
which greatly impressed the quick imagination of the
novelist. Then they returned to Haworth, and to the
quiet of a home-life which was unspeakably happy. We
can permit ourselves but one glimpse of it.

' We have had many callers from a distance,' she
writes, ' and latterly some little occupation in the way of
preparing for a small village entertainment. Both Mr.
Nicholls and myself wished much to make some response
for the hearty welcome and general goodwill shown by
the parishioners on his return; accordingly, the Sunday
and day scholars and teachers, the church-ringers, singers,
&c., to the number of five hundred, were asked to tea
and supper in the school-room. They seemed to enjoy
it much, and it was very pleasant to see their happiness.
One of the villagers, in proposing my husband's health,
described him as a "consistent Christian and a kind
gentleman." I own the words touched me deeply, and
I thought (as I know *you* would have thought had you
been present) that to merit and win such a character was
better than to earn either wealth, or fame, or power. I
am disposed to echo that high but simple eulogium......
My own life is more occupied than it used to be ; I have
not so much time for thinking: I am obliged to be more
practical, for my dear Arthur is a very practical as well
as a very punctual and methodical man. Every morning
he is in the National School by nine o'clock ; he gives

31st, the solemn chime of the bell of Haworth announced that Charlotte Brontë was no more.

Yet she, being dead, still speaketh ; speaketh in those admirable works of hers, the product of a genius singularly pure, strong, and true,—of a heart alive to all generous impulses, and touched with the finest and tenderest emotions ; and speaketh in the story of her life, which teaches to all who read the lesson of duty and the nobility of self-sacrifice.   Among English women of letters we know of none whose life-theory was more elevated or more thoroughly worked out ; and we may justly conclude with the eulogium of Miss Martineau, which describes her as endowed with 'the deep intuitions of a gifted woman, the strength of a man, the patience of a hero, and the conscientiousness of a saint.'

[Authorities :—' Life,' by Mrs. Gaskell : ' Biographical Sketches,' by Miss. Martineau : articles in *Macmillan's Magazine*, 1876. by T. Wemyss Reid : *Edinburgh Review*, 1847. &c., &c.]

Young Lady's Library.

Self-Effort Series.

••

Crown 8vo, cloth extra. Price 3s. 6d. each.

Lives Made Sublime by Faith and Works. By Rev. ROBERT STEEL, D.D., Ph.D., author of "Doing Good," etc. Post 8vo. *New Edition.*

A volume of short biographical sketches of Christian men, eminent and useful in various walks of life, as Hugh Miller, Sir Henry Havelock, Robert Flockhart, etc.

Noble Women of our Time. By JOSEPH JOHNSON, author of "Living in Earnest," etc. With Accounts of the Work of Misses De Broen, Whately, Carpenter, F. R. Havergal, Sister Dora, etc. Post 8vo.

A handsome volume, containing short biographies of many Christian women, whose lives have been devoted to missionary and philanthropic work in our own and other countries—Sister Dora, Mrs. Tait, Frances Havergal, etc.

Self-Effort ; or, The True Method of Attaining Success in Life. By JOSEPH JOHNSON, author of "Living in Earnest," etc. Post 8vo, cloth extra.

This book of example and encouragement has been written to induce earnestness in life, the illustrations being drawn from recent books of biography.

"In a pleasant style the author discourses of self-culture and the way and means of self-improvement, of the best means of securing health and success in business, of industry and early rising, of habits and manners, of books and companions. Mr. Johnson's illustrations are chiefly drawn from biography, and include many pleasing anecdotes."—MANCHESTER EXAMINER AND TIMES.

The Young Huguenots ; or, The Soldiers of the Cross. A Story of the Seventeenth Century. By "FLEUR DE LYS." With Six Illustrations. Post 8vo, cloth extra.

General Grant's Life. (*From the Tannery to the White House.*) Story of the Life of Ulysses S. Grant; his Boyhood, Youth, Manhood, Public and Private Life and Services. By WILLIAM M. THAYER, author of "From Log Cabin to White House," etc. With Portrait, Vignette, etc. Reprinted complete from the American Edition. 400 pages. Crown 8vo, cloth extra, gilt side and edges.

Torch-Bearers of History. A Connected Series of Historical Sketches. First and Second Series in One Volume. From the Earliest Times to the Beginning of the French Revolution. By AMELIA HUTCHISON STIRLING, M.A., Edinburgh, formerly Lecturer in the Ladies' College, Cheltenham. Post 8vo, art linen, gilt top.

Volumes I. and II. of the "Torch-Bearers of History," bound together, make a handsome book. It embraces the great men of the world from the Earliest Times till the French Revolution.

The Great Authors of English Literature. Their Lives, and Selections from their Writings. *In Three Divisions:*—FIRST, From Chaucer to Pope. SECOND, From Goldsmith to Wordsworth. THIRD, From Macaulay to Browning. By W. SCOTT DALGLEISH, M.A., LL.D. With Thirty-two Portraits. Crown 8vo.

T. NELSON AND SONS, London, Edinburgh, and New York.

Self-Effort Series.

long**Crown 8vo, cloth extra. Price 3s. 6d. each.**

Architects of Fate; or, Steps to Success and Power. By ORISON SWETT MARDEN, author of "Pushing to the Front; or, Success under Difficulties." With Eight Illustrations. Crown 8vo.

A book of inspiration to character-building, self-culture, to a full and rich manhood and womanhood, by most invigorating examples of noble achievement. It is characterized by the same remarkable qualities as its companion volume, "Pushing to the Front," which passed through more than a dozen editions the first year, has been adopted for use in the Boston and other public schools, has received hearty commendation from other countries, and is pronounced by the press one of the greatest success-books ever published.

Men Who Win; or, Making Things Happen. By W. M. THAYER, author of "From Log Cabin to White House," "Women Who Win," etc. Crown 8vo.

"The works of Mr. W. M. Thayer are second only to those of Dr. Samuel Smiles as encouragement (or dissuasion) to boys."—ACADEMY.

"Though many books have been written upon the subject, we feel that this volume will easily rank among the best of its kind."—PRACTICAL TEACHER.

Women Who Win; or, Making Things Happen. By W. M. THAYER, author of "From Log Cabin to White House," "Men Who Win," etc. Crown 8vo, cloth extra.

"A better gift for girls than 'Women Who Win,' by W. M. Thayer, is not to be found. The perusal of the lives of such great and good women is calculated to arouse girls to a sense of their responsibilities, and to give them high ideals of character and usefulness."—DUNDEE ADVERTISER.

The Achievements of Youth. By the Rev. ROBERT STEEL, D.D., Ph.D., author of "Lives Made Sublime," etc. Post 8vo, cloth extra.

A wholesome and stimulating book, in which the subjects of the biographies are shown to have in large measure developed their greatness in the days of their youth. It treats of men famous in the departments of Literature, Science, Art, Music, etc.

Doing Good; or, The Christian in Walks of Usefulness. Illustrated by Examples. By the Rev. ROBERT STEEL, D.D., Ph.D. Post 8vo.

A series of short biographical sketches of Christians remarkable for various kinds of usefulness, for example and encouragement to others.

Earnest Men: Their Life and Work. By the late Rev. W. K. TWEEDIE, D.D. Crown 8vo.

Contains biographical sketches of eminent patriots, heroes for the truth, philanthropists, and men of science.

Famous Artists. Michael Angelo—Leonardo da Vinci—Raphael—Titian—Murillo—Rubens—Rembrandt. By SARAH K. BOLTON. Post 8vo, cloth extra.

Interesting biographies of Michael Angelo, Da Vinci, Raphael, Titian, Murillo, Rubens, and Rembrandt. Also critical and other notices by Vasari, Passavant, Taine, Crowe and Cavalcaselle, etc., which are both interesting and instructive.

Heroes of the Desert. The Story of the Lives of Moffat and Livingstone. By the Author of "Mary Powell." New and Enlarged Edition, with numerous Illustrations and Two Portraits. Crown 8vo, cloth extra.

T. NELSON AND SONS, London, Edinburgh, and New York.

Tales of History by E. Everett-Green.

Crown 8vo, bevelled boards, cloth extra, gilt top.
Price 5s. each.

A Clerk of Oxford, and His Adventures in the Barons' War. By E. EVERETT-GREEN, author of "The Young Pioneers," "In Taunton Town," "Shut In," etc.

The Young Pioneers ; or, With La Salle on the Mississippi. By E. EVERETT-GREEN, author of "Shut In," "In the Days of Chivalry," "In Taunton Town," etc.

"A thrilling tale of a persecuted French family of two hundred years ago, who joined La Salle in seeking to found a new France on the shores of the mighty Mississippi. Stories of love and war are blended with the records of the 'Home of Peace' established by Father Fritz among the friendly Indians."—SWORD AND TROWEL.

Shut In. A Tale of the Wonderful Siege of Antwerp in the Year 1585. By E. EVERETT-GREEN, author of "In the Days of Chivalry," "The Lost Treasure of Trevlyn," etc.

"A vigorous and lively picture of the siege of Antwerp in the sixteenth century. Scenes of love and of fighting alternate to give a charm of variety to the life of the sturdy burghers whom the tale depicts."—SCOTSMAN.

The Lost Treasure of Trevlyn. A Story of the Days of the Gunpowder Plot. By E. EVERETT-GREEN, author of "Shut In," "In the Days of Chivalry," etc.

"A romantic plot, full of incident and changing fortunes, set against an interesting historical background."—SCOTSMAN.

In the Days of Chivalry. A Tale of the Times of the Black Prince. By E. EVERETT-GREEN, author of "The Lost Treasure of Trevlyn," "In Taunton Town," etc.

"A historical romance of substantial merit, telling a story full of adventurous movement, and valuable for the idea it gives of feudal England."—SCOTSMAN.

In Taunton Town. A Story of the Rebellion of James, Duke of Monmouth, in 1685. By E. EVERETT-GREEN, author of "Shut In," "In the Days of Chivalry," etc.

"A historical romance, charmingly written."—SCOTSMAN.

"'In Taunton Town' is another of Miss Evelyn Everett-Green's admirable historical tales, and is marked by the author's usual graphic descriptions and historic fidelity, while infused with romantic interest."—GLASGOW HERALD.

Loyal Hearts and True. A Story of the Days of "Good Queen Bess." By E. EVERETT-GREEN, author of "In Taunton Town," "The Church and the King," etc.

"This is admirably told by Evelyn Everett-Green, who in a picturesque manner brings before us the court and time of the Maiden Queen and the stirring incidents of the Spanish Armada."—GLASGOW HERALD.

The Church and the King. A Tale of England in the Days of Henry VIII. By E. EVERETT-GREEN, author of "Loyal Hearts and True," "In Taunton Town," etc.

"The plot involves many romantic situations of love, adventure, patriotism, and religious zeal; and the spirited interest is well maintained throughout."—SCOTSMAN.

T. NELSON AND SONS, London, Edinburgh, and New York.

www.ingramcontent.com/pod-product-compliance
Lightning Source LLC
Chambersburg PA
CBHW020845020726
47497CB00005B/1266